CW01497375

DARK THREADS OF VENGEANCE

AN ASHMOLE FOXE GEORGIAN MYSTERY

WILLIAM SAVAGE

RIDGE & BOURNE

For Jenn as ever

∼

This is a work of fiction. All characters and events,
other than those clearly in the public domain,
are products of the author's imagination.
Any resemblance to actual persons, living or dead,
is unintended and entirely co-incidental.

∼

*"To me belongeth vengeance and recompence ...
for the day of their calamity is at hand
and the things that shall come upon them make haste."*

The Bible (Deuteronomy, 32:35)

1

"THE DAY OF THEIR CALAMITY"

IT WAS FINISHED. THE MURDERER CROUCHED OVER THE BODY, HIS breath coming in gasps, his stomach heaving. Who would have thought it so hard to kill? It had been the work of a moment to slip the leather strap around the man's neck, lean back, cross the ends and pull as hard as he knew how. If the victim had allowed himself to fall backwards, they would both have fallen over. The fellow might even have escaped.

Instead, the man had twisted and writhed, trying to throw off whoever had come from behind. Strained to get his hands under what was choking him. Pulled forward against the murderer. Put even more pressure on his windpipe.

The actual struggle lasted perhaps a minute. It felt like thirty. Then the victim lost consciousness and both of them fell forward onto the ground, the murderer still pulling hard on the ends of the strap. How long would it take the man to die? Since the murderer was unsure, he kept up the pressure long after all resistance and movement had ceased. Two minutes? Four? It might have been longer, had not the dying man voided himself. That was what caused the murderer to loosen his grip and jump away. The stench was nauseating.

Straightening up, the murderer peered around. There was no one in sight. What now? All his plans had ended with the man's death. Then his gaze fell on the bottle of cheap spirits laid on the ground for safety in the struggle. Pouring that over the corpse should be enough to convince whoever found it that the man had been drinking heavily. There, it was done. He laughed to himself. The final insult!

After a moment or so, the murderer realised he faced a problem. To make the death look like robbery, he must empty the dead man's pockets. But to do so meant leaning close over the body again, subjecting himself to the foul smell of alcohol mixed with faeces. Touching the soiled breeches. He dithered, trying to steel himself.

What was that? Voices, for certain. Men coming along the quay, perhaps heading for Fye Bridge or returning to sleep on one of the boats moored alongside. Time to hide or get away. The murderer slipped into the shadow of a nearby pile of boxes and barrels awaiting loading.

"Gar! Wha's that god-awful stink then? Christ, it's a drunk! You can smell the booze on 'im, even through all the rest. Stupid bugger's shit 'isself."

Two men, young and full of bravado. They bent over the dead man. Just not too low. The smell was too bad for that. Perhaps that, and the dim light, explained why neither noticed the strap driven deep into the flesh of the neck, the bulging eyes or the tongue hanging from the mouth. They might have straightened up and wandered on, for they had seen plenty of drunks before and dismissed them as simpletons not worth their notice. But that night, some devil of mischief stirred in the mind of one of them.

"Serve 'im right if 'e wakes up 'alf-way to Yarmouth," he said to his companion. "Do you take 'is feet an' I'll take 'is arms. Pitch 'im into that wherry.'

"Bloody 'ell! I'll get shit all over me 'ands."

"Nah! Not if you be careful. Quick grab now and … over 'e goes."

The two of them lifted the body, swung it once for momentum and sent it flying out over the deck of the wherry. As luck would have it, the corpse fell neatly through an open hatchway into the hold. There it settled on top of a pile of grain.

"Do you sleep it off there," one of the men called out. "Teach 'ee to get so sozzled you messes yourself."

The men walked on then, laughing and congratulating themselves on their joke. The murderer slipped along behind, well pleased with what they had done. But, as time proved, it would have been better to have staged a robbery after all.

THE TWO CREWMEN told to load the last of the barley found the body the next morning, while the wherry was still at its mooring. Its captain, furious at the mess ruining his cargo, snapped at them to leave all as they found it and stamped off to find the harbourmaster. The magistrate was duly informed and two constables were set to guard the boat and the dead man.

All this time, the reek of drink and the smell of faeces kept everyone from making a close inspection of the corpse. The coroner, called to examine it in situ and arrange for a post-mortem, was the first to look into the distorted face. What he saw caused him to call the magistrate across. After a single glance, the magistrate hurried back to the quay and sent an urgent message to the mayor. The mayor at once summoned his most trusted allies amongst the aldermen of the city.

This was a crisis.

One by one, the aldermen came together, incredulous at the news. Shock and disbelief marked every face. They gaped at one another, unable to comprehend the scale of the disaster before them. Once all were present, the mayor called for order and shared what he knew. Sailors had found the body early that morning, but only now had it been recognised. The man was strangled, but not robbed. His clothes and corpse reeked of brandy.

That was when the questions began.

The victim had never touched alcohol. Everyone knew that.

Preached against it whenever he could. How could he have been drinking enough to smell of it in that way?

What was he doing in that part of Norwich, and at night? It was asking to be robbed. Yet his purse, his fine pocket watch and the silver buckles on his shoes were still there. Why kill him and take nothing?

And why leave the body in the hold of a wherry? If he was killed ashore, it must have taken at least two strong men to put him there. If he was killed on the wherry, what had he been doing on board? Was he too drunk to know what he was doing? But he never drank at all …

On and on the questions continued. Round and round went the guesses at what had happened. No answers were found. All the while, no one voiced the most pressing question at the forefront of their minds: is our money safe?

Finally, the mayor called a halt.

"This is getting us nowhere," he said. "We all have questions. What we need are answers. I don't need to tell any of you what this might lead to if word of the details gets out. A run on Morrow & Son's Bank would be barely the start. None of the banks would be safe. Our first need is to keep as much as we can secret. We know the man wasn't robbed, but no one else does. Let the world assume this is a straightforward case of a rich man attacked by ruffians. It won't do a lot for the city's reputation, but it's a great deal better than the alternatives. Do you all agree?"

All did.

"Next, we have to know who did this and why. Does this murder have anything to do with Morrow & Son? Do they have a problem we don't know about?"

"They'd better not," someone said. "I have two thousand pounds on deposit with them." Others nodded and mumbled numbers of a similar size.

"Yes, yes!" The mayor was tetchy now. "We all stand to lose money if the bank is in trouble, gentlemen, myself included. What we need to do is make sure it isn't; or if it is, see how we can rescue as much as possible. I'll talk to Ezekiel Morrow myself on that score.

For the rest, there needs to be a quick, thorough and above all confidential investigation. One preferably followed by a trial at the next assize and a welcome hanging to keep the mob happy."

Heads nodded in agreement.

"Well, Halloran," the mayor continued. "Do you agree this is a job for your man Foxe?"

"Usual terms?" Alderman Halloran asked. "Bonus for speed?"

"Whatever is needed," the mayor said. "He'll know at once what's at stake. It would be stupid to go to him pretending this is an ordinary killing. Let's just hope he isn't too greedy."

"He won't be," Halloran said. "I've never known Foxe concerned about money."

"Where does he get his wealth from?" someone said. "Got a share in Gracie's brothel? That tin-pot shop of his wouldn't earn enough to pay for one of his foppish waistcoats!"

That remark raised several laughs.

"Well, I'm sure you of all of us know Gracie's establishment best," Halloran said. That shut the fool's mouth. He scowled at the assembled elite of Norwich's business community. "We need Foxe's help, gentlemen. I therefore suggest we treat him with decent courtesy." He turned back to the mayor. "I should be able to find Foxe at home at this hour."

"Good," the mayor said. He glared at the rest of the aldermen. "Off you go, Halloran. The rest of you as well. We've wasted enough time. Action is what we need, not foolish remarks. I'll call another meeting when it's required. Meanwhile, remember this. If you want to see your money again, keep your mouths tight shut. If you're pressed, say as little as you can. Talk vaguely about cut-purses and robbery. Don't say he was robbed, just let it be assumed. If any of you let a word of the real story get out, you'll need somewhere exceptionally good to hide. I'll soon know who opened his mouth ... and I'm a dangerous man to cross. Now go! I have much to do."

Mr Ashmole Foxe was a bookseller by trade, though his shop was a puzzle. Its neat frontage adjoined his house, not far from the great Market Place of Norwich. The rest stretched back along a narrow lane that led to the street behind. From there, nothing could be seen of house or shop, now hidden behind a high wall. Only wooden doors across the carriage entrance suggested a dwelling.

The shop itself was spacious, clean and well-kept. Outside, there were splendid glass bow-windows for displaying prints. Inside, the walls were lined with book stacks made from polished oak. An oval counter dominated the centre of the space. In Mr Foxe's father's time, he or his assistant would stand there to take their customers' orders.

The shop was close to the heart of the city and should have been well-patronised. Yet today few of Norwich's prosperous merchants or their wives had ever been inside. Indeed, for a long time, 'Foxe & Company, Booksellers and Printers' rarely opened at all. When it did, its contents seemed scanty. Even if all were sold, they would not furnish sufficient profit to pay for the premises, let alone the fine house next door. Yet certain customers did come. All were recognisable as wealthy men; all were welcomed by Mr Foxe himself, wearing one of the richly-embroidered waistcoats for which he was famous; most were at once ushered into a rear room, away from prying eyes. When these men re-emerged later, they would be carrying a parcel neatly wrapped in cloth or heavy paper.

Since Mr Foxe was undoubtedly prosperous, the conclusion seemed obvious. He must be a dealer in pornography for the rich, brought from countries notorious for low morals such as France or Italy. And although this characterisation of his business and stock was wrong, the man himself did nothing to correct it. He seemed more amused than insulted.

Of late, however, Mr Foxe's shop had taken on a new lease of life. It now opened at regular hours. The stock was being increased to include all anyone would expect to find in a good bookseller's. There were even prints and pamphlets for sale; and a substantial range of patent medicines too.

The source of this change was the woman now to be seen rearranging the newest books and laying some out on tables for inspection. Mrs Susannah Crombie's husband had also been a local bookseller. Though he and Mr Foxe had not quite been friends, their acquaintance had been amiable and of long-standing. Then, a little over three months before, Mr Crombie had finally succumbed to a passion for gambling. In short order, he ran through his capital, followed by his credit. When he finally grasped he was ruined, he killed himself rather than face what lay ahead, leaving his much younger second wife destitute.

Word of Crombie's death soon reached Mr Foxe and he hurried to offer his condolences. He found Mrs Crombie in tears, trying to decide whether to seek a position as a housekeeper or try her luck as a streetwalker. He stepped in at once.

Now her self-respect was intact and her joy in life had returned. For the past month, Mrs Crombie had been acting as the manager and guiding light behind Mr Foxe's revived shop. Foxe had even found her a suitable dwelling, above a cobbler's shop off the marketplace, at a rent he knew she could afford. This was not so surprising, since he owned the building, as he did many others throughout the city. Mr Foxe's investments were many and substantial. As well as owning property, he was a sleeping partner in several successful business enterprises. Those who thought him prosperous, underestimated him. Mr Ashmole Foxe was really rather rich.

So it was that on that fine day in early April, when Alderman Halloran stepped into Foxe's shop, he found, not Mr Foxe, but a strange young woman standing alone near the oval counter.

"Mr Foxe about?" he asked her.

"I believe he is in the stockroom, alderman," the young lady said. "Shall I tell him you are here to see him?"

"Please do, madam," Halloran replied.

Though he was one of Mr Foxe's longest-standing and best customers, the alderman had not visited the shop for several months, preferring to summon Mr Foxe to his own home to discuss the needs of his library. When he saw before him a handsome, well-dressed young woman—one certainly worth more than a cursory glance—his thoughts were predictable. Foxe was well known to be a ladies' man. This must be yet another of his many conquests.

Mrs Crombie was absent only a few moments. When she returned, she was followed by her employer and benefactor, Mr Ashmole Foxe.

"Good day to you, alderman," Foxe said. "Is it not a remarkably fine day? My morning walk furnished me great satisfaction, not least because so many people in the Market Place showed smiling faces to the world. Now you have come to visit us too, which is a further pleasure. May I present to you Mrs Crombie, who is my new assistant?"

Halloran was impolite enough to take a further lengthy look at the young woman, eying her from head to toe. Good Lord, he thought to himself. Are the city's young ladies queuing up to throw themselves at Foxe's feet? He supposed it must be so, even if they knew what to expect from such a confirmed philanderer. Yet in this too, the alderman was mistaken. Foxe and Mrs Crombie had done nothing even the most rigid moralist could find worthy of disapproval.

Startled by Alderman Halloran's sharp stare, Mrs Crombie looked away. Foxe, suspecting what might be going through the man's mind, suppressed a smile and continued speaking. He knew how to distract Halloran from displaying any more breaches of polite behaviour.

"I have new books for you, sir," he said. "Books which I'm sure will be of great interest. If you will but step into the storeroom"

The mention of new books would normally have driven all other thoughts from the alderman's head. Collecting rare books was more than an indulgence to him. It was his major passion in life.

"Not today, Foxe," he said, his voice sad. "I have come here about a most serious matter. Mayor sent me. Bad business in the city. Need you to help us."

"What kind of bad business?" Foxe asked.

"Can we go somewhere less public, Foxe?" Alderman Halloran said, looking at Mrs Crombie.

"If you wish," Foxe said. "Mrs Crombie. Please excuse us for a few moments." He hadn't forgotten his manners, even if the alderman seemed to have abandoned his.

Once the two men were seated in the chairs Foxe kept in his stockroom for his more eminent visitors, Alderman Halloran began.

"There's been a murder, Foxe. Man strangled last night and dumped in the hold of a wherry down at the old wharf by Fye Bridge. The one where the smaller boats tie up. It's behind The Maid's Head Inn."

"Most likely a wherryman's brawl. Why should one more distress the mayor?"

"The dead man is Joseph Morrow."

"Ezekiel Morrow's son?"

"Yes. That one."

Now it was Foxe's turn to be startled. "Now I see why the mayor's concerned. Strangled, you said? What in heaven's name was he doing there—unless he was killed elsewhere and taken there to be dumped? Was he robbed? Was the body deliberately hidden?"

"No and no, so far as I understand things. He certainly wasn't hidden. His body was thrown into the hold of a wherry, right on top of a pile of grain. Someone was bound to find it as soon as they started work again."

"Not robbed either?"

"No. That isn't generally known, by the way, so keep your hat on it. Mayor thinks it best people assume he was the victim of some ruffian."

Foxe smiled. "No run on Morrow & Son's Bank, then. I assume someone is still going to look at their books thoroughly?"

"You don't strangle yourself with a leather strap, Foxe. If he'd hanged himself or blown his brains out, things would look very different. As it is, no need to panic … yet."

"Very well. Strangled and put where the body is bound to be found quickly."

"There's more. The body stank, I was told."

"You said he was killed last night. No body would stink after such a short time."

"This one did. For a start, he'd fouled his breeches. Then he reeked of drink, I'm told."

"Drink? Surely not. The man was totally adamant against any kind of alcohol. He was always going on about the evils of the bottle. As for the … the other smell … emptying the bowels is a commonplace accompaniment to hanging or strangling. But Joseph Morrow smelling of drink? It would be easier to accept the Bishop smelling of a whore's perfume."

"Drink it was. Cheap brandy, the coroner said. He smelled as if he'd been drowning in it. He must have been roaring drunk to smell like that."

"If that gets about, you really will have a financial panic. No one will let their money stay in a bank where the principal partner gets blind drunk and wanders along by the river in the dark."

"You see why we need you. We'll work to keep the whole predicament quiet to stave off any problems in the marketplace. You find out what's been going on. Why a notorious puritan and self-righteous bigot on all matters of morality gets himself killed while wandering about, late at night, totally sozzled."

"I still find it hard to believe," Foxe said. "His father, Ezekiel Morrow, is puritanical enough, but Joseph made him look almost liberal. The man was the most narrow-minded, rigid Calvinist in this city. If you worked for him, he gave you a list of forbidden actions. Break one of his 'commandments', even once, and you would be dismissed without a character. Right at the top of that list was abjuring alcohol, even in your own home when you had finished for the day. The man petrified his workers. No Sabbath-breaking. No frivolity on Sundays. No gambling. Definitely no adultery or enjoyable sex of any kind. Joseph Morrow raised self-righteousness to levels seen nowhere else. Pride too, though he couldn't see it. He was one of God's Elect, and don't you forget it. What a loathsome creature!"

At that moment, Mrs Crombie knocked at the door.

"I'm sorry to disturb you both, but there's a message for Alderman Halloran. The mayor wants to see him urgently."

"Better go," Alderman Halloran said. "The fellow panics when I'm not there."

"Oh, Mrs Crombie," Foxe said. "Do you know if Charlie is hanging about outside?"

Mrs Crombie smiled. Childless herself, she had quickly grown fond of the cheeky urchin who ran errands for her employer.

"Charlie is always hanging around here, Mr Foxe. Your cook feeds him far more often than his mother does."

"His mother is too often unable to feed herself, Mrs Crombie," Foxe said. "Without the few pence Charlie earns from me, the whole family would be in the House of Industry—or worse. If you can, please find the boy. Tell him to ask Captain Brock to come here as soon as he can. Remember, the rate for errands to the other side of the river is two pennies. Don't allow Charlie to trick you as he did the last time."

"I had been here but a few days then, Mr Foxe," Mrs Crombie replied, "and was not yet wise to his stratagems. I fear that, as he gets older, that look of innocence, coupled with barefaced lying, will become his stock-in-trade."

"As I do," Fox said. "Never fear, Mrs Crombie. Brock and I have plans for young Charlie, once he's grown somewhat. He needs to learn an honest trade in place of living on his wits."

"Whom do you speak of?" Alderman Halloran asked.

"An urchin boy who serves me as a messenger, alderman. Soon he will reach that point when the course of his future life will be set. Then it will be either a short life of crime and danger, or a longer one of honest toil. I do what I can for him. His mother has other mouths to feed and little to feed them with. Such work as she can get pays paltry wages. She also drinks intemperately. By paying him, I help to keep her family together, for she will not accept charity. I suspect doing so in her past has reduced her to her present state of destitution. Many who profess concern for the poor do not mean what they say—unless the poor repay their kindness in some tangible manner. Not every woman forced to become a whore walks the streets."

"Very commendable of you," the alderman said. "Enough criminals in this city already."

"To business then. I expect the coroner has had the body
removed by now. I will speak with him as soon as I can, certainly
before he holds an inquest. I must also try to find out why Joseph
Morrow was in that area."

"You're accepting our commission?" the alderman said. "I am
very glad of it. I am also authorised to offer you a bonus for a quick
result, should that be possible."

"Let's not worry about money. Other things are far more important. You need to hurry back to the mayor, and I must speak with
Brock as soon as he comes here."

"Yes, the mayor will be waiting impatiently, I have no doubt."

"Time to be off. Farewell to you, alderman."

Mrs Crombie came back into the shop soon after the alderman
had left. She had found young Charlie and sent him on his errand.

"Ah, Mrs Crombie," Foxe said. "We need to have a short discus-
sion. I had hoped we might have had longer before this sort of thing
happened, but there we are."

Mrs Crombie was alarmed. "Is anything wrong?" she asked.
"Business is getting better all the time. The word is spreading that
your shop is open again. Even if a good few of those who come are
driven by curiosity, they still buy."

"No, nothing is wrong. It is just something you need to understand now, not some time hence. Do you feel confident in the shop?
Would you be able to do all that needs to be done without me being
here?"

"I think so," Mrs Crombie said. "Are you going away?"

"No, but I will not be able to pay much attention to you or the
shop for a while. The mayor and his aldermen have once again
engaged my services on a delicate question."

Mrs Crombie looked puzzled, but waited for Mr Foxe to
continue.

"For several years," he went on, "I have assisted them in certain
confidential investigations. I enjoy the challenge; they find it convenient to wait until a matter is cleared up, then take the credit for the

solution. No one, save a few of my most trusted friends, knows of this. I must now ask you also to stay silent."

"Of course, Mr Foxe," Mrs Crombie said. "I would not dream of discussing any business that passes between us with others, let alone any confidential topics. You may trust me not to divulge your business."

"Good," Mr Fox said. "Whatever you see or hear within these walls must stay here. However …" He grinned at her now and the easy atmosphere between them returned. "Whatever you see or hear outside—anything you think may be of use in my investigation—is another matter. With your agreement, I will keep you informed of my progress. Thus you may use your eyes, ears and curiosity to best effect. Will that be acceptable?"

"Oh yes … yes indeed, Mr Foxe. I feel as if you have looked into my very soul. I dearly love a good mystery."

"I suspected as much. We are kindred beings in that respect. It was indeed a fortunate day for me when I found you crying in your old shop and invited you to help me here."

"As for that Mr Foxe, let us wait and see. I may not be as clever or as perceptive as you think I am. However, you will never find me guilty of ingratitude. You saved me from a dreadful fate, sir. I can never repay you. All I can promise is that, whatever you ask of me, I will undertake without question and to the best of my ability."

"Great heavens! Be careful what you promise, Mrs Crombie. I'm sure you have heard that my reputation in this city is of a person not much bound by the conventions of society."

"I have indeed heard that, Mr Foxe. It does not worry me. I have found you to be the kindest, gentlest and most thoughtful of men. For the rest, I care not a whit. For a woman who has come near to seeking her bread by walking the streets, you can ask little of me that would be any worse."

2

THE INVESTIGATION BEGINS

"Joseph Morrow you say. That is a surprise. I know his father a little, old Ezekiel, but not the son. Nasty piece of work from all I've heard." Brock had little time for moralists or preachers. "Full of cant and self-righteousness. Hard to imagine him drinking, though. Certainly not enough to get stinking drunk, whatever that medical examiner says."

"I'm inclined to agree with you," Foxe said. "But then, none of it makes sense."

They were sitting in Foxe's small parlour beside the fire. It wasn't really cold, but the wind was strong enough to find its way through every crack and chink. No house in Norfolk, it seemed, could be made proof against the east winds that blew over the German Ocean.

Captain Brock was one of Foxe's oldest friends. He had been in the Royal Navy for a time, then master of several merchant vessels and privateers. Lately, his business was running wherries up and down the River Wensum between Norwich and the ocean port at Yarmouth. A big, bluff man with the rolling walk typical of all seafarers, for a long time he affected the speech and manners of the Norfolk countryman. That was what his forebears had been and none the worse for it. However, since Foxe had almost forced him into attending the Mayor's Ball last year, his life—and his speech—had been transformed. That ball was where he met Lady Julia Henfield, the widowed sister-in-law of the Earl of Pentelow. The earl was a spendthrift and a rake. Lady Julia, on the other hand, was both well-spoken and discerning, with no time for nincompoops like her brother-in-law. She and Brock had struck up an unlikely friendship that evening; one that had continued ever since. As a result of her influence, Captain Brock now seemed quite the gentleman.

"What could have taken Morrow—at night—to that part of the city?" Foxe said.

Brock considered the question for a while.

"Had to be meeting someone, I imagine. A woman? A boy?"

"Neither seems much more likely than finding him drunk," Foxe said. "Besides, there would be rumours if a man like him was making the rounds of the brothels or molly-houses. You heard anything?"

Brock shook his head.

"Nor have I."

"Shame Gracie isn't about," Brock said. "Her girls would know for sure. Any idea when she'll be back?"

"No. Being engaged for the season at London's Drury Lane Theatre, and in leading roles, is Kitty's big chance. From what I gather, she's a prodigious success. She won't want to come back to Norwich after this—at least, not for a long time."

"Not even to see you?"

Foxe shook his head. "Not even for that. Oh, I don't doubt she's fond of me—even loves me a little—but the theatre is her life. No, Miss Kitty Catt is fast becoming the toast of the London stage, and that will matter much more. Imagine her giving it up to return to a mere lover in Norwich."

"Why did Gracie have to go as well?" Brock asked. "I can see the reason for Kitty to throw you over in favour of fame and fortune, but not Gracie."

"Those two sisters have been inseparable since birth," Foxe said. "Neither can be happy without the other close by. Besides, I think

Gracie wanted a change. Running the bagnio was enough for a while. It fitted in with her fancy to scandalise the dull folk of the city. There she was, the daughter of a wealthy and respectable merchant, acting as the madam of a fashionable brothel. That was flying in the face of convention in almost every imaginable way."

"So why change now?"

"Ah, Brock. You underestimate the power of respectable society to wear someone like Gracie down. No one would receive her. I was the only person willing to be seen with her in public settings. Being a rebel can be exciting for a while. Later it means isolation and rejection."

"It's never bothered you."

"Men have an easier time of it. Being thought of as something of a rake adds glamour to a man in the world's eyes. No, Gracie had had enough. By going to London, she hopes to escape from her reputation. Rumours may filter there from Norwich, but Londoners rarely pay much attention to anything that happens in the provinces."

"But I thought Gracie truly loved you, as you loved her," Brock protested.

"I believed she did," Foxe replied, his voice sad. "Then I spoiled it."

"How? Another woman?"

"No. Far worse than that. Gracie knew I was faithful to her—except for sleeping with her sister, of course, which didn't count for either of them. What sent Gracie away was her growing desire to get married and settle down into domestic life and motherhood. The years are passing. She calculated she needed to do it sooner rather than later."

"Gracie? Get married?"

"Why not?" Foxe said. "She will make a marvellous wife and mother. The only trouble is that she knows I'm not ready for such a step—if I ever will be. I'm not much attracted by marriage, Brock. I have no interest in getting heirs for my estate, nor in tying myself down. Gracie knew if she stayed with me, things would remain more or less as they were. I remained deaf to her hints, so she gave up."

"So she won't come back either?"

"She may. If she does, I suspect it will be as a respectable, married woman, though her reputation in Norwich is likely to be something she will never fully overcome. Far more likely that she'll settle down somewhere else, where she can stress her family's solid background and forget she ever had anything to with a brothel."

"So what will you do?" Brock asked.

"Find someone else, I expect. There's no rush. I haven't ever been much desirous of copulation without affection, but if I need a woman for a night, there's no lack in this city. No, I'll take my time and let my feelings settle. There aren't that many women willing to be a long-term mistress to an unmarried man. Marriage always looms in their minds sooner or later."

On this melancholy note, both men stared into the fire, shaking their heads over the bizarre ways of the female of the species.

"What about you and Lady Henfield?" Foxe asked after several minutes had passed. He had noticed over the past months how Brock had changed from a rugged sailing-master into a prosperous merchant of the middling sort. The effect of Lady Henfield, he assumed. Tidying the man up a little.

"What about us?" Brock said. "I like her very well and I believe she likes me. We've met several times since that ball given by the mayor. Always very proper, with someone else present and so forth. The trouble is the gap between our status in the world. She's one of the nobility and I'm a nobody."

"Hardly that, Brock. I strongly suspect you could lay your hands on a good deal more cash that that feckless brother-in-law of hers, the Earl of Pentelow. The way he's going he'll be facing bankruptcy before long."

"Makes no difference, does it? He's still an earl, whatever he does. I could be rich as Croesus and still be a nobody in their eyes. A tradesman."

"By that criterion, the mayor is a tradesman and so are all the aldermen. How many wherries and keels does your business run nowadays?"

"You should know. You're a partner."

"A sleeping partner. You do all the work and direct the business. So how many?"

"Four keels, nigh on a dozen wherries, two schooners out of Yarmouth and one out of Wells."

"There you are. You're a man of substance and significant wealth. Cheer up, Brock. To my mind, you underestimate Lady Julia. She strikes me as a gifted and determined woman, with a remarkable need to get her own way. If she wants you, she'll have what she wants, whoever stands in the way. If she doesn't, you can plead your love till Hell freezes over and it will do no good. No, my friend, she will make the decisions. All you need to do is wait and says yes to whatever she determines."

"For Heaven's sake, Foxe! You make her sound like a gorgon."

"No. Just a woman with confidence in herself. Why not? I hear she has her own money and depends on no one. So long as the man she decides on is respectable and wealthy enough, society will tut-tut a little, then accept it. You fit the bill, Brock."

"Enough of this," Brock said. "We're far from what we ought to be talking about. How are we going to find out who killed Joseph Morrow and dumped his body in that wherry?"

"You're right," Foxe said. "I wandered away from the matter in hand because it seems so impossible. We haven't enough information and speculation is pointless at this stage."

"So … what do you want me to do?"

"Start with the wherrymen. Do they know anything? Was Morrow lending out large amounts of money in that area? Was he worried about some debt that was likely to remain unpaid? If that fails, see if they know why he was wandering about the wharves. Plenty of whores there, as well as young sailors who might be willing to accept his money and his attentions."

"Still can't see it," Brock grumbled.

"No, I can't either. But we'd be foolish not to check. I'll find out about his businesses more generally. Then there's his private life and recreations. I don't much like the woman who's taken over as madam in Gracie's bagnio, so that source is one I'd prefer to leave unless there's no alternative. No … I'll try someone else first. Yes … someone who keeps his eyes and ears very much open to whatever goes on in this city, even if he keeps what he finds to himself. Now, will you dine with me?"

FOXE DIDN'T HURRY the next morning. It was the day before the next edition of *The Norfolk Intelligencer* would be published, so he knew the person he wished to talk with—Mr. Brandon Seager, the editor—would be much too busy to give his attention to anything else. So, despite his frustration at the delay in approaching his best hope for useful intelligence, he breakfasted in his normal expansive style, took his usual walk around the great Market Place of the city, and spent an hour or so drinking coffee and looking over the latest editions of the London newspapers.

As he expected, there were several mentions of Kitty. She was the talk of the fashionable theatre community. Gracie had sent him one or two letters, carefully worded, but he had not heard from Kitty in weeks. Too busy, he supposed. He was now part of her past. Her future was opening out before her and she wasn't going to miss any of it.

Thus it was that he walked back towards his home full of gloomy thoughts. He would have indulged in self-pity for some time longer, had he not been surprised by the sight of several tables set outside his shop and a substantial throng of people looking over them. Turning aside, he went in through the shop door to find out what was going on.

There he found Mrs Crombie serving one gentleman, while a small queue of women waited their turns, each holding one or more books in their hands. Since his shop had for many years attracted scarcely a single customer in a day—save for the special ones who came by appointment—the sight almost overwhelmed him.

Catching sight of him lurking by the door, Mrs Crombie called out, "Mr Foxe, can you help me serve these customers for a moment? I hate to keep people waiting, but I am here on my own, as you see."

Bemused, Mr Foxe did as he was asked. The next hour and more passed with both of them taking money, giving change and accepting the eager assurances of many customers that they would return, "as soon as new stock had been announced". Only when the throng subsided—largely because few books remained—did Foxe find an opportunity to ask what was going on.

Mrs Crombie looked alarmed.

"Have I done wrong, Mr Foxe? Have I exceeded the freedom you allow me? I thought only to increase the sales from both old and new stock and produce a greater profit by doing so. If I have been presumptuous, I can only apologise and promise not to do it again. I never thought to get your permission first, perhaps because I worked for too long with a husband who made every decision himself. Asking permission usually resulted in being blocked. Being allowed to run things as I think best has gone to my head."

"No. No." Foxe said. "You have done no wrong. Far from it. I have never seen this shop so busy, not even in my father's day. I was merely somewhat taken aback. What do these people mean by promising to come back when new stock is announced? What books are on the tables outside? I took money and thanked people for their custom, but I did not look at what they were buying."

"Most were buying the latest novels which arrived three days ago from London," Mrs Crombie said. "I know I did wrong by spending your money without your express permission, but word reached me that a bookseller my husband used to deal with was in need of money quickly. He would sell all his stock to the first person who might buy it. Everyone in London already had the same titles, so there were no takers. Here nearly all the titles have never been available before. So I sent him a letter and promised to buy all he could send for a single sum of £25.00. To be plain, it brought more books than I expected, some good and some not so good. So I placed an advertisement in the newspaper announcing new stock. You saw the result. The titles already well-known in this city I set on the tables outside and offered at one half of the usual price."

"You see," she went on. "I watched my husband ruin his business and gamble or drink away such few profits as he made. Yet he refused to let me help. To his mind, I—a mere woman—was there to cook his meals, wash his clothes, keep his house clean and bear his children ... though I failed badly in the latter respect. I had no place in the shop. When you offered me the chance to manage your business here, I was too flabbergasted to stop and consider. All those months watching our business fail and knowing how I could have improved it. All the wakeful hours at night planning what I would do, if only he had allowed it. Suddenly, there it was—the opportunity to put my ideas into practice. You told me to do as I thought fit and I took your words literally. I fear my newfound freedom has run away with me, sir."

Mr Foxe was amazed. He had imagined he was offering refuge to a woman crushed by events, seeking nothing more than peace, quiet and a way to earn a respectable living. Now he found he had obtained a shrewd businesswoman with a quick mind and the confidence to seize an opportunity. He did not quite know what to say.

Mrs Crombie became still more alarmed by his silence.

"Mr Foxe! Mr Foxe!" she cried. "Don't cast me out, I beg you. I could not bear it. I would rather throw myself into the river to drown than leave knowing I had so abused your charity and trust! If I have done wrong, I will amend. If I have spent your money unwisely, I will pay it all back, I promise."

"Cast you out?" Foxe said, coming to himself at last. "Cast you out? What on earth for? Oh, Mrs Crombie, what a marvel you are proving to be! I approve of all you've done, believe me. Nor do you need to ask me first on such matters. No. Unless you wish to spend very large amounts of my money—say a hundred pounds or more —I will accept whatever you say is needed."

Now it was Mrs Crombie's turn to look stunned.

"But ... Mr Foxe, I beg of you. Do not lay so much responsibility upon me."

"Is it too much, then?"

"Well … no. But it is so sudden."

Foxe grinned at her. "I make up my mind swiftly, Mrs Crombie. Besides, I have much else to worry about at the moment. If I know the shop is in safe hands, it is worth a good deal to be able to set all that aside and concentrate on this vexing problem of the mayor's. There is one thing, though …"

It amused him to see Mrs Crombie's face take on the worried frown again. He did not wish her to take his approval entirely for granted in all matters. There was also a certain imp of mischief that sometimes sat on his shoulder and whispered in his ear.

"Today I happened to be here to assist you. Otherwise you could not have managed so many customers. If you agree, I will let you find an assistant and employ them on whatever terms you think fit."

"An assistant! But surely, that will be a considerable expense?"

"If you attract as many customers as I saw today, it is essential."

For a while, both of them were silent. Foxe was rearranging his ideas of how he should deal with Mrs Crombie in the future. What she was considering, he could not guess—until she made the subject of her thoughts clear.

"Mr Foxe," she began. "I have been thinking a good deal about the matter you mentioned regarding the sad death of Mr Morrow and your involvement in seeking his murderer. You asked me to keep my eyes and ears open, in case any useful information might arise from gossip in the shop. Now … if you will to trust me enough to use me as your assistant in wider ways, ways outside this shop, I believe I could prove of yet further worth to you."

"How so?" Foxe asked.

"If I knew precisely the information you might need, I could employ my own means to seek it out. Once this shop is busier for more of the time, I know that it will become a regular calling-point for many of the better-off people of the city. Women mostly, I would guess, for I propose to build a reputation for having a good stock of the latest novels and romances for sale. They will also like dealing with a woman. Many will become friends. It has probably not escaped your attention …"

Here she paused for effect and smiled shyly at Foxe's rapt attention.

"… that some women like to gossip and exchange news. What better place than in the quiet and proper environs of a bookseller's shop? Should I also prompt them … point them in the right direction, so to speak … who knows what they may find themselves telling me?"

She paused again, then plunged forward to make her final point.

"You are a wealthy gentleman, Mr Foxe. As such, you will intimidate many people of the middling sort or artisans. Oh, not intentionally! But your fine clothes, your exquisite manners … your reputation. I am a nobody. I can talk easily with those who would be too afraid to speak openly in your presence."

Foxe could have kissed her, had not that been so very much against all propriety. Instead, he contented himself with earnestly endorsing her plan. Then he walked to the door, closed it and pulled down the blind to indicate the shop was shut.

"No! No!" Mrs Crombie cried out. "Let us keep regular hours, Mr Foxe. That way, people will be assured of finding us open if they make their way here. If we do not, they will be the less inclined to come. Unless it will vex you greatly, let me suggest instead that we meet in the shop after the time for closing and before I make my way to my lodging. You can tell me of anything I should be seeking from our customers, and I can tell you how much money we have taken today."

Mr Foxe agreed at once. Whatever her confidence, Mrs Crombie needed to be reassured of his support. If he wished her to free his mind of business matters, save for his special clients, he must, in return, give her ample encouragement and praise. It would scarcely be a hardship.

With all settled between them to their mutual satisfaction, Mr Foxe finally made his way into his own part of the building and settled down to make two lists: one of what he must ask the editor of *The Norfolk Intelligencer* the next day; the other of what he might ask Mrs Crombie to seek out from the bookshop's customers.

Neither list proved easy. He had so little information. It was hardly possible even to choose a direction in which conversation might be steered. In the end, Foxe determined the best course in both cases must be to raise the subject of Morrow's death and note what the other person might say. At least that might fill in some gaps in understanding how the man was seen in the city and how his death was seen. Was it put down to simple robbery, or were people considering more complex motives for murder?

LIKE MOST BOOKSELLERS of his time, Foxe's father had been a printer of pamphlets and newsletters. When the first newspapers were produced in the city, sixty years before, he had been one of those who helped set up the necessary printing works. Foxe was therefore familiar with the operations of any newspaper, and found the all-pervasive smell of ink and paper in the building more nostalgic than oppressive.

To be sure of engaging Mr Seager's attention fully enough, Foxe had sent young Charlie round first thing to enquire what might be the best time to make his visit. Now Foxe made his way through the jumble of papers and printer's paraphernalia towards the editor's desk, set on a small dais at the rear of the room. From there, Mr Seager could survey his small domain and make sure everyone was attending to their duties, as befitted one of the county's leading journals.

When Foxe entered the room, he found Mr Seager hidden behind one of his own newspapers, probably checking that his sub-editors had done their job. It was their task to remove as many as possible of the misprints and errors common to all typesetters. They had to work with tiny letters against short timescales. Seager always held back some of the typesetting to the very last moment, in case some important story arose during the early part of the night.

This wasn't the first time Foxe had seen Mr Seager that day, of course. They shared the same favourite coffeehouse. Once Seager knew the new edition was as complete as it could be, he retired to drink a dish or two of coffee, read the latest London papers and—

most important of all—to keep his eyes and ears open for whatever enticing gossip was in circulation. More than once, Foxe had used this habit to his advantage. He would discourse on something he wanted made public loudly enough to be sure Mr Seager would pick it up. There it would be in the newspaper the next publication day, usually prefixed by the phrase "We have it from a reliable source that …" Foxe was fairly sure Mr Seager knew what he was doing. However, he always played fair and ensured the 'news' he was airing had enough basis in fact to avoid the paper embarrassment.

When Foxe reached Mr Seager's desk, he seated himself in the chair set before it and prepared to interrupt the editor's reading.

"Morning, Foxe," came from behind the paper. "What do you want to know this time?"

"How did you know it was me?" Foxe asked.

"Simple. I smelled that awful pomade you put on your wig. Besides, I'm not expecting anyone else and none of my employees would dare sit down before I asked them to. Well?"

"Well what?"

"What do you want to know? We've known each other for most of our lives, and I've never known you call just to pass the time of day. Morrow, is it?"

"As it happens …"

"Nothing just 'happens' around you, Foxe. I expect the mayor and his cronies are soiling their breeches with fright. They've called you in to clear up the mess."

"You put it somewhat inelegantly, Seager, but you are correct in essence. What I want to know is all you can tell me about the Morrow family."

"Not enough time in the day for that. Nor would I ever tell anyone all I knew. Not even about you, Foxe."

"Somehow that comment doesn't give me the reassurance it ought, my friend. So … tell me as much as you are prepared to give away."

"Give? Who said anything about giving?"

Foxe sighed. He had anticipated this.

"Trade then."

"What are you offering?"

"An opportunity to print ahead of your competitors whatever I find and can make public."

"How far ahead?"

"Far enough for your paper to be on the streets with the news before it even reaches them."

"Fair enough. Very well. Sit quietly and learn from the master."

Foxe nodded. "No questions till the end? Very well."

"Ezekiel Morrow deserves his success," Mr Seager began. "He's a first-rate man of business—honest and fair, even if he tends towards the grim puritan on Sundays. He knows yarn and he knows how to spin and sell it. Thus his business grew until he retired as one of the leading yarn merchants, not just in East Anglia, but in the whole kingdom. As the fine worsteds of Norwich have dominated the market for rich fabrics, his firm has helped keep all those weavers supplied with the yarns they need. That's how he became a rich man."

"He has two sons," Seager continued. "Joseph, his heir, and James. Joseph grew up to copy all the worst aspects of his father's manner. He became ever more puritanical and self-righteous. Paraded his virtue all around the city. Used every opportunity to criticise anyone who fell below the standards he set. James and he fought all the time when they were boys, since his younger brother refused to be dominated. That's why James never joined the family business. He asked for his inheritance as soon as he was old enough to leave home. Then he went to Yarmouth and used it to apprentice himself to a brewer. A brewer! And his brother so loud against all who took alcohol in any form! Everyone saw it as a slap in the face, even old Ezekiel. They more or less disowned him."

Seager was an outstanding storyteller and in the Morrow family he had a first-rate subject. Foxe was entranced as he unfolded their complex and often contentious history.

After the break with James, Ezekiel took it into his head to let Joseph run things. Like numerous wealthy businessmen before him, he bought an estate on the edge of the city. Then he stepped aside from active participation in the firm and attempted to turn himself into a country gentleman. However, there was a great difference between the two Morrow sons. Mr James, Seager said, worked hard to be successful. He was willing to do even the most menial tasks to ensure he knew as much as possible about the business of brewing and the supply of wines and spirits. When he completed his apprenticeship, he took jobs with several different brewers in the area. He went as far away as London to learn more of managing dealings on a large scale. He was also careful with his money against the day he would want to set up in business on his own.

Joseph, on the other hand, seemed to find everything about the yarn trade distasteful. Maybe he thought himself too fine for the small weaving operations he had to sell to. He certainly alienated a good number of them by pressing for higher prices and quicker payment. The firm's yarn was still good, but many chose to go elsewhere to avoid dealing with Joseph. Gradually, sales and profits fell.

Joseph would have sold out, if he could, but his father was still a partner and wouldn't agree. So Joseph left the running of the yarn warehouse to managers and busied himself with a different venture —banking.

"Morrow & Son soon became significant in local banking," Mr Seager explained. "It's not the largest lender, but it's generally reckoned to be the most secure. Joseph Morrow's puritanical approach means he won't make loans to anyone he thinks 'unworthy'. That includes anyone engaged in speculation or without the safest kinds of security to offer. By these means he has been able to take all the deposits he needs, while paying at least a half-percent less in interest. There are many about the city who are happy to get $4\frac{1}{2}$ percent interest with safety, rather than 5 percent with more risk."

Brother James' opportunity to set out on his own came sooner than he expected. The brewer he had served his apprenticeship with in Yarmouth died without a male heir, so his widow approached James to help her run the business. He accepted. Soon he had considerably increased its sales and added a number of tenanted public houses to the estate. Finally, he married the widow's daughter and bought out his mother-in-law's interest with a generous annuity. Thus he became the owner of the most successful brewing business in Great Yarmouth and soon extended his business into Norwich as well.

Seager fell silent.

"Is that it?" Foxe asked.

"More or less."

"What about the manners and character of each of them?" Foxe said.

"Ezekiel makes an unconvincing gentleman. He lacks the right education and has little interest in learning or culture. He isn't an outdoor kind of person either. He never learned to ride well enough to take part in a fox hunt and he shoots indifferently at best. Wounds the birds, if he hits them at all. Most of true gentry see him as an upstart and avoid his company when they can. The result is that he must spend a good deal of his time on his own, wandering around his estate and getting under the feet of his servants. In short, Ezekiel Morrow is what he has always been, a blunt man of business. Now I hear his health is failing, so he can only leave his grand house to go to Bath or some other spa to seek a cure."

"James?"

"Excellent businessman, good father and husband. Generally well liked by everyone. He can be hard on debtors, I hear tell, but so can almost anyone in business. No major vices."

"What about the dead man, Joseph?"

"Widely disliked, even loathed. Said to be a tyrant within his household, but almost nobody visits, so that could be wishful thinking. Difficult to tell how good he is at business. The yarn firm is dying slowly, as I said. Never a good idea to leave it all to managers. They have little interest beyond doing as well for themselves as possible. Still, I doubt any of them would try outright embezzlement. Joseph would be delighted to see anyone who did that hang. Indeed, he'd probably hang them himself, if he could. All the time he would sigh over their wickedness and promise them everlasting torments in Hell. The banking side? I don't know. It seems sound enough."

"Only seems?"

"Show me a bank and I'll show you a business that's rumoured to be in trouble. Let's just say there are twenty or more merchants acting as bankers in this city. Nineteen of those will have a shakier reputation than Morrow and Son."

It seemed that Foxe had come up against a blank wall. Most of this information he already knew. Either Seager was holding back something more interesting, or he knew little more than Foxe did. It was probably the latter. Brandon Seager was a clever operator in the world of newspapers, but Foxe had never found him to be dishonest in his personal dealings.

Brock too returned more or less empty handed. When he and Foxe met later that afternoon in a corner of the main room of The Maid's Head Inn, he had little to offer beyond some confirmation of their current knowledge.

"Morrow was comprehensively hated, so far as I can tell," Brock said. "The only ones who supported him were puritanical bigots like himself. Even they seemed to find him something of a trial. I could find plenty of people who supposed him a hypocrite, but none had firm evidence to back up their suspicions. Most distrusted him on the principle that someone who protested his virtue so much must have something to hide."

He took a long pull at the tankard of beer Foxe had set before him and shook his head sadly.

"The only strange thing I found was the extent to which Morrow preserved his privacy. No one I met had ever been able to cross the threshold. He didn't entertain. His wife—yes, he has one, but no children—didn't receive visitors either, or wasn't allowed to. Indeed, she rarely goes out, except to that Independent Calvinist Chapel he makes so much of. Even the servants are kept on such a close rein they don't mix with other servants. I was told he has a deep hatred of gossip. That he is furious with any from his house who spread word abroad of what goes on inside. I also learned he has difficulty getting and keeping servants in the normal way. Those who work there rarely last long. He manages to intimidate them so much none will talk about their experiences either. Either that or they move to other towns."

"That sounds odd to me," Foxe said.

"To me too," Brock replied. "Even so, it works. I couldn't find a single person who would admit to having worked for him."

"So how does he manage for servants?" Foxe said.

"Get's 'em from the Houses of Industry and the orphanages. He pretends it's for the sake of showing charity to poor children who need a start in life. The reality seems to be he can pay them nearly nothing. They're also young enough to be browbeaten into obeying his household rules."

"And these hapless children survive and learn in his household?"

"Maybe. I managed to pick up one rumour that any of the boys who show signs of rebellion are quickly 'persuaded' to enlist in the army or handed over to the Press Gang. Either way, they're unlikely ever to return. I haven't heard about the girls."

"Don't be downhearted, Brock. Tomorrow may bring better fortune to us both. You have done better than I have today. It's almost as if Joseph Morrow anticipated people might try to find out about the details of his life and took action beforehand to prevent that happening. I'll spend some time this evening trying to work out some new avenues we might follow. You and I are not defeated yet, my friend. Not by a long way!"

3

THE STORM BREAKS

WHEN FOXE RETURNED FROM HIS MORNING WALK THE NEXT DAY, HE entered through the bookshop to speak to Mrs Crombie. He was not just being polite. He wished to observe the changes she was making in his name without appearing to be snooping on her.

As he came into the shop, he was amazed to see young Charlie Dillon, the urchin boy he used to take messages about the city, struggling with a broom larger than himself. Mrs Crombie must have set him to sweeping the shop floor. Now he was brushing away with a will and sending clouds of dust up to the ceiling.

"Good morning, Mr Foxe," came a voice from the lady herself. She was temporarily hidden from sight by the dust cloud Charlie was raising. "Stay there for a moment, if you please. Let me tell Charlie how to sweep the floor without making the whole shop dirty while he does it."

Foxe stood still as he was told. To his surprise, Charlie listened attentively, then nodded to show he understood. It seemed Mrs Crombie knew how to change a wild, unbiddable child into a model servant. Foxe was impressed.

"Now, Mr Foxe," Mrs Crombie said at last. "I think it will be safe to proceed without covering your fine clothes in dirt. Was there something you wanted to speak to me about? I hope you don't mind me spending a few pence of your money on paying this boy to do some cleaning? I noticed him hanging about and thought his hands would be better employed in useful work than getting into mischief. I imagine his family will be glad of the extra."

"I'm sure they will," Foxe said. "I applaud your action. You're a marvel, Mrs Crombie. It has always been as much as I could do to send young Charlie on my various errands. I never thought to see him with a broom."

"I'm good at sweeping," Charlie said proudly. "Missus Crombie say I be."

"Says I am, Charlie," Mrs Crombie said. Foxe was taken aback to hear Charlie repeat the correct words, then get an approving nod.

"Now, Charlie," Mrs Crombie continued, "Mr Foxe and I need to talk for a few moments. You can either go back outside until I call you, or sit quietly in the corner on that stool."

"Outside," Charlie said. "Then I can take the dirt with me. Just wave when you wants … want … me again."

"Now, what did you require of me, Mr Foxe?" Mrs Crombie said.

"Merely to wish you a good morning," Foxe replied. "However, the miracle you have wrought with Charlie Dillon has near taken my breath away."

"Having him hanging around outside the shop isn't good for trade, Mr Foxe. He won't go away in case you have a job for him. So I thought it better to give him a job inside and make him look less of a budding criminal."

Foxe shook his head in wonder. It had never occurred to him that a boy like Charlie would come in off the streets, even for a few moments. What else had never occurred to him, he wondered; about this frustrating murder case, for example. Was he getting too set in his ways?

"Before you leave, Mr Foxe," Mrs Crombie said, "I have one or two minor pieces of information about Mr Morrow to pass on."

"Already?"

"The topic is widespread in conversation amongst the people of the city, Mr Foxe. The gentleman was not well liked, but he was well known. There is much conjecture about whether his death was caused by robbers or due to some different reason."

Halloran would not like to hear this, Foxe thought. The mayor was adamant that everyone should be encouraged to accept the notion of a robbery. If that ruse was failing so soon …

"Have you heard what is being suggested instead?" Foxe asked, as casually as he could.

"Nothing specific yet, as I hear it. Robbery is still seen as the most credible explanation. However, several persons have recounted a strong rumour going about. It seems the man could be brutal in dealing with servants who defied the rules set in his household. Few would stay long, save those unfortunates from the House of Industry who had little choice. Even some of those ran away."

"He was a man who liked firm discipline, Mrs Crombie."

"A little more than that, sir. Tales exist, it seems, of beatings and locking offenders in cupboards for days at a time with neither food nor drink."

"Surely exaggerations."

"Perhaps. Still, there must have been something to start such rumours going abroad. Shall I keep listening?"

"By all means, Mrs Crombie. Even if such tales are false, they show how people's minds are working. Since Mr Joseph Morrow was so disliked, maybe any discreditable rumour will be seized upon."

"I was also told that Mrs Morrow is rarely, if ever, seen abroad. She brought him a considerable dowry at her marriage, I believe. She was also thought to be a little too free in her behaviour for the godly Calvinist family to which she belonged. Rather than risk scandal, her father married her off at the first opportunity. Mr Joseph Morrow was an acceptable husband, given his family's wealth and his father's connection with several groups of Dissenters. It was not expected he would become the austere puritan he now seems to be."

"You have discovered more of use than Captain Brock and I have, Mrs Crombie, even with our combined efforts. Pray continue as you have begun. If you will, listen especially for anything bearing on Mr Morrow's dealings with the sundry tradespeople of the city. His family must buy food and clothing. Did he pay his bills promptly? Did tradespeople care to deal with his household? The rich are prone to treat tradespeople without the regard for politeness and propriety they apply with one another. Thus one may sometimes glimpse what goes on behind the mask presented to the world."

Mrs Crombie promised to do as she was asked. It seemed a good number of ladies who had investigated the shop were the wives of small shopkeepers and traders. They would know what their husbands thought of Joseph Morrow.

Foxe had just gone through into his house proper, when he heard the doorbell ringing. Alfred, his manservant, hastened to answer it, then brought Foxe a message. Alderman Halloran was most eager to speak with him and had sent a servant to ask how quickly Mr Foxe could attend him at his home.

Something new must have arisen.

Such was his haste that Foxe did not stop to change his waistcoat for something more appropriate to a visit to the mayor's right-hand man. Nor did he suffer the delay of waiting for a chair. Instead, he replaced his coat, seized his third-best hat and set out at once to walk the modest distance from his shop, behind the grand church of St. Peter Mancroft, to Alderman Halloran's house across the water in Colegate.

It was obvious the alderman was in a distraught state. He barely attempted the usual pleasantries. Instead, he blurted out the news which had caused him to call for Foxe's presence without delay.

"It's the Morrow bank," he said. "Old Ezekiel has been forced to step back into running the Morrow businesses. He knows yarn— though it's clear that side of Morrow's trade has been declining for some time. What he does not know is banking. Out of his depth. Trouble is, his son kept everything about that business in his own hands. Even his chief clerk seems to be at something of a loss. No one knows which loans are outstanding, what interest is due to be paid, and which debts—if any—have gone bad."

"That's only to be expected, I suppose," Foxe said. "Still, everyone knows it's a sound business. Given time, those who must now run it will find out what they need."

"That's the worst part, Foxe. You and I—and the mayor and just about everyone else—assumed the business is solid. It never occurred to any of us it might be otherwise …"

Oh, Good Lord. That troublesome phrase again. Was Foxe doomed to find it haunting him at every turn?

"Trouble is, it might not be. Ezekiel Morrow has sent word to the mayor. He wants someone discreet, with sound banking knowledge, to help them unravel the state of the banking business. Quietly, of course. No one wants to start rumours flying, or we'll have a run on all the banks right away. The mayor has asked a Mr Allday, a merchant and banker from King's Lynn, to step in and help. That's fair enough. However, some of us are now questioning what he might find."

"Do you expect any problems?"

"That's just it. No one knows. Business is mostly a matter of trust. Undermine that trust, even with tittle-tattle, and things can run away from you. Any progress at your end, Foxe? If I could tell the mayor you were on the track of, say, a common thief, it would lay most of these rumours to rest. Uncertainty, see? Business thrives on certainty, not its opposite. Anything that suggests things may not be as they seem is seen as grounds for panic. A group of businessmen is like a gaggle of spinster aunts coming upon a brothel. They can't see inside and nothing is happening outside, but the mere idea of it is enough to give 'em the vapours and send them running for home."

"I've known men kill themselves to avoid a business scandal, alderman, but that can't be the case here. You cannot strangle yourself, not even on a wherry—and he didn't hang himself or we would have found the noose around his neck. Even if there are problems with Morrow & Son, they are unlikely to have any bearing on the man's murder."

"Never said they did. It's just a damned inconvenient coincidence. Fellow gets murdered and draws attention to himself. His business may or may not have a serious problem. Stands to reason the one will affect the other. Hard to keep everything quiet when people are already wondering about the robbery."

"Hmm …" Foxe said. "I hear that some haven't accepted that explanation. It seems there's a good deal of speculation about the man's family and personal life."

"God in Heaven, it gets worse!"

"Calm down, alderman. The best thing will be to say nothing. That goes for the mayor as well. If you're seen to be doing anything out of the ordinary it will add to the speculations. Wait until Mr Allday can find out for certain what state the bank is in. There's nothing for the rumour-mongers in an experienced banker being called in. Everyone knows Ezekiel Morrow is a yarn merchant, pure and simple. An outside expert will calm nerves, not inflame them. What is more sensible in this situation than for Ezekiel Morrow to seek help from other bankers? When you put it like that, the news should calm a good many fears."

"Foxe, you're a gem! I'll tell the mayor what you have said. He's such a simpleton! You would scarce believe how perturbed he had become."

"I'm sure you can reassure him, sir. He trusts you implicitly, as I hear."

The alderman preened himself.

"He does, Foxe," he said. "Without my imperturbable advice, he would be lost. So, do you have any other news?"

"Not really," Foxe said. "These are still early days. As yet, all seems as it ought to be. Joseph Morrow was not liked, but no one seems to have wished him dead. Nor is there any evidence that might help us fathom what he was doing by the wherry wharves."

"Could he have been killed elsewhere and taken there afterwards?"

"He could, but why? He was a man of at least normal height.

No single person could carry such a dead weight far. Two men could, but again, why would they? If the body had been concealed in some way, it might make sense of a kind. His body was there, almost in the open, exactly where it must be found the next morning —as it was. Besides, if he died somewhere else, where was that? Such imaginings take us no further."

"Oh well, I must be patient again, I suppose. Now, Foxe. Another matter. What is this I hear about your shop being so busy? I hope you will not be distracted from the task the mayor has given you?"

"You need not worry. Mrs Crombie will be running that whole side of the business."

"But she's a *woman*, Foxe. I mean … I am as fond of the fair sex as most men, but they do not have the … manner … no … wherewithal …"

"Brain?"

"They are best suited to domestic matters. Their minds are not as … er, robust … as a man's."

"I can assure you, alderman, that Mrs Crombie is equal to any man in running a bookseller's shop. Probably superior to most. You may remember her husband's shop. It was in one of the courts off King Street."

"That place? I went there but once and found it poorly stocked and the owner surly and unpleasant. That is hardly a recommendation for this woman."

"On the contrary. Her husband drank and gambled away the profits and refused to allow her any part in the business. While she watched him destroy their livelihood, she considered ways in which she could have done things better. Three months ago, her husband killed himself rather than face the public shame of bankruptcy. I found her in despair and offered her the chance to work with me. I wanted to restore her self-respect."

"An act of charity, then."

"Yes. That was how it began. However, I am now finding my reward for that common kindness. It is far greater than any benefit she has derived from me. She has been involved with the shop for scarcely a month and has transformed it out of all measure."

"My wife and nieces are eager consumers of novels and suchlike feminine trash, when they can find them. They read so quickly they soon exhaust such funds as I allow to buy those trifles. Without my restraining them, they would seek out new titles every week."

"As would many other ladies in this city and its environs, I imagine. Mrs Crombie recently bought a large consignment of the latest novels from a London bookseller. That is why the shop was thronged with purchasers. She is not such a poor hand at business as you suggest."

"By God, Foxe! It never occurred to me …"

"Don't say that!" Foxe interrupted. "That phrase is starting to haunt me, I swear. Every time I hear it, it reminds me how narrow my outlook has become; how swiftly I ignore important matters that fall beyond its reach. I am thinking those few words may even hold the key to this mystery of Joseph Morrow's death."

The alderman stared, perplexed.

"I will be on my way, with your permission, alderman," Foxe said. "There is much to do. Do you know if anyone has spoken with Mr James Morrow, the dead man's brother?"

"Not to my knowledge, Foxe. He lives in Great Yarmouth, I believe."

"Then I will send him a message at once, requesting a meeting. Someone must know more about Joseph Morrow's life and business dealings. I hesitate to bother his grieving father at such a time. The brother will have to do. Good day to you, alderman. I pray you, when you have the leisure, talk with Mrs Crombie and discover for yourself the miracles she has accomplished."

FOXE AND BROCK met to exchange news at the end of a long day. The light was failing. Molly, Foxe's maidservant, had just been in to light the candles. Now they reflected in the mirrors set between the windows to the street and from the fine, polished wood and glass of the two cabinets. The soft light, plus the flickering from the fire, made the room feel suitably comforting.

They were sitting in the small parlour. Each held a glass of fine brandy as an aid to pondering what little they knew. The perfumed smoke from Foxe's expensive cigar mingled with the ranker smell of the tobacco in Brock's pipe. Like most sailors, he had taken to a pipe early in life. He still considered it superior to what he called "those fancy things" that Foxe smoked.

"You know, Brock," Foxe said, "I'm beginning to believe we're looking in the wrong places to find clues to this murder."

"You may be right," Brock said. "So far, I've found little more than we knew already. There aren't any wherry or ship owners who used Morrow & Son for loans. Joseph thought seafaring too chancy a trade to risk money on it. One bad storm and all his loan security would be at the bottom of the ocean. Even wherries have been known to be sunk in bad spots along the rivers. You can get 'em up again, of course, but the cost's often more than the boat's worth."

"What about the tradesmen who supplied Morrow's household?"

"They hated him, most of them, but he was too important in the city to upset. The usual story. Complaining all the time, then taking months to pay his accounts. One small thing, though. Several I spoke with said the delays in payment had been getting even worse. They used to be able to get something once a quarter. Recently, he'd taken to paying some only twice in the year."

"Interesting. That's the kind of behaviour you usually associate with a man who's running out of funds. But Joseph was a wealthy man. Was he simply mean?"

"Maybe. Then again, everyone assumed he was wealthy. It never occurred to any of them …"

Foxe groaned and banged the heel of his right hand on his forehead.

"Are you feeling ill, Foxe?" Brock said.

"No, Brock. Just infuriated by that phrase. It hadn't occurred to either of us to suspect Joseph Morrow was in financial trouble. It hadn't occurred to me to reflect whether he was involved in dealings with people we wouldn't expect. More hasn't occurred to me than has! I am being driven distracted by those words. Each time I hear them, they reproach me for my stupidity."

"Calm down, old friend. I made no accusations …"

"Not you, Brock. I'm condemning myself. The only thing we have found so far is an inkling that Joseph Morrow's finances might not be as sound as they appear. Why didn't I consider that from the start? Because suicide was clearly impossible and …" He groaned in frustration. "It never occurred to me that he might be in need of funds. This might be the breakthrough we need, Brock."

"How so?"

"Well, it opens the possibility of blackmail, for a start. What if Joseph Morrow had some dark secret? Suppose someone found out about it. Given his constant harping on his righteousness and godly ways, proof of wrong-doing would fall on him like a thunderbolt. You said yourself that no one liked the man. Imagine what the gossips would do with some mud to soil that spotless image."

"But you said yourself you couldn't imagine the man using whores. Molly-boys? Even less likely. The word would soon have got about in either case."

"Not every cause of blackmail has to be about sex, Brock. What about doubtful financial dealings, embezzlement or even fraud? Then there's wife-beating, abusing your children …"

"He has none."

"Don't be pedantic, Brock. These are just ideas."

By now, Foxe was feeling elated. At last he had some notion of what to do next.

"We need to look amongst the lower classes, Brock. Servants, those who toil over the books in Morrow's bank, the workers in his yarn warehouses, even delivery boys."

"I'll start tomorrow."

"No. That won't work. Like me, you've become too fine a gentleman to move easily amongst such people. They won't speak freely to either of us. What we need is someone who will be accepted among them. Someone who can ask questions and not raise suspicion."

"That's a tall order. This city is plagued by government spies. Start asking questions and you'll be marked down as an informer for the Revenue—or one of those busy sniffing out sedition."

"Not if you're already well-known and generally liked. A stranger would be useless. So would someone who had never been disposed to gossip before."

"Gossip? You need a woman, then," Brock said.

"Men gossip just as much. Sit quietly in any inn or coffeehouse and what you'll hear will be either gossip, boasting or a mixture of the two."

For a few minutes, both men sat silent, enjoying their tobacco and taking sips of brandy. Then Foxe sat upright.

"Mrs Crombie!" he cried. "Of course. She told me so herself."

"The lady in your shop? Surely not, Foxe. She couldn't wander into inn tap-rooms or gossip over ale with cobblers and market traders."

"Not her in person, but I'll bet she'll know someone who could —or even several people. Her husband was a freeman, but certainly not a gentleman. She's lived among the middling sort and the artisan class. We don't want to go right to the bottom, Brock. I can't see some day-labourer or humble servant being able to blackmail a man like Joseph Morrow. Any accusation they made would be ignored the moment he denied it—even if it was true. No magistrate or judge would accept the word of a labourer against that of a wealthy, upstanding member of the city elite—even if they found the man as offensive as the rest of us."

"True enough, I suppose."

"She already offered to speak with any ladies she thought might be useful. Now we need someone to talk with their menfolk in the same way."

"Do you think Mrs Crombie would be willing to suggest anyone?"

"It's worth asking, Brock. I'm beginning to believe she can perform miracles."

"She's a handsome woman too," Brock mused. "Not quite beautiful, but nicely put together, as they say. I wouldn't mind …"

"Keep your hands and ideas to yourself, Brock," Foxe warned. "I need that lady free to run my shop. Stick to trying to win over Lady Julia."

"No chance," Brock said in a morose tone. "Beyond my reach, whatever you say."

4

THE BOOK THIEVES

NEXT MORNING, FOXE WENT ONCE AGAIN TO SPEAK TO MRS Crombie before setting out on his walk to the coffeehouse. He had no need to go outside. Instead, he used the narrow passageway that ran from the far right-hand end of his hallway to a door opening directly into the shop. He was feeling sluggish and out-of-sorts, probably as a result of too much brandy shared with Brock the previous evening. If he didn't do it right away, he feared he would forget.

Mrs Crombie, in sharp contrast, appeared full of energy and eagerness. She had reordered several book stacks, she told him. Next she would sit down to draw up fresh orders to the London booksellers and publishers. She wanted to add to the stock of novels, books on cookery and housekeeping and other useful sources of information for the housewives of Norwich. It made Foxe exhausted to watch her hustling and bustling around the place.

Asking her to stay still for a moment, Foxe explained his need for someone—maybe several people—who could move easily amongst the petty tradesmen, shopkeepers and market traders of the city.

"And their families," Mrs Crombie added. "Don't forget them. The men may be ready to gossip of an evening over a pint or two of ale or porter, but the women will be open to a chat almost any time during the day. Try to talk to their husbands then and you'd be told they're too busy for such stuff."

She didn't know at once of someone suitable to talk with the menfolk, she told Foxe, but she would look around. Of course, it might take several days to pick on the right person, talk with them and secure their co-operation. A generous scale of payment might speed things a little.

Foxe offered to pay whatever she thought necessary, so long as it was not outrageous.

"Might I use the services of young Charlie?" she asked. "If I could send him with messages, it would save waiting until I had time myself."

"Please do," Foxe said. "Just beware of his natural tendency to try to cheat you. One penny is the amount I have agreed with him for carrying a message within this part of the city. Two pence if he must go into the Great Ward over the river. No more than that, save in special circumstances when he must run both ways. He'll probably try to convince you I pay him more."

"I'll be careful," Mrs Crombie said, smiling. "He's not entirely the rapscallion you think he is, Mr Foxe."

"Maybe, but he has the makings of a successful market trader. They usually fit their prices to the outfit worn by the customer. Look well-dressed and the price doubles."

"That sounds like bitter experience," Mrs Crombie said with a laugh. "I suspect when you come along in one of your fancy waistcoats, they multiply their prices by at least four."

"I would be hurt if they did not," Foxe said. "Those waistcoats cost me a pretty penny."

"And worth it I am sure. Now, sir. If you have completed what you wanted to tell me, perhaps I might give you my own news. It's thin fare, I'm afraid, but it may lead somewhere in time. You know that Mr Joseph Morrow was a leading light in that Independent Calvinist Chapel?"

Foxe said that he did.

"Well, one of the customers yesterday afternoon was a regular chatter-box. I encouraged her, naturally, and it wasn't long before she was recounting most of her life story. She attends the Octagon Chapel every Sunday. I'm sure you know it. The congregation call themselves Presbyterians, but they're really Unitarians. Being a Unitarian openly is still illegal, as I hear. Stuff and nonsense!"

Foxe hoped this was heading somewhere useful. He had little interest in any kind of religion and Mrs Crombie's enthusiasm for life was making his headache worse.

"Last Sunday—that's only a day or so after Mr Morrow was killed—everyone at the Octagon was shocked to see Mrs Morrow, his wife, joining the congregation for the morning service. She had never been there before. I think they all assumed, as you would, that her husband required she attend the same place of worship as he did. Those Calvinists see every other congregation as foul heretics. They don't allow the members of their congregation to mix in any way, on pain of expulsion."

"It's certainly curious behaviour," Foxe said. Despite his apathy, he knew many took their allegiance to a specific church or sect earnestly.

"No one made a fuss, of course, though the minister did make it his business to express his condolences when the service ended. One or two of the ladies—including the one I was talking to, I expect—tried to strike up a conversation with Mrs Morrow, but she slipped away as soon as she could."

"Hmm," Foxe said. "I wonder if she'll be there again next Sunday?"

"Exactly my thought, Mr Foxe. That's why I thought I might be there as well. Two strangers together, as you might say. What could be more natural than sitting together to give one another support? Two recent widows too. It would be no lie to remark that I know what she must be going through. Aye, and how tired you become with strangers offering well-meaning but unwanted advice and company. All you really need is a sympathetic ear and a shoulder to weep upon."

"Heavens, Mrs Crombie," Foxe said, "You have as much cunning as any fox—and I should know. I was wasting my breath in warning you about young Charlie's nose for opportunity. You are by far his superior in wiliness. Mine too! I shall need to take care that you do not take over my whole business and put me onto the street!"

"How you exaggerate, sir!" Mrs Crombie said. "You know I would never consider such underhand behaviour. Nor would I do anything to harm you. No, Mr Foxe, I am your most humble servant and will never forget it, I assure you."

"I was only jesting," Foxe said. "Press on with your plan, Mrs Crombie. If it works, you will have proved yourself as clever in the business of seeking out information as you are in the matter of selling books."

FOXE WAS NOT sure what to do next. He had sent a letter to Mr James Morrow, the dead man's younger brother, by the first available carrier, but it could not arrive until late in the day. It might not even be opened before the next morning. He was unlikely to receive a reply before the day after that at the earliest. No, even if James sent a letter by the fastest means, Foxe would not get it before evening. That made three days from now. Foxe could not be in Great Yarmouth until late the following day—probably too late for a visit. Four days then—perhaps five. He was not even certain James would agree to talk with him; or give the arrangement anything like the level of urgency Foxe wished.

There was no option but to wait with whatever patience he could muster. That was not much at present. Could he find some way of occupying his mind in the interim?

At length, after considering and rejecting a range of options linked to the death of Joseph Morrow, Foxe decided he might as well turn to something connected with his own part of the bookseller business. The more he considered this, the better it looked. In dealing with the purchase and sale of rare books to collectors, Foxe had few peers, even in London. It would be good to remind himself of that. Over the past few days, he had been feeling superfluous. Mrs Crombie needed no help from him to run a shop devoted to the normal stock a bookseller handled. Indeed, she was grasping the opportunity to act independently with such ardour that Foxe found himself hesitating to step through the doors of his own shop, in case she might feel herself spied upon.

It would be best to stick to the areas where she could not go and content himself with that. After all, he was the one who had given her her head. It would be churlish to go back on it, just because he was feeling melancholy.

That decided, Foxe pulled himself together and pondered where he could be of greatest use. Of course! He'd promised the spendthrift Earl of Pentelow he would go to the earl's mansion as soon as he could to see if he might be able to raise the latest sum the earl needed.

The foolish man was always in debt, generally to pay for more losses at the gambling tables in London. He cared nothing for literature, learning or anything, it seemed, beyond whoring and gambling. Now he was a regular user of Foxe's services to sell valuable books from the last earl's outstanding collection.

So frequently was the present earl in need of money, he had given his staff a general instruction to allow Foxe to enter the house and bear away whatever he chose from the library, even in their master's absence. It would take Foxe only two hours to reach Kelham Hall. There would be plenty of daylight left to find enough books to bring back.

Foxe spent two happy hours in the earl's magnificent—but already sadly depleted—library. Though Pentelow cared not a whit what he took, so long as it raised a good sum, Foxe had set himself the task of selecting the smallest number of books needed to raise the desired amount. To exercise his mind and judgement still further, he had long ago determined never to purchase any book without knowing, in advance, who would be willing to buy it.

As he had hoped, this dual exercise of mind and memory occupied all his attention. He didn't return home until just before the time for dinner. When he did not have visitors—which was most of the time—Foxe never bothered to change into formal dining dress.

Provided he reached his house in time to remove his coat and hat
and wash his hands, he was ready to eat right away.

On his return that day, however, he found an urgent message
from Halloran asking him to visit the alderman at his home as soon
as possible. Damnation, Foxe thought. There must be something
unusual afoot.

Foxe considered the time. The alderman would probably be at
table now, as Foxe hoped to be shortly. Better to allow enough time
for the meal to be completed properly before presenting himself.
Foxe was feeling hungry—a state made worse by the delicious smells
emerging from the kitchen to the rear of the house. He would send
Alfred, his manservant, with a message that he had only just
returned from business outside the city and would attend on the
alderman promptly at 7:00 pm.

FOXE FOUND Halloran in a shocking state. The man looked haggard
and declared he had not slept a wink the night before. Had someone
close to him died? It seemed that was not the case. What had
destroyed the alderman's peace of mind—and seemed set to destroy
his health as well—was the discovery that some books had been
pilfered from his library.

"Last night," the alderman said, "I decided to spend a little time
with my books before retiring to bed. I do that quite often. It helps
me to calm my thoughts. Especially when my colleagues or the
mayor have been more than usually tiresome. At first, I noticed
nothing amiss. It was only when I tried to take one of my favourite
books from its place that I found it missing. Missing, Foxe! As you
can imagine, I searched everywhere I thought I might have set it
down and forgotten it, but to no avail. I could not find it."

"No one in the house might have borrowed it?" Foxe asked.

"Certainly not! All know that I protect my books with the
greatest vigilance. Even my family will not enter the library without
my permission."

"A servant?"

"Even less likely. I once caught a new footman going in there without asking me first. He swore he had touched nothing, but I still dismissed him on the spot."

"Hmm," Foxe said. "Even so, it was dark. Searching with a candle is never too effective."

"Exactly what I told myself, Foxe. This morning, as soon as it was fully light, I returned to the library, fully expecting to establish that I had simply missed the book before. It was not so. I searched and searched, but could not find it."

"Hmm," Foxe said.

"It was this diligent searching that produced the next blow," Halloran continued. "At least a dozen more books are missing. A dozen! Some of my choicest volumes! I felt as if I had been stabbed in the heart. You must set everything else aside, Foxe, and find my books. Let it be your highest priority. You know how I love my library. I feel as you would if your wife had been violated by some intruder while you slept. It's intolerable!"

Foxe reminded the alderman that he was already engaged fully in investigating the death of Joseph Morrow. He pointed out that Halloran had told him the mayor had made that the greatest priority. That the prosperity of the city and its businesses would be at stake if Morrow & Sons bank were to collapse. None of this weighed a jot with the alderman. He brushed each objection aside with a grunt of contempt.

"Look, Foxe," he said. "I've said what I want. I'll deal with the mayor, if he complains."

Foxe doubted this would work, but it was useless to argue further with Halloran in such an emotional state. He allowed himself to be led into the library to examine the scene of the crime.

"See," Halloran said, pointing to one of the many book stacks that filled the room. "The damned thief was cunning. He's replaced the missing books with others, so the gap they left wouldn't be noticed. He even chose books of roughly the same size and colour of binding. If I hadn't been looking so carefully, it would have been weeks before I noticed what he had done."

"Can you give me a list of what has been stolen, alderman?"

Foxe asked. "If I contact my friends in the trade, we should be able to catch the thief in the act of trying to sell what he has taken. Were they taken at random, or can you see any pattern to the theft?"

"Pattern?" the alderman shouted. "Of course there was a damned pattern! He's chosen some of my finest books, the scoundrel!"

"Odd," Foxe mused. "A common thief would hardly know which books to steal amongst so many. What of the books he used to replace those missing?"

"See for yourself," Halloran said. "There … and there … and there, for example."

"That's peculiar," Foxe mused. "These books are quite desirable in themselves. Assuming the thief brought them along specially—itself a further risk—you would expect him to have gone to some seedy store and selected anything that might appear roughly the same on the outside as those he took. Yet now I think of it, that's equally hard to explain. How did he know what the bindings of the volumes he stole looked like? Many purchasers of important works have them bound specially to order. They want their shelves to show a uniform appearance. Even if the thief had seen the exact same title in some other library, it would be no guide to how your copy might be bound. Have you had any visitors to your library recently? Any collectors not well known to you? Any strangers expressing an interest?"

"None," the alderman said sadly. "As you can imagine, I do not trumpet abroad that I have so many books of value. There are a good many collectors quite well known to me who have never set foot in this room."

"Even so," Foxe said, "our thief must have been able to come and view these shelves in advance. Note down which books were where and how they were bound. Any other visitors to your house recently, sir? Perhaps he took care not to reveal his interest in your collection, lest he be suspected later."

"Again, none," Halloran said. "My wife and I rarely entertain. Just the typical rotation of dinner parties amongst the better-class merchants of the city. Nor, before you suggest it, could any of them have found an occasion to slip in here unnoticed. I keep the door locked at all times. There are only two keys. One I keep myself and the other is held by my wife. She assures me she gives the key to no one, save by my instruction."

It so happened that, as Foxe was leaving, the lady herself came to bid him farewell, accompanied by two young girls. Mrs Halloran had known Foxe for many years, even before she married the alderman. She would have considered it most impolite to allow him to come and go without a kindly greeting. Her husband, being entirely caught up in his own troubles, had whisked Foxe into the library almost as soon as he had arrived.

Mrs Halloran greeted Foxe warmly and introduced her two nieces, Miss Maria and Miss Lucy Halloran, the daughters of the alderman's younger brother. Their parents were abroad, she explained, residing in Leghorn for several months in connection with the business of The East India Company. They had therefore sent their daughters on a visit during their absence. After that, she enquired of Foxe's health and business, as befitted a polite hostess. She had, she told him, been curious enough on hearing of the unusual activity at his shop to go there herself. Thus she had encountered Mrs Crombie and her inquisitiveness had been aroused still further.

"She seems a most capable and obliging young woman, Mr Foxe," she said. "Where did you find her?"

That naturally drew forth a suitably edited version of Mrs Crombie's previous troubles, to which Mrs Halloran responded with genuine distress.

"It is a harsh world, Mr Foxe," she commented, "especially for women. I have told my nieces here it is vital they develop their minds and capabilities to the full. However well they marry, you never know when they may be thrown unexpectedly upon their own resources."

At her remark, the girls blushed prettily and glanced at each other, the way young people do when some adult has spoken about them in an embarrassing way. They appeared to Foxe to be polite, well-behaved young ladies, so he smiled at them indulgently. That produced still more blushes.

"Like having 'em here," the alderman barked. He had recovered a good deal of his normal manner; probably because he had managed to dispose of the problem of the lost books to Foxe. "Decent girls, though I say it myself. Bright too. Lucy, the younger one, has a solid interest in literature and history. Maria's interests lean more towards scientific matters. She has such an orderly and mathematical mind! Twice the little minx has persuaded me to take her to some incomprehensible lecture on so-called Natural Philosophy. All numbers and symbols and stuff about gases and the like."

"It was an opportunity to learn about phlogiston and what is termed inflammable air, sir," Miss Maria explained. "It is lighter than normal air and burns very easily. Of what benefit this discovery may be to mankind, none can yet tell. However, it is undoubtedly significant."

Lucy was not to be excluded by her elder sister.

"Uncle took me to a lecture too, sir," she said. "It was very interesting. I heard an elderly gentleman talk about discovering ancient bones turned to stone and hidden in the earth. I once read a story about the giants of ancient times. Do you think these might be their bones?"

"Possibly," Foxe said. "Though, as I recall, most of the bones found appear to have belonged to giant animals. But you have the advantage of me, Miss Lucy. It is long since I heard an up-to-date exposition of such findings."

"Is it true that you sell important books, sir?" Lucy said. "I would find such work of great interest. My sister's passion is for numbers and calculations, but I love books and reading. To be caught up in a story is the greatest pleasure I know."

"Yes, I do sell books," Foxe replied, "and I agree with all you say of reading. If your uncle and aunt allow it, you must come to my shop. There I will show you some of what I have on sale. I may even let you see some of my own, special books."

Lucy's eyes shone at the prospect. Then, so that Maria should not feel left out, Foxe quickly added, "And you might find my small collection of mathematical writings and works of Natural Philosophy of interest, Miss Halloran. Indeed, you can help me understand some of them more clearly, for I freely admit my mind is not disciplined and logical enough to grasp all they contain."

"We will indeed avail ourselves of your great kindness, Mr Foxe," Mrs Halloran said. "But now it is time for these two to retire for the night and for me to take a dish or two of tea in the withdrawing room. Will you join us?"

Sadly, Foxe felt he had to decline the invitation. He was sorely fatigued after a long day and two journeys. He wanted nothing more than to retire for the night himself. Thus, with mutual expressions of warm regard on both sides, he took his leave of the alderman and his wife.

Yet even when he had reached his bed, Foxe lay awake for a long time, his mind going round and round these two new mysteries. How did the thief get inside the alderman's house and make his way to the library unseen? Especially when Halloran had stressed he would not even allow a servant inside to clean and make up fires, unless he was present. More puzzling still, how did any thief know to make off with only those particular books? They were clearly not taken at random, from what the alderman had said.

Sleep came before either matter was anywhere near to being solved.

5

FAMILIES AND DECEPTIONS

Despite Foxe's gloom, things were about to take a turn for the better. Next day, when he returned from his morning walk, he found a message waiting. James Morrow was already in Norwich. Foxe's letter had reached Morrow's home in Great Yarmouth as the man himself was about to leave. On his arrival the night before, he had therefore prepared a note to say he would call on Foxe next day at 1:00 pm. He hoped Mr Foxe would understand that it was not presently convenient to invite him to Ezekiel Morrow's house.

James Morrow arrived punctually. Foxe could not recall seeing him before, but that was not surprising since he lived more than 20 miles away. That day, James Morrow looked far from his best. There were dark circles under his eyes, his shaving had been cursory and his overall appearance was slightly unkempt.

Foxe had decided the small parlour would be the best place to talk. The drawing room was rather large. It was also close enough to the shop on that side for some sounds to penetrate the walls. Here, on the opposite side of the hallway, they would not be disturbed. The dining room on the first floor was too large for two people to feel comfortable in it.

"Forgive me for being so blunt," James Morrow began, "but I

need to know one or two things before we talk about my brother. I realise this is not what politeness demands, but I hope you will understand my need to turn at once to matters of substance. I have slept little in the past few days. Even now I have much that I must attend to when our meeting is ended. My father's health was frail before this dreadful event, sir. When I arrived last night, I found a man I scarcely recognised. One who is barely clinging to life. His doctor agrees with me. It falls to me to lift whatever I can from shoulders now too old and weak to bear so much grief. My mother died when I was born, Mr Foxe, and my father did not marry again. He must face what has happened alone."

Naturally, Foxe agreed to waive the courtesies and answer whatever questions his visitor had. The death of a child must be a frightful blow to any father. The murder of a child in such puzzling circumstances would be even worse.

"So …" Morrow said. "Why does a bookseller show a close interest in my brother's death? I hope it is more than simple curiosity. If that is the case, I will be upon my way. I will not be questioned by any hoping to turn my brother's murder into the kind of scurrilous broadsheet the mob delight in."

"Your question is a fair one," Foxe said. "I would have explained in any case. I have been asked by the mayor of the city to take on an investigation on his behalf. I have performed similar tasks for him and his predecessors on several occasions. The city constables are mostly good men, Mr Morrow, but better fitted for dispersing mobs and apprehending thieves than dealing with people of the better classes. I can offer both intelligence and discretion."

"So why is the mayor so interested? I know he is a magistrate, but magistrates usually rely on the family to bring malefactors before them."

"Your brother was an important man. Not only was he in charge of one of the larger yarn merchants, he was a banker as well. It is not in the interests of the other merchants and professional men who govern this town to preside over a run on the funds of Morrow & Son. Should it fail—even if only through fear —their own businesses would be affected. So far, they have been able to keep the details surrounding your brother's death from becoming public. However, in time the facts must surely emerge. Better for them—for your family too—if by that time the murderer is in custody and awaiting appearance at the next assizes."

Foxe's words left Morrow looking yet more stricken, if that were possible. His features had paled to an almost greenish hue. His eyes stared at Foxe with anguish.

"Murderer," he said. "An ugly word for an uglier deed. You are the first who has used it to my face."

"That is what it was, Mr Morrow. The question now is why was he killed. Once we understand that, we may move further towards discovering the perpetrator. That is why I wished to speak with you. I have dealt with such crimes before. Very often, the clue to why they are committed lies in the life and character of the person killed. Anything you can tell me may be of immense usefulness."

"I was stunned and amazed by my brother's ... murder," Morrow replied. "We weren't close, yet remained in touch in a general, family way. I have not had much direct contact with Joseph for a good many years. I may not be able to help you as much as you hope."

"You didn't follow your brother's progress in the business?"

"No. I had my own affairs to worry about. Nor would he—or my father—have welcomed it. I had been cut off, you might say. Not completely, but enough to seem an outsider. My father has taken Joseph's death very badly. Now he must attempt to resume involvement in a firm he retired from some years ago. He is totally lost in trying to deal with the banking business, for he was never more than a nominal partner in that. We are told someone—the mayor I now suspect—has arranged for a Mr Allday, a banker from Lynn, to assist us. I am come from Yarmouth to do what I can to help. Nothing more."

He swallowed noisily and wiped his eyes with a grubby handkerchief he had taken from some pocket.

"Your words make me wonder if there is not worse to come. What are these circumstances surrounding my brother's death that have been kept from public notice? For God's sake, tell me! I fear for my father's life if he must cope with still worse news."

"Your brother's body was found in the hold of a wherry moored at the wharf behind The Maid's Head Inn. He had been strangled with a thin piece of leather. What he was doing there, we do not know … nor why his clothes and body reeked of cheap brandy."

"No! No! No!" Morrow shouted. "That cannot be! It cannot be true! The subject of taking alcohol almost broke our family apart. My father, like many of his religious outlook, did not use strong drink himself. He naturally urged others to follow his example. Then my brother, as in so many other matters, went to extremes on the topic. He claimed to hate alcohol in any form. He railed at those who drank even a glass of ale on a hot day. He preached and fulminated against anything to do with wine or spirits. When I determined on the brewing trade—for I had no problem with drinking in moderation—my father was saddened, but accepted my choice. My brother, on the other hand, tried to cut me from his life. Oh, we spoke with sufficient civility at my father's house, if only to save a parent's feelings. Yet, from that day forward, I was forbidden to cross the threshold of my brother's dwelling."

"We are all puzzled, as you are," Foxe said quietly. "However, the coroner's medical examiner is adamant. The mayor wishes for any investigations to be undertaken as discretely as possible. If this aspect of the murder becomes known, no one will benefit."

"I cannot tell my father," Morrow said.

"Nor should you. We will be able to keep it quiet for a while longer yet. No one wishes to cause your family still greater pain. Nor to run the risk of any collapse of confidence amongst the business community."

"How can I help?" Morrow said. "I told you my brother made me a stranger to himself and his family."

"Your brother has not proved an easy man to investigate," Foxe said. "Though his religious and moral views were noised abroad plainly enough, in all personal matters he seems to have been a most private person."

"Aye, that's Joseph. Always ready to pry into another man's life and conscience, but secretive to an extreme degree about his own. Let us be plain, Mr Foxe. I did not like my brother. Even from our earliest days together, he wished to know my every thought and action, so that he could criticise them. For himself, he made sure none knew more than he was willing to show. He took the injunction in the bible literally—that one that says your left hand should not know what your right is doing."

"So you have no idea why any should want to kill him?"

"None at all. Brother Joseph was disagreeable and rigid, but we all assumed him to be honest. The word amongst the merchants and traders was that he was not a pleasant man to do business with, but he wouldn't cheat you."

"No family problems?"

"None that I know of, though that is saying little. If Joseph had been facing problems of any kind, large or small, he would have hidden them. He had to appear perfect, you see. One of God's Elect, destined for Heaven. He would not have suffered the slightest breath of scandal to touch him."

"And he did not become reconciled to your choice of profession?"

"Not in the smallest degree. As the younger son I knew I had to make my own way in the world. Joseph and I could never have worked together. Yet I would not set myself up to compete with my own father's business. I will not bore you with the details, but an opportunity arose unexpectedly to learn the brewing trade from a most successful man. I decided to take it. Not because it was a trade I especially wished to enter, but because my master would be a person I admired almost above all others. A kind, open-hearted, generous and wise man, who managed also to be extremely clever in business matters."

"There are few such," Foxe said.

"Few indeed. I had no expectations of a substantial inheritance on my father's death, so I asked for my small portion right away and he gave it. That I used to pay my way while I learned the brewing trade. As I said, my father and I had almost become reconciled. He was proud of my determination and effort. Joseph was never willing to forgive me. I knew he was fanatical before, but his actions then and since amply confirmed my view."

"Do you know anything of his recent state of mind—or his business position?"

"Nothing, I'm afraid. My brother did not even allow me to attend his wedding. I have met his wife only on rare, family occasions. She kept very much to the house and was completely subservient to her husband. I know my brother regretted not having an heir, but only because my father told me. What will happen to his wealth now, I cannot imagine. He has probably left it all to his church."

"You do not approve of his religious views?"

"No, I do not. I quarrel with no man for choosing a path in religious matters that differs from my own. What I could never stomach in that sect, however, is their readiness to condemn all who do not follow them. That and their narrow-mindedness. During our own lifetimes, Mr Foxe, great discoveries have been made which must be to the benefit of all mankind. Yet those people refuse all and cling to their peculiar notions of what is written in the bible."

They talked for a few more minutes, but it was clear Morrow could add nothing further. Foxe thanked him and allowed him to go on his way.

As he was leaving, however, Morrow had one last thing to add.

"Mr Foxe. I pray you will forgive my suspicion at the start. It is now clear to me that we of the Morrow family should be grateful that you have undertaken this task of investigation. I cannot imagine anyone else would be so careful of our feelings. Nor so thorough in probing for the truth. I believe I am speaking for us all, including my father, in saying that we are glad to associate ourselves with the mayor's choice. For myself, I will promise now to help you in any way that I can. You need only ask."

With those words, Mr James Morrow stepped through Foxe's door and hurried away to whatever awaited him next.

∽

FOXE SEEMED DOOMED to have no time to concentrate on anything for long. Next morning, before he had finished his breakfast, Alfred, the manservant, came with the news that Alderman Halloran was in the bookshop. He would be most obliged if Mr Foxe could present himself there with all speed.

If there was one thing Foxe hated above all others it was being hurried over his morning routine. He therefore left the table with a bad grace to go through the passageway to the shop. He did not even stop to change his old morning gown for something more suited to receiving a guest. If the alderman was in such a hurry, he would have to take Foxe as he found him.

Foxe found the alderman deep in conversation with Mrs Crombie. It appeared he could talk of nothing save his lost books, since Foxe heard her express surprise at the nature of the books used as replacements.

"So they did not resemble the stolen books in content, or even age?" she was saying. "It was simply that they looked similar from the outside. Similar binding, page size and thickness. How very extraordinary."

"That's correct," Halloran told her. "But the worst is that the volumes the scoundrel stole were particular favourites of mine. That's why I kept them in the two stacks closest to my reading desk. No point in having to search for something you're always wanting to read."

"And what of those put in their place?" Mrs Crombie asked. "Were they books you might have been interested in—in other circumstances, of course."

"You know, Mrs Crombie," the alderman said, "I believe I might have been. They were not of the first rate, you understand. Not titles I would have paid a high price to obtain. Certainly not the extortionate prices your ... employer? ... friend? ... Mr Foxe charges." The alderman was clearly fishing. Mrs Crombie's presence still puzzled him.

"That's a very old tune," Foxe said, deciding he needed to make his presence known before Halloran was carried away by Mrs

Crombie's attentiveness. "It's also one you know to be a good way off key, alderman."

The alderman had the grace to blush.

"Ah … um … Foxe. Didn't hear you come in. Just explaining to your …"

"Business partner?"

"Um … business partner … about the theft of my books. Well? Are you on the trail of the thief?"

"Not quite yet. I have been somewhat occupied."

"Never mind that, Foxe, whatever it is. I shall have no peace of mind until my books are restored to me. I am relying on you to let me see the fellow who robbed me dangling at the end of a rope."

Foxe's temper, already turned sour by the time at which the alderman had arrived, rapidly worsened.

"Let that be, alderman, I beg of you. The mayor is expecting me to work wonders over Mr Joseph Morrow's murder, while you are telling me to ignore that and find your books. I cannot be in two places at once, nor can I be expected to …"

Fortunately for Foxe's longer term relationship with the alderman, Mrs Crombie intervened.

"May I ask you a question, sir?" she said to Halloran. "Do you allow any of the servants into the library or only certain ones? I know you told me you are always present when they come in. Still, I am sure you must have many matters on your mind and cannot watch them the whole time."

"Good to see someone is paying attention to what I need and asking sensible questions, not just bleating about being overworked," Halloran growled. "As it happens, dear lady, I am most particular on that point. There are but two trusted servants who look after the library. Both have been with me for many years. Neither would, I am certain, dream of touching any of the books."

"I'm sure they would not," Mrs Crombie said. "However, if they have served you for many years, they must have become familiar with everything in the house. If they had come into the library at any time and found something moved, surely they would have mentioned it to you?"

"I imagine so … but what is in your mind, madam?"

"It seems to me that someone might speak with them—someone they would trust—to discover if they had noticed anything different in the days before the theft. If, as you imagine, the thief must have found a way to enter the library earlier to note where certain books were placed, he may have left some trace. After all, he could not have chosen suitable replacements without first noting the look and dimensions of what he planned to steal."

Alderman Halloran stared at her, then turned to Foxe with a look of triumph.

"You need to beware, Foxe. I declare this lady may soon prove your equal in matters of investigation. She has already shown a better temper."

He turned back to Mrs Crombie.

"Dear lady," he said. "You will be welcome in my house at any time. I will speak with the two servants involved and ask them to answer all your questions."

"Don't you think that is more a matter for Mr Foxe, alderman? I mean …"

"No, I do not. In his present surly mood, he will frighten them. You, however, have the rare gift of being one of the easiest people in the world to talk to. They will trust you at once, of that I am certain. Now, I must hasten away to try to calm another bad-tempered fellow—our worthy mayor. He has demanded my presence—demanded, I say—at 10:30 without fail. I cannot imagine he knows any more than he did yesterday, but still I must dance to his tune. Farewell, dear lady. I will look for you soon. Goodbye, Foxe. I can't imagine how Mrs Crombie copes with your moods."

As soon as the alderman left, Mrs Crombie started to apologise for her trespass on what was clearly Mr Foxe's personal business. Foxe smiled and raised his hand.

"It is I who should apologise to you, Mrs Crombie," he said. "I am never at my best early in the morning. Thankfully, you saved me from upsetting our crusty alderman still more than I did. I do believe you have captivated him. By the time he left, he seemed to dote upon you. I hope he is wary in singing your praises to his wife."

If anything, Mrs Crombie appeared more flustered and confused by these remarks that she had been before.

"Oh, Mr Foxe. I try so hard to do what is right, yet it seems all my efforts come to naught. I am truly grateful for all you have done for me. Most truly. Yet I repay you with muddles and embarrassments and by constantly stepping beyond my place …"

"Mrs Crombie," Foxe said. He tried to keep a serious face, but he could not. "Dear lady—to copy a phrase the alderman delighted to use of you—you have done nothing erroneous. You kept your head where I did not. You asked sensible questions and offered suggestions that sent the alderman away happy. I was in danger of dispatching him for good. Even better, he has conscripted you to help him find his books, which leaves me free to deal with the minor matter of the murder of a leading citizen."

"Oh, but Mr Foxe! I know nothing of investigation. Nor would I dream of interfering in your business in that regard. You must believe me!"

"Indeed I do. Calm yourself. If you look at me properly, you will see at once that I am not annoyed. Rather the opposite."

"Oh!" Mrs Crombie started, as if she had noticed some new threat. "You called me your business partner. I remember now. Why did you do that, if not to rebuke me for my presumption?"

"Because it is true—or will be, if you agree. To treat you as an employee or a servant is an insult. And the alderman's use of the word 'friend' was deliberately ambiguous, I dare say. It implies … well, you can guess what he was implying. No, if you accept, I will call on my attorney and ask him to draw up papers to turn this shop into a partnership, with you as my partner."

"But I have no money," Mrs Crombie almost wailed. "How can I purchase a partnership?"

"I did not ask for any money. Later, we will, I am sure, reach a satisfactory agreement. One that will prevent anyone suggesting this is not a genuine business arrangement. Do you agree?"

"Mr Foxe! Mr Foxe! Why do you do this to me? I just begin to imagine I know how matters stand between us, when you throw all into the air and leave me breathless and confused."

"All you have to do is say yes," Foxe said.

"But what am I agreeing to? What do you expect of me? How will I know whether I am doing what you want?"

"You are not a gambler, then?"

"Indeed I am not, sir. I saw what it did to my husband!"

"My apologies, Mrs Crombie. That was a most tactless remark. Look. Please agree and put me out of my misery. I need to be able to turn all my thoughts to the matter of the murder. If you relieve me of concern for some part of what presses upon me, I will be extremely grateful. Do not fear. I will not leave you without assistance in dealing with the alderman—or his stolen books. But if you would consent to talk to his servants, it would be of great use."

For a moment, Mrs Crombie still hesitated, then she took a deep breath and said, "Yes" rather more loudly than she had intended.

"I do declare," she added after, "I was not so frightened of what I was agreeing to when I accepted my husband's proposal of marriage."

"Thank you, Mrs Crombie," Foxe said. "I will do my best to ensure you do not regret your decision. Now I too must leave if I am ever to return to my proper routine for the day. By the time I am dressed correctly, it will be too late to take coffee, but I may still have my usual morning walk. When I return, you may tell me how … yes … our business is developing."

DESPITE HIS BEST INTENTIONS, Foxe was not destined to enjoy a quiet walk around the Market Place that day. He had scarcely gone thirty paces from his front door when young Charlie Dillon rushed up to him.

"I got a message for you from the captain," the boy blurted out. "He say he'll go to the coffee 'ouse, 'cos 'e expects that's where you'll be. If you ain't there, 'e'll stay till you comes. Thass a penny you owes me!"

Foxe looked down at the boy, trying his very best to appear severe.

"And what did Captain Brock pay you for bringing me this message, eh? I warrant you've already received a penny from him."

Charlie grinned.

"Worth a try, though, eh? Anyhow, I got to be on my way. Missus Crombie might 'ave summat for me to do."

With that, he was gone.

Brock was indeed waiting at the coffeehouse when Foxe arrived. He, at least, seemed to be relaxed and cheerful that morning. Foxe decided he must have found out something important.

"The look of smugness you're wearing tells me you've discovered something at last," Foxe said. "Out with it, then, for I need some better start to the day than finding Alderman Halloran in my shop soon after nine."

"It's not much," Brock said, "but it's something at least. I've had some people I know nosing around Morrow's yarn manufactory. It seems Ezekiel Morrow was well enough liked by the people there, as well as by the spinners in their homes. He was firm—wouldn't stand for any shirking or other nonsense—but he was fair. Besides, his vast knowledge of every aspect of the yarn trade gave him an authority few could match."

"And the son, Joseph?"

"Exactly the opposite. Seems he's heartily disliked all round. Invents petty rules—like taking no alcoholic drink even in your own home—and sacks those who infringe them. No warning, just dismissal. A typical tyrant."

"Why do people stay?"

"Because there aren't too many other places to work in that trade. Anyhow, Joseph isn't interested in yarn. Leaves the running of the business to his general manager and the foremen most of the time. They've got more sense than to enforce his silly rules—unless he turns up of a sudden. Then it's chaos for a time. Worst thing, the workers say, is that Joseph Morrow understands about as much about yarn as a whore about chastity. Knows what it is, but hasn't the slightest intention of having anything to do with it. His father they respected; him they despise."

"Enough for someone to kill him?"

"Who can say? I wouldn't have thought so, but anger is a powerful incentive to kill; especially if you've been turned out of work for some absurd reason and your family are starving."

"It's been going on since he took over from his father, I expect. Why kill him now?"

"Again, I can't answer that. What I did hear is that the Morrow yarn business has problems. Either the general manager and his cronies are raiding the till, or they aren't bothering to do their jobs. Whatever the cause, people are being laid off—not for want of orders, but simply because there's no money to pay them. My people found some workers owed three and four weeks' wages. The out-workers, who are all on piece-rates paid for what they spin, haven't been given their due for nearly two months. Some are being forced onto parish relief."

"You said you hadn't discovered much, Brock, but this is important. Even if Joseph had lost interest in yarn—or never had any, more likely—it makes no sense to drive the firm into ruin. You could get a good price for it as a going concern. Our worsted producers have rarely been busier than they are right now. They must be buying a great deal of yarn. A firm with angry workers and problems with cash is going to be impossible to sell for anything but a knock-down price."

"That's what I thought," Brock said. "But where's the money going? As you said, demand for yarn is high, so it can't be lack of orders. My bet is that Joseph's neglect has been letting those set in charge help themselves. If he started taking a closer interest, one of them might have decided to strike first. It might seem preferable to facing what would happen when he discovered what they'd been doing. A man who'll sack someone for having a drink in his own home and his own time isn't going to be soft on thieves, is he?"

"No. Anyone stealing from him would hang for certain. Do you think you could find a way for me to talk to the general manager? I doubt he'll confess, but we might be able to trip him up somehow."

"I'll do my best," Brock said. "By the way, what brought Halloran knocking on your door so early? I never had him marked down for someone who would leave his bed much before ten o'clock."

"Someone's been stealing books from his library."

Brock let out a whistle.

"How in God's name did they do that?" he said. "I thought he protected his books more carefully than his wife's honour."

"That's what I have to find out. That and get his books back for him. Oh … and seize the thief, or thieves, and hand them over so he can see them hang. All of it quickly, of course."

"Any ideas?"

"Not one. Now he's lost some books, the matter of Morrow's murder can wait, as far as he's concerned. I doubt the mayor would agree with that, but Halloran simply waves the objection away. There's only one tiny glint of sunlight through all the clouds of fury that follow him about."

"What's that?"

"While he was waiting for me to hurry in to discover what he wanted, he started talking to Mrs Crombie. I don't know how she did it, but by the time I arrived he was fawning over her as if he'd never seen a woman before—and purring like a cat being stroked."

"Halloran? That woman must be a witch! She's put a spell on him. He's a crusty old bugger, who goes about the city looking as if there's always a bad smell near him. He's also famously devoted to his wife. You'd better be on your guard."

"Me?"

"Cross her and I'll be finding you turned into a toad!"

"Stuff and nonsense! She's … she's …"

"Too damned persuasive, if you ask me. She'd better not try her wiles on me."

"You're talking about my new business partner. I'll thank you to show greater respect, sir."

"Business partner? Since when?"

"Since this morning. I've offered her a share in the bookshop business and she has accepted."

"And you claim she isn't a witch? That's two of you under her spell—and it isn't noon yet. Whatever she has, if I could bottle it I could make a fortune. Noticed any black cats lurking behind the bookshelves? Any brooms propped up in corners?"

"Young Charlie Dillon had a broom yesterday and was sweeping out the shop under her direction."

"This gets worse! Charlie too, and he's barely …what? … nine or ten years old. I'm keeping away from your shop, Foxe, in case she turns me into something."

Foxe regarded him solemnly for a few moments, then said, "A walrus, I think. Big, whiskery and prone to bellowing. I've never seen one, but that's what I've read in seamen's tales."

"At least you're smiling now," Brock said. "When you came in, I thought your execution had been set for this afternoon."

At that point, they were interrupted by the entry of Charlie Dillon.

"You're to come back to the shop as quick as you can, Missus Crombie say … says," Charlie began. "That fat alderman's there creating a stink and wanting to speak to you secret-like. Oh, and Missus Crombie wants to tell you summat too. She gave me tuppence, cos I had to run all the way."

"I'll give you a thick ear if you're cheeky about the alderman again, my lad. Go back and tell Mrs Crombie—politely—that I am on my way."

"Does I … do I … have to run?" Charlie asked.

"Yes, I suppose so."

"That's tuppence then," the boy said, holding out a grubby palm.

"Three ha'pence," Foxe said. "It's not very far."

"Tuppence, or I dawdle all the way," Charlie replied.

"Oh, give the lad his tuppence," Brock growled. "You know you're going to. He won't give up until he gets it. While you two are bickering here over a ha'penny, the … slightly overweight … visitor in your shop will be working himself into a rage. Either that, or that witch you've got in there will have him rolling on his back, begging to have his belly rubbed."

"'Ere!" Charlie said. "Don't you be calling Missus Crombie no witch! I mayn't be big enough to punch yer face, but I can kick yer shins."

With that, the boy matched action to words, catching Brock a sharp blow to the shin with his boot. Brock yelled in pain and tried to hit the boy in return, but Charlie dodged his hand with ease. He was well used to avoiding clumsy attacks by adults.

"Stop it, you two!" Foxe snapped. "Charlie, here's tuppence. Off you go. The Captain was only joking, so there's no need to defend Mrs Crombie's honour. Brock, stop using that word, even in jest. There are plenty in this city who still believe in witches. Before you know, they'll be all around my shop and the poor woman will never have a moment's peace. Now, be off with you too. No arguing. Charlie gave you no more than you deserved. I've enough problems today in dealing with angry aldermen to want to be keeping the two of you from attacking one another."

6

MONEY PROBLEMS

FOXE EXPECTED TO FIND THE ALDERMAN IN THE BOOKSHOP, MAKING the further acquaintance of Mrs Crombie, but she was alone when he entered.

"Ah, Mr Foxe," she said. "Thank you for coming so quickly. I'm sorry to have interrupted whatever you were doing, but the alderman insisted. I took the liberty of speaking to Alfred and asking him to take Mr Halloran through into your house. He's also to offer him something to drink. The man looked so ill when he arrived, I was concerned for him."

"Ill?"

"Deadly pale, perspiring about the face. He looked like a man who has just suffered some ghastly shock. You will treat him gently, won't you? I know he is something of a nuisance with his fretting about his books, but I believe they are as dear to him as children. Anyway, he was swaying on his feet and I thought he should sit down immediately. I hope I did right."

Foxe agreed that she had done what was appropriate and hurried through to find where Alfred had put his visitor. Alderman Halloran was sitting in the small parlour, sipping at a glass of wine. When he saw Foxe, he started to get up, but Foxe waved him to stay where he was. Alfred followed his master into the room to take his outdoor clothes. Foxe sent him to fetch a second glass of wine.

"Mrs Crombie tells me you seemed unwell when you arrived, alderman," Foxe said. "I hope you are now recovered."

"Better, thank you," Alderman Halloran replied. "Good wine this. To be honest, I'd just come from the Guildhall and probably walked a far faster than I should for a man of my age. It's the mayor, you see. He sent me. He's in a thoroughgoing panic."

"Yes, I see. Now, take it slowly and tell me what has happened to make the mayor so apprehensive."

Halloran took a large gulp of wine and a deep breath.

"It's what we dreaded most," he began. "Mayor had a visit first thing from Mr Allday. I told you he'd agreed to look over banking affairs at the Morrow business. Seems he's been greatly hampered by old Ezekiel Morrow flying into a rage and dismissing his chief cashier. The man had been with the bank since it was established a dozen years ago, I'm told, but nothing would content Ezekiel but to throw him into the street at once."

"What on earth for?" Foxe said. "Losing access to the chief cashier is certain to disadvantage everyone. What had the man done?"

"Here's the worst part, Foxe. Mr Allday told the mayor there's something very wrong with the banking business. Substantial sums of money are missing. When Allday asked Ezekiel about the losses, the old man called the chief cashier and demanded to know who had authorised such payments. When the cashier said it was Mr Joseph, Ezekiel seemed to go completely mad and ordered the man out of the building at once. Accused him of embezzlement to his face. Said he was trying to cover up his own crimes. Of course, without help from the chief cashier, it's going to take everyone far longer to hit upon the precise problem."

"But that's stupid," Foxe said. "Didn't he even allow the man to explain what his answer meant?"

"Not a word. Mr Allday says Ezekiel is completely out of his depth in dealing with the banking side of things. He also thinks the death of his son has unhinged him. Anyhow, Allday sent word at once to the other son, James, and asked him to come and escort his father home. He's planning to return to the bank later in the day, hopefully with Mr James Morrow present, to see what he can find in the books to explain the losses."

"That makes good sense."

"Naturally, Allday thought the mayor should be warned at once. Then the mayor sent for me and started yelling about bank crashes and the ruin of the city and heaven knows what other disasters. Next he wanted to know why you were being so slow. What was I doing to persuade you to give the matter the proper priority? Don't take any notice of that, Foxe. The mayor needs people to blame and you and I were at the head of his list. I don't doubt he's railed at most of the other aldermen by now. I got out and hurried here. This news is bound to get out. If we're not ready with a suitable state-ment, there's going to be panic enough to start the financial crisis the mayor is so afraid of."

Foxe sat and pondered these new developments for a while. From what Brock had told him earlier, he had expected to find the yarn business was not the only part of the Morrow family businesses to be in trouble. What wasn't clear was whether Joseph Morrow had been engaged in something dishonest or was simply incompetent. Brock said the man knew nothing about yarn. Was it possible he knew nothing about banking either? That the air of solidity at the bank had been little more than people's assumptions about a man always proclaiming his own virtue?

He needed time to work out what this meant. Yet as soon as the news of problems at the bank leaked out, there would be immediate panic. Many in the city would face ruin. How could he gain enough time to understand the nature of the problems at Morrow's, formu-late a plan and explain to the mayor what to say; all before they must face a furious populace?

"Here's what I suggest, alderman," Foxe said at last. "The mayor must ask Mr James Morrow to assume temporary control of the family business, on the grounds that his father is too over-whelmed with grief to cope. If he agrees—and I believe he will—the mayor should beg him to send word to the chief cashier and get him to return. Again, he can say his father is not himself and is not fully responsible for his actions. If that works, Mr James and Mr Allday have a chance to discover what's been going on. In the meantime, let all of you put the word about that Ezekiel Morrow is prostrated by grief over his son's death. His doctor has advised him to take a complete rest. Meanwhile, his second son is in charge. Aside from that, all will proceed as normal."

"Will that do it?" the alderman asked. "What if the cashier has already started telling people what happened and why he was sacked?"

"We'll simply have to hope he hasn't. It doesn't seem likely to me. He'll be be shut in his house, trying to explain matters to his family and worrying in case the constables come to arrest him for embezzlement."

"In case the mayor asks, why am I advising we take this course?"

"To buy time. Captain Brock has already picked up rumours that the yarn business is laying off employees and delaying payments and wages. Looks as if it's running out of money too. We have to know what is behind it all."

"The yarn business as well? Surely not. After my own, Morrow's is the largest yarn supplier in East Anglia. They should have more money than they know what to do with."

"That's what Brock's been told."

Alderman Halloran shook his head in wonderment.

"I'm amazed, Foxe. Dumbfounded. The city and our woollen trade are riding the crest of a wave of prosperity. Then one man gets himself murdered and all our hopes and plans lie in ruins."

"We're not beaten yet," Foxe said. "Tell the mayor this also. You and the other wealthy gentlemen and merchants in this city should ready yourselves to rescue the bank, if that is what is needed. It sounds like throwing good money after bad, I know. But I assure you it will prove far better than watching Morrow & Son go bankrupt, taking everyone's deposits with it. See if the Gurneys would be willing to assume the debts and deposits and merge them with their own. Collect pledges of cash to ensure people can withdraw their money in an orderly fashion, if that is what they wish. Make it clear you and your colleagues will be leaving your own deposits untouched."

"You ask a great deal, Foxe."

"I ask you to help save yourselves, that is all. Oh … another thing. I cannot imagine Mr James Morrow will wish to run the yarn business in the longer term, especially under his father's watchful eye. If one son proves to have strayed from the straight path, why not the other? If Morrow's Yarns remains a viable business, consider whether the best way to provide the money needed to prop up the bank might be for you to buy Morrow's yourself."

"Me? Well … it used to be a sound business, I suppose. But, in Heaven's name Foxe, you run so fast I can hardly keep up. You do not decide to buy another business in an instant."

"An instant may be all we have, alderman. My plan to conduct a quiet, orderly investigation now lies in ruins. Events have run ahead of us and we must struggle to keep up. Now, if you are recovered, I suggest you return to the Guildhall at once, before the mayor can do further damage. Say we have discussed all we both know. No alternative course of action is open to him. Urge him to act immediately. If it goes wrong, I will accept the blame."

"No need for that, Foxe. I know I often annoy you, but I won't ever be accused of disloyalty to my friends. This is *our* plan. If we must face ruin and disgrace, we'll face them together."

"Thank you." It was all Foxe could manage to say.

To the casual glance, Mr Foxe's house was like those owned by many merchants and professional men in the city of Norwich. True, it was a house of some size. The original builder had been a prosperous man. The walls were made of trim red bricks, well bonded and set, with facings and quoins of good ashlar stone. The roof was covered with Dutch pantiles, as were many homes in Norwich. It had large sash windows and a front doorway with an arched glass fanlight. Yet there was nothing superfluous in the design. No grand portico with columns. No bands of decorative stonework. Just seven steps, edged with curving iron handrails, leading up to the front door. The whole was neat and harmonious in style and design; a solid Palladian villa some fifty years old, or a little less.

If an observer crossed the street to see the elevation better, he might note the half-basement for the usual domestic offices, topped by three principal floors, then dormer windows in the roof to indicate attics. Perhaps the most unusual feature was the bookshop, which adjoined the house to the right as you looked at it. Most buildings in the city associated with shops had a shop-front set into the house. Mr Foxe's shop occupied a separate building to the side, so that the house itself need give over no internal space to the demands of commerce.

As a result, the bookshop too was spacious, with fine bow windows either side of the entry door. On the ground floor, the shop took up the front half of the building with what was now a storeroom to the rear. The second floor consisted of a single large room, long silent and unused, with benches and tools for bookbinding. There were no attics. The building holding the shop was, in fact, somewhat older than the house. It had once been the office of one of Norwich's first newspapers, with the printing-shop behind. A few years ago, when two newspapers combined, the owners sought larger premises. Foxe's father had bought the place they left. Since he was originally a printer of pamphlets and broadsheets, not a bookseller, he had kept the presses and made part of the office area into a shop. It was Foxe himself who had the printing equipment removed and the shop extended to focus entirely on book sales. Then, after his father's untimely death, he sold both his parents' home and his own to buy the former newspaper owner's house next door.

Few had ever seen beyond the shop area, save for Mr Foxe's special customers. They might penetrate into the storeroom to view the purchases Mr Foxe laid out for them there. They never went up the steep stairs to see what might be above.

Thus it was that Mrs Crombie, her head whirling with the possibilities opened by Mr Foxe's sudden offer of a partnership, decided, on a whim, to explore the whole of what was now to be their shared domain.

The rear room, she thought, or part of it, would make an excellent space for a circulating library. To reach it, patrons would be obliged to pass through the shop, where their eyes might be caught by items they could be tempted to purchase. Such an arrangement would also serve to separate the books available for subscribers to borrow from those on sale. She would need to find a suitable person to remain in the library during the times it was open. Their duties would include making a suitable record of all borrowings and returns, collecting payment and generally keeping the place tidy. She would also expect them to engage customers in polite conversation, so that she might discover which titles they might wish to borrow in the future. All in all, it would be a substantial position for a trusted person—and she knew exactly who that should be. All that was required was to convince Mr Foxe of the importance of adding a circulating library to the bookshop.

The upper room—dusty and somewhat neglected now—could be swept out and given some fresh decoration. Part would then become the space for Mr Foxe's antiquarian and similar books to be held. If some good chairs were added, it would make an elegant room for receiving his wealthy customers. The rest would serve as room for general stock.

It was while she was trying, mentally, to lay out the whole area to make it look less like an empty workshop that she heard the bell from the shop below. Being on her own for the moment, she had no alternative but to hurry down to see who had entered.

She found a stocky, heavily-built man of some forty or fifty years of age, well-dressed but retaining the clear appearance of a person used to an outdoor life.

"May I assist you, sir?" she said, advancing towards him.

"Not introduced myself properly before," the man said. "Brock's the name. You'll maybe hear folk refer to me as The Captain. Foxe and I have known each other these many years. He's been singing your praises so loudly I thought I should take a look at you myself."

Mrs Crombie was torn between pleasure that Mr Foxe had

mentioned her kindly to this friend of his and a certain degree of irritation at the man's manner. His words suggested he viewed her more as a phenomenon to be observed than a person worthy of better acquaintance.

"Indeed, sir," she said, somewhat coldly. "I have heard Mr Foxe mention your name. Well, here I am. You may look as much as you wish, for I assure you I shall not improve in appearance from what you see today."

"Apologies," Brock growled. "Didn't mean any offence, madam. Not much of a hand at fine manners."

"In my experience," Mrs Crombie said, "fine manners, as you call them, are generally assumed to deceive. I would far rather have plain good nature, Captain Brock. I am, as I'm sure you know, Mrs Susannah Crombie. Mr Foxe has been my rescuer from great ill fortune. In return, I am doing the best I can to turn his book-selling business to profitable ways. He seems to have somewhat neglected it, though I understand he has a good many other calls on his time."

Brock stared at her for a moment, then his face relaxed into a grin.

"You and I will get on famously, I fancy," he said. "I like a woman who speaks her mind and doesn't hide behind claims of fragility and decorum. You put me in my place, Mrs Crombie, which is what I deserved. To be honest, I expected to find someone a lot more …" Brock groped wildly for words that would not be insulting.

"Modish?" Mrs Crombie said. "Fashionable? Decorative? Believe me, Captain Brock, I have heard many tales of Mr Foxe's taste in ladies. But I am here to work, not adorn his arm. I leave that to the likes of the Catt Sisters."

"Ah …" Brock said, thoroughly taken aback by this woman's confidence and honesty. "In a manner of speaking, it's because of them I wanted to … um … look you over. I'll try to put this delicately, Mrs Crombie, but I have been a wherry-master and seafarer for more years that I've worn a gentleman's frock-coat."

"Don't apologise, Captain Brock," the lady said. "I doubt you will approach me in any way I have not encountered previously."

It added the final seal to Brock's amazement at the woman before him that he now found himself talking with her as if they were of long acquaintance.

"I'm worried about Foxe," he said. "As I said, we've known each other many years and I regard him as one of my family. Don't like to see him as miserable and hurt as he is now. You mentioned Kitty and Gracie Catt."

"They were both his mistresses," Mrs Crombie said. It was not a question. "Though I gather there was a good deal of genuine affection on both sides, not just a man willing to bestow presents and women willing to earn them with their favours."

"Aye, you're right again. Foxe loved 'em both, different as they are. That's why he misses 'em so bad."

"Are they gone away?"

"They are—and not likely to come back, as I hear. Kitty is making a grand career on the stage in London. Gracie has gone with her. What you probably don't know is this. Kitty provided Foxe with the kind of amusement you would expect, but her sister did much more. She offered Foxe a shoulder to cry on and a welcoming refuge when things got on top of him."

"And useful information for his investigations too, I imagine," Mrs Crombie said.

Brock started.

"You know about those?" he said.

"He has mentioned it to me, since I might be useful in collecting gossip and rumours from those who come to buy books," Mrs Crombie said. "Besides, I have already made the acquaintance of Alderman Halloran. He, like you, made it his business to come into the shop to "look me over". He also tried to fish to discover the exact terms of my relationship with Mr Foxe."

"Aye, he would," Brock said, laughing. "Our worthy alderman gains a good deal of pleasure, I think, from wondering what Foxe is up to and who he is doing it with. I hope you served him as you did me."

"I responded to all his polite enquires, Captain Brock. For the others—which were implied rather than spoken—I developed a sad affliction of deafness."

"That I would love to have seen," Brock said. "However, back to our mutual friend Foxe. Without the Catt Sisters, the man is lost. So far, he's been too honourable—and too fond—simply to walk out of an evening and find someone else to supply Kitty's place in his ... activities. That's what he needs to do, since there's little chance Kitty is depriving herself of similar recreation. Gracie cannot be replaced so easily. A man in this city can find bed-fellows aplenty, but it takes trust and long acquaintance to find a woman to whom you can open your heart. Haven't you noticed how irritable and morose Foxe has become?"

"To be honest, Captain, I have hardly known him long enough to be aware of his manner and moods. But, now you mention it, I have certainly noticed a degree of distraction. I put it down to worry about the death of Mr Morrow."

"Foxe has investigated more troubling situations than this, but I have never known his good humour and calmness of mind to be as agitated as they are today. What are we going to do about him, Mrs Crombie?"

"I hope you aren't going to suggest I should offer Mr Foxe my bosom to cry on," Mrs Crombie said.

"He'd be a fool to turn it down! No, Mrs Crombie. I do not suggest anything beyond the bounds of strict propriety. It's just that I am lost in matters of the heart—especially Foxe's heart. I love the man. There, I have confessed all. I simply hope you too might hold him in affection enough to wish to see him restored."

"Indeed I do," Mrs Crombie said. "His kindness to me demands no less. Yet I feel unsure what either of us may do, other than try to bear with his moods and wait for time to heal his wounds. I suppose ..." she looked sad now "... I should not bother him at present with all my ideas about this business. It's just ... I hate to see waste, Captain Brock, and this business as it stands is wasting opportunities for improvement and extension. Perhaps the best we can both do is try to help him with his present investigation as much as we can. That way, he may regain some sense of his own worth. I do not have the … nocturnal resources, shall we say? … that Grace Catt could call upon, but I have a good ear for gossip."

"You have much more than that," Brock said. "You have the rare gift of listening. I came here determined either to command you to leave Foxe alone or convince myself you were no more than a pleasant distraction of the kind he has found before. Instead, I find myself telling you many of my deepest thoughts and seeing you for what, I believe, you are; a fine young woman with a most capable head on her shoulders. It's a miracle!"

"No miracle, Captain Brock. You may try to present yourself as a rough mariner used to battling against the winds and waves, but I was not deceived, even at the start. You have a soft heart, sir, and a great kindness within. So, let us agree to be friends and do what we can to help Mr Foxe in his time of need."

"Amen to that," Brock said. "Now I must be off next door. Young Charlie Dillon told me Foxe was calling for me urgently a good two hours ago. I dread to imagine what temper he may have worked himself into since then."

"Remember, Captain Brock. It is still the same man beneath the moods and the passions. If you keep that in mind, I am sure you will not go far wrong in responding to your old friend, whatever he may do."

BROCK'S WORDS to Mrs Crombie were, of course, accurate. In such a situation of tension and impending doom, Foxe's response in the past had always been the same. He would go immediately to Gracie Catt's bordello. There she would make a fuss of him, soothing his fears and anxieties with her soft words and warm caresses. But Gracie was more than a hundred miles away in London. Foxe had never felt so wretched and alone.

Now, sitting in the small library of his house—a room severely masculine in layout and decoration where he did most of his thinking—he stared through the windows as the light dimmed and the shadows lengthened. Soon it would be time for dinner, yet he had no appetite. He lacked even the energy to snap at Brock when his old friend finally put in an appearance. Instead, he recited the fresh developments and rumours linked to the bank, his voice dull and his words without emphasis or vigour.

This limp, disheartened Foxe alarmed Brock more than any angry or hectoring version could have done. It was also much harder to think how best to stir him from his lethargy. Brock had no cheering news to bring him—nothing beyond some confirmation of what he already knew. Joseph Morrow had been a demanding and tyrannical master in the workplace, preaching the same theme of absolute obedience to strict rules of life that he had thundered from the pulpit when he preached.

Finally, just as he was about to leave in near-despair, Brock had an idea.

"Have you heard?" he said. "The Norwich Company of Comedians present a new programme at the theatre this evening. Why don't you rest your mind by going along to take a look at what they have on offer? You always enjoy the theatre. It will take your mind off the problems we are facing. Who knows? You may even pick up one or two useful fragments of gossip?"

Foxe's response was to wave a hand.

"I appreciate your concern, Brock," he said. "Don't imagine I don't. It's just …"

He lapsed into silence again.

Yet after Brock had left, the idea of going to the theatre refused to leave his mind, even as he picked with listless application at the food Mrs. Whitbread, his cook, had prepared for him. In the end, he called Alfred and sent him to enquire at what time the evening's performance would be starting.

Finding he had just time to change into something more appropriate for appearing in public, Foxe decided to follow Brock's advice. It could do no harm. Besides, if Kitty ever returned to Norwich, she would be angry if she found he had deserted the theatre in her absence.

Norwich's fine new theatre had been built by Mr Thomas Ivory in 1757 as the "Grand Concert Hall" to avoid the need for a licence

from the Lord Chancellor. There were several other theatres in the
city, including the one behind the "White Swan" close by the
looming bulk of St Peter Mancroft Church. That had been the
previous home of the Norwich Company of Comedians. However,
this new building was better arranged and able to hold a larger
audience, so the Company now held most of their performances
there. It was also in the most modern style, with an interior layout
modelled on London's Drury Lane Theatre. As a result, it attracted
more than one London company to put on plays at the busiest times
of the year, like Assize Weeks.

When Foxe made his appearance that evening, he found to his
surprise that he made quite a stir. He had forgotten how many
weeks had passed since he was last a member of the audience. The
theatre manager bustled up, full of compliments and subservience,
and insisted on personally ushering Foxe to a seat in what he
claimed was the best box in the house. It was probably simply one
that had not yet been reserved, but Foxe could not bring himself to
puncture the man's obvious pleasure at having such a regular—and
wealthy—patron back again.

"After the performance," the manager said, "you must let me
take you backstage and introduce some of the new members of our
company. No, I insist! To lose Miss Kitty to London was a hard blow
—I admit it—but we have done the best we can to find people to
take her place."

Foxe had to admit to himself, as the evening progressed, that the
new group of players had some promising members. The prologue
was spoken well, if without much flair and the principal item—a
tragedy called "The Duchess of Genoa"—produced some choice
acting. Only in the burlesque was Kitty's absence clearly causing the
manager problems. The woman who played the part Kitty would
have taken lacked both the looks and the wicked gift for flirtation
that had made Kitty Catt the darling of the Norwich beaux.

At the end of the evening, Foxe decided to slip away unnoticed,
but the manager seemed to have anticipated that. Before the curtain
had descended for the last time, the man entered the box and gently
took Foxe's arm. It would have been most impolite to draw back, so

Foxe suffered himself to be taken along the aisles and through the doors he knew so well. Before, he had always gone straight to the principal dressing-room, where Kitty would be found. Now, the manager took him instead to the general tiring-room for all the junior ladies of the cast. The man had clearly been busy backstage, for no less than five young women were lined up to await Foxe's arrival. If it was not quite as blatant a case of take your pick as he would have found in a bordello, it was not far short. Foxe's reputation as the very devil for young actresses had survived even the three years of his exclusive attendance on Kitty.

Again, Foxe would have drawn back, if he could, but these ladies were as eager for him to lavish his patronage upon them—if that was the word—as the manager. They pressed around Foxe, admiring his fine clothes, seeking his praise for their individual performances—though, to be blunt, he had noticed only two of them—and trying to arrange themselves before him in ways that would best display their physical assets. That it was all about his wealth and his reputation for generosity towards his protégés, he did not doubt. Still, it was undeniably enjoyable and he felt his spirits rising again.

Finally he was allowed to take his leave, sent on his way with numerous kisses and a promise he would return the next week.

Since the hour was late, the streets around Norwich's vast Market Place were not safe for any dressed as richly as Foxe. So he allowed the manager to call him a chair and two men to light his way. Thus he returned to his house feeling almost, if not quite, his old self.

Later, as he composed himself for sleep, he reached a grave decision. It was no use, he told himself. He had to accept the likelihood that Kitty was not going to return. Her last letter, weeks ago now, had mentioned Dublin and Bath as future venues alongside the capital, not Norwich. Where Kitty went, Gracie would follow. It was time for him also to move on with his life.

That night, he slept soundly for the first time in many weeks.

7

STIRRING UP TROUBLE

THE NEXT MORNING, FOXE DRESSED IN AN EVEN MORE FLAMBOYANT manner than usual. It was time to stop moping and get on with his life, he told himself. First he must call into the bookshop before leaving for the coffeehouse. This was, of course, purely to give Mrs Crombie encouragement. Had he been totally honest however, it was at least as much to see what effect his exquisite plum-coloured velvet coat, with the matching breeches and pink silk waistcoat and stockings, all heavily embroidered, would have upon her.

On that score at least, the result was all he could have hoped for. Her eyes widened as he entered, then she looked him up and down, sighed several times and slowly shook her head. Foxe felt sure she was, in her own, restrained way, indicating unbounded delight. He was not to know that her true response to this vision of high fashion so early in the day was more one of bewildered concern than admiration. After her talk with Captain Brock, she was wondering whether Mr Foxe's sudden leap from downcast misery to somewhat overdone exuberance was not another sign of her new business partner's desperation.

Mrs Crombie had been hoping Mr Foxe would appear that morning, if not in those clothes. She still had to try her luck approaching one or two of the servants at Mr Joseph Morrow's house to see if they were willing to talk with her. That meant leaving the shop, perhaps for several hours. Keeping regular hours was, in her view, important to building business and she had, as yet, no one to assist her. So she was wondering whether she could persuade Mr Foxe to take her place behind the counter for a time.

At the sight of him in this dandyish clothing, she almost lost her nerve. He looked more like someone bound for one of the city's pleasure gardens than a serious shopkeeper. Nevertheless, she stuck to her plan and explained what she needed him to do.

To her surprise, he agreed at once. He even suggested that he might take over from her as soon as he returned from his morning walk. She could only hope that he would have the good sense to change into more sensible clothes before he did so.

Quite unaware of Mrs Crombie's concerns, Foxe walked purposefully towards his favourite coffeehouse, enjoying the stares of those he passed. But when he arrived, his mood darkened. There was somebody seated at the table he usually claimed as his own, private domain. Why had the proprietor not asked the man to move? Was he so much taken for granted in this place that they assumed he would accept what had happened and choose another seat? It was not to be tolerated! He was about to call for the owner when he realised it was Mr. Brandon Seager, the newspaper editor, sitting there.

What could he want?

Seager, it appeared, had been waiting for Foxe to arrive, spending his time in the interim scanning the London papers of two days ago. Foxe was intrigued. Seager was not quite such a devotee of this establishment as Foxe was. Perhaps for good professional reasons, he tended to divide his time between several of the better coffeehouses around the Market Place. Yet he came often enough for most people to know he and Foxe were, if not quite friends, then amiable acquaintances. That was why no one had asked him to take a seat elsewhere.

The moment Foxe sat down, Seager took a grubby piece of paper from his pocket and slid it across the table towards him.

"This was pushed under the door this morning," Seager said. "My title is written on the back, not my name. Seems the writer may not know that. Read it."

Foxe took the sheet and read what it contained. It was poorly written, badly spelled and barely understandable, so it took him a few moments to grasp. The writer was challenging the editor of what he called "The Inelligencer" to ask the authorities about the state of Joseph Morrow's body when it was found.

"I knows," the note stated, "as how that ranting poritan blagard Morrow was out drinking and horing the night he got kilt. Ax the mayor. He knows too. Ax him what he be hidding from the peeple of this city. Vengeance is mine, saith the Lord. I will repay."

Foxe read it over twice, then looked up. Seager was watching him closely.

"Bit hard to understand what the writer means, isn't it?" Foxe said. "I suppose 'horing' means 'whoring' and 'hidding' should really be 'hiding'."

"Never mind the spelling," Seager said. "It's clear enough that whoever wrote this thinks the mayor and his friends are covering up something about Morrow's murder—or at least his state at the time of his death. What do you know about it, Foxe? You saw the body."

"Ah," Foxe said, choosing his words carefully. "There you are wrong. I didn't see it. I was told about what had happened, just as you were."

"I'd take a good wager you were told much more," Seager said. "Out with it, Foxe. You promised me the whole story. Now it seems you haven't even told me the first paragraph."

"I promised to share all I could with you, when …" Foxe paused to stress that word, "… when I was free to do so. Nothing has happened to change that."

Foxe didn't wish to dismiss the accusation in the letter out of hand. That would involve a blatant lie. Instead, he tried to deflect the conversation into less treacherous areas.

"Look, Seager," he said. "It's obvious someone is trying to make trouble for the Morrow family. This is probably no more than that. Given Joseph Morrow's reputation as a puritan—or 'poritan' as the writer spells it—the accusation of drinking and whoring seems barely credible. Why choose that line of attack? Hardly anyone would believe it for a moment."

Seager look at Foxe for several moments, then he rose to return to his newspaper office.

"Keep the note," he said. "You're a wily fellow, Foxe. Aye ... Foxe is the right name for you, even if today you look more like a strutting popinjay. I won't push the matter further—for now. You owe me two favours. Don't imagine I'll forget. For all your tricks and evasions, one day you'll have to deliver on your promises—be sure of that."

Then he left.

Foxe carefully put the paper in his pocket. Halloran would want to see it. However, that would need to wait a while. Foxe was certain Seager would try to see whether he now took his accustomed walk. If the newspaper man were to see him rushing off to talk to Halloran, it would prove what was in the note was true.

It cost Foxe a great deal to remain in his seat, drinking his coffee with an air of total unconcern. He hoped it would be worth it. If nothing else, the inactivity gave him time to think. Who had sent the note? The obvious answer was the murderer, but was that correct? Why had he done it? Why draw attention to something most people would dismiss as inconceivable? Foxe knew Morrow's body had reeked of drink, but he doubted any who had not been there would believe it—not even if all the aldermen, plus the mayor, swore to it on the bible. Why drag in the nonsense about whoring? If Joseph Morrow had approached a single harlot in this city, the word would be everywhere in half an hour. The man was wealthy. If he needed quick sex for money—which in such a bloodless, canting bible-waver was also beyond credence—all he needed to do was travel somewhere he was not known.

No, there was more to this than met the eye. Best to say nothing to anyone until he understood Morrow's life better. In the meantime, he would take his usual walk, then make good on his promise to take Mrs Crombie's place in the shop.

Wait a minute! What was that Seager had said about looking

like a popinjay? The fellow was confounded insolent! He was nothing like a popinjay. These clothes had cost a small fortune and were in the very peak of fashion. Well … fashion in the best parts of London anyway. But if the rustic nincompoops of Norwich were going to laugh at him …

Foxe quickened his pace. He needed to change before going into the shop. There was no way he would allow the folk of the city to make *him* the butt of their humour!

IT WAS A SOBERLY-DRESSED Mr Foxe who entered his shop half-an-hour later to allow Mrs Crombie to go on her errand of snooping. He had convinced himself there was no point worrying further about the strange note. Better let the matter rest until he had further information. Showing it to Halloran right away would only cause more panic at the Guildhall.

Once Mrs Crombie had left, Foxe wandered about the shop, noting with satisfaction how much better it looked. The two large windows onto the street, either side of the entrance, had been washed. No one could make window glass in large enough pieces for the whole space, so each window was made up of small panes set in thin frames. Now some of the latest satirical prints and caricatures had been attached to the inside of these frames. They almost filled the lower half of the window. Passers-by could stand and gawp at them, those who could read telling the rest what the characters were supposed to be saying. A few people, better-off than the rest, might even buy one to take home.

The shop floor had been swept, thanks to the efforts of Charlie Dillon. A strong smell of beeswax proved many of the inside surfaces had received attention as well. When he went to take his place in the open centre of the oval counter, Foxe ran his hand along the counter surface to enjoy the delicate feeling of newly polished wood.

Bookshops were rarely crowded with people eager to buy the volumes displayed. Books were too expensive for that. Insufficient sales also drove up the price, since each purchase needed to bring the seller a considerable profit for him to stay in business. Only people with significant incomes could afford to buy on a regular basis—or any basis at all. Foxe, like most booksellers, sold books unbound, so the cost of bookbinding added to the overall price. In his father's day, there had been a book binder working away in one of the workspaces above the shop. The bench and tools were probably still there. Perhaps one day he would seek them out, if only to satisfy his curiosity.

To counteract the meagre trickle of book customers, nearly all booksellers added other items to the goods on sale; things that were cheaper and in more demand. Mrs Crombie had given over nearly half of the shelves opposite the left side of the counter to patent medicines and salves. Sick people—or their relatives—wanted some alleviation of their symptoms right away. They didn't quibble at the cost either, provided it was not too prohibitive. Physicians charged high fees and apothecaries were suspected of selling what was most expensive, not what worked best. Ordinary people relied mostly on patent remedies because they were inexpensive and easily obtained.

In a city like Norwich, with a high population of artisans, tradesmen and shopkeepers, demand for such medicines was constant. Indeed, the only two people who had so far entered the shop had come for those, not books. Even so, there were bound to be lengthy periods of solitude between customers.

To distract himself—and fill his time usefully—Foxe turned his attention once more to the mystery of Halloran's stolen books.

Try as he might, he could make no sense of the theft. How did the thief get in and out unnoticed? Why did he take those particular books? They were neither the most valuable in the alderman's collection, nor the most finely bound. Foxe estimated the eight books taken would fetch barely ten or twelve pounds in the second-hand market; less if sold to a dealer. A tidy sum for a poor man. Yet hardly enough to justify the risk involved in robbing the house of an alderman and a magistrate.

Had the books been taken at random? Surely not. The thief had been too careful in replacing them with books that matched those he carried off. The only thing the alderman had told him was these books were amongst his favourites—those he consulted most often. That was why he kept them close to his desk.

Foxe realised he had forgotten to ask Halloran exactly how he decided where to shelve his books. Was it by size, by title, by subject-matter, by author or some other means of categorisation? Until Foxe knew that, he couldn't even guess why those particular books had been selected. He would have to return to the alderman's house at a convenient time to find the answer to his question. Perhaps he should also examine the library again, preferably on his own. Halloran had been in such a state the last time he had given Foxe no opportunity to make a thorough inspection.

Now several servants came to the shop while Foxe was mulling this over in his mind. They came for their masters or mistresses, carrying specific orders for medicines. Once or twice, the wife of someone of the middling classes came herself. Foxe worked hard to charm such ladies. He couldn't help noticing, however, that several of them seemed disappointed to find him rather than Mrs Crombie behind the counter. He suspected the shop was already becoming a good place to exchange the gossip of the day. For all his fine manners and flowery compliments, as a man he was not likely to know—or share—anything worth hearing. He therefore made a point of telling these customers he was only there because Mrs Crombie had to attend to an urgent matter. If they returned tomorrow, they would doubtless find her once again in her usual place. In no way did he wish to stop them offering their gossip in return for titbits from others.

In another gap between customers, Foxe noticed several of the shelves on the right side of the counter as you entered were empty. Was that simply a matter of insufficient stock, or did Mrs Crombie intend yet another innovation? It was true that those shelves received less light than those to the left. Most of the available light in the shop came through the big windows onto the street, then was reflected back by two large mirrors placed either side of the door that went through to the working spaces and storeroom. The left side of the shop abutted Foxe's house of course, so no windows were possible there. The right-hand wall, however, gave onto part of the garden of the neighbouring house and contained two small windows, set high up between the shelves. Mrs Crombie had obviously noticed this, placing the medicine packets and bottles where this extra source of light would pick them out.

Though the right-hand shelving was in a more shadowed area, there seemed no reason to ignore it. There was still plenty of light from elsewhere. He must remember to ask Mrs Crombie why she acted as she had. He would not, of course, interfere, provided she had a sound reason, but he was undeniably curious.

While he was puzzling about this, Mrs Crombie herself returned, her face showing him at once that she had news to share. In such a circumstance in the past, Foxe would simply have closed the shop and settled down to hear what it was. Mrs Crombie would have none of it.

"Regular hours, Mr Foxe," she said. "I believe I did mention how important this is. We need our customers to prefer us to other shops selling similar goods. If a servant is sent for a powder to help with a headache, or ward off more pains from the gout, and finds us closed when we should be open, you can be sure next time that servant will be directed elsewhere. Be patient, sir. We will close at four, as usual. Then, with your agreement, I will delay my return home long enough to tell you all. We must both perhaps wait a little longer for our meal, but I think it will be worth it."

Try all Foxe could, the lady would not be moved from her resolution. All that was left was for him to retire through the door into his house and try to remain calm for two more hours. His attention was so occupied with this that he even forgot to ask about the empty shelves.

∾

At four o'clock precisely, Mr Foxe went back through the door into the shop, determined to make Mrs Crombie stick to her promise to tell him all. The lady herself was just bolting the shop door.

"Right," Foxe said, all business. "What did you discover?"

"Should we perhaps go somewhere else, Mr Foxe, where we cannot be seen from the street? If people come and see us still here, there is a danger they will bang on the door and expect to be let in, even though we are closed for the day. If we went through into the storeroom, perhaps …?"

"No," Foxe said. "It will be cold in there and soon it will begin to grow dark. Come through into my house, Mrs Crombie. My small parlour is warm, the candles will soon be lit, and I can offer you at least a dish or two of tea to help offset the delay to your dinner. No, come through. Remember you are now my partner, not an employee. With my servants about, there will be no impropriety."

Mrs Crombie allowed herself to be persuaded, despite her reluctance to enter such a wealthy man's home. Soon they were settled comfortably on either side of a small, cheerful fire. The candles had been lit in the wall-sconces above the fireplace, and Foxe's maid, Molly, brought them tea. It was time to begin.

"I had a stroke of great good fortune, Mr Foxe," Mrs Crombie said. "The housekeeper in the Morrow household had been sent several times to my late husband's shop. Her mistress at that time suffered badly with sick headaches and swore by Dr Lampeter's Chlorodyne Powders as the best cure. Of course, the lady I met again today, Mrs Whateley, was not a housekeeper then, though she was plainly a superior kind of servant, destined for higher things. She remembered my name."

"Several servants came to the shop today for medicines," Foxe said.

"Precisely. It's good business. Also, from your point of view, perhaps another source of fruitful gossip. The servants in any household know everything that goes on, however hard their employers try to hide it."

"You're right," Foxe said. "I hadn't looked at it in that way."

"To return to Mrs Whateley," Mrs Crombie continued. "Sharing recollections made gaining entry to the servants' area easy.

Of course, as housekeeper, Mrs Whateley has her own room. There we would not be disturbed by anyone else."

"How did you explain your visit?" Foxe asked.

"I fear I lied," Mrs Crombie said. "I told her I was seeking out the most valued of my husband's past customers to encourage them to visit me in my new location. I think she was flattered. She even accepted the unlikely idea that I noticed her in the street one day and marked the house that she entered."

Foxe couldn't help smiling.

"So," Mrs Crombie continued, "after we had exchanged the usual pleasantries, Mrs Whateley started to commiserate with me over my husband's death. It was exactly the chance I needed. What was more natural than for me, in turn, to express my own concern over the death of Mrs Whateley's former employer. That opened the flood-gates. Mrs Whateley had probably been dying to talk to someone about her situation. Indeed, she talked almost non-stop."

The burden of Mrs Whateley's tale was simple. Mr Joseph Morrow had been a tyrant and a bully, as well as a puritan of deepest hue. He constantly invented fresh rules of behaviour for the members of his household, enforcing them with threats of instant dismissal. Mercy and tolerance were unknown to him.

The only saving factor was Mr Morrow's wife. If the staff loathed the master, many of them soon became devoted to their mistress. They did all they could to lighten her burden at being married to such a man. Those who left—and many did—tended to leave quickly. Those few who stayed were those whose pity for Mrs Morrow outweighed their disgust at how the household was treated by the master.

"She doesn't quite trust me fully, as yet," Mrs Crombie told Foxe. "I noticed she was holding one or two things back. I suspect one was that Mr Morrow was known to strike his wife if she disobeyed him—even beat her."

Being so devoid of mercy, Mrs Crombie went on, Mr Morrow treated those who did leave—or those he sacked—with mean and thoughtless cruelty. None received a reference. Any whom he especially disliked might find themselves accused of theft. Of course, he never reported such thefts to the magistrate. He claimed this was a matter of 'Christian mercy', but it was more likely because he had no evidence to back up his charges. Nevertheless, the mere threat of being taken to the court and facing severe punishment was usually enough to send the person on their way.

"Not only that," Mrs Crombie added. "They kept quiet about whatever was happening in that house. Mr Morrow's reputation was such that no magistrate was likely to believe the word of a servant against his. Especially if our good puritan Mr Morrow raised a counter-charge of theft."

That there was something badly amiss, Mrs Crombie felt sure. What it was, she had yet to discover. She had tried to press Mrs Whateley on the point, but found, once again, a strong resistance to further explanation.

"I am sure there is more to find out, Mr Foxe," she said. "If you wish, I am ready to return to see if I can build on today's conversation and increase the trust Mrs Whateley feels in me."

"You are surely right that there is more to know, Mrs Crombie. However, I think we should move carefully. This whole matter is wrapped in a cloud of suspicions. We need facts to clear it away. You have already done wonders. I would be loathe to ask you to take the risk of frightening Mrs Whateley by questioning her too closely. Did you discover any more?"

"Not really. Only that Mrs Whateley herself was on the point of handing in her notice to leave next Michaelmas, reference or no reference. But now Mr Morrow is dead, she feels it would be an act of treachery to abandon Mrs Morrow. Besides, things in the house have changed greatly, she told me. No more petty rules. No more bullying and threats. It is as if a dark cloud has been lifted from them all."

"What of Mrs Morrow?"

"She has, of course, assumed the required mourning. Yet Mrs Whateley feels sure she can be feeling nothing but relief. The only matter that remains is money. According to her, Mr Morrow was fond of boasting to his wife, even in the hearing of the servants, that he intended to make a will leaving almost everything to his church.

He would, he said, leave her only enough to live in a most modest manner, since he knew she would fritter any more away. Whether this threat will be proved correct, Mrs Whateley does not know. Only that the man was mean enough to do it—and enjoy imagining the result."

"I am coming to feel reluctant to seek out Mr Morrow's murderer," Foxe said. "I cannot help thinking he has rid this world of a truly hateful man. The fellow should be congratulated, not taken to the gallows. If it were not for all the other issues that would remain —and the threat to the city as a whole—I would go to Alderman Halloran and tell him as much. I suppose the law is the law, but there are times when ignoring it seems more just than seeing it enforced."

"So what now?" Mrs Crombie asked.

"I think everything through again," Foxe replied. "You have produced more useful information in barely two hours than I could have imagined possible. You have also helped me to set aside at least one line of enquiry."

"What is that, if I may ask?"

"There is a suggestion Mr Morrow's businesses have money problems. Naturally, that caused me to consider he might be facing a blackmailer and need money to pay him off. Yet what you have found, while confirming there might be domestic issues inviting blackmail, has made such an explanation less appealing. The servants may have hated him. One may have discovered something that could lead to blackmail. But what you have told me proves Mr Morrow would refuse to pay. No, he would be far too confident of his ability to have potential scandal dismissed as spite. If blackmail is still involved—which I consider less and less likely—it must be concerned with his business dealings, not his behaviour in private."

"So I do no more?"

"By no means!" Foxe exclaimed. "I only suggest that you perhaps should step back a little. Let the information come to you for a time, instead of seeking it out. Invite gossip. Listen to what others ask and what the replies might be. For example, Mrs Whateley may already be feeling nervous about telling you so much.

If you return too quickly, she will stop confiding in you altogether. But if time passes and nothing untoward results from her disclosures, the next time you seek her out may be even more productive. Events are moving too quickly for us to plan very far ahead. The best we can do it to stay alert and take full advantage of whatever opportunities arise."

Mrs Crombie agreed this made good sense. Besides, she now had a better idea what type of gossip in the shop might be most useful.

"What about Charlie?" she asked.

"Charlie Dillon?" Foxe was confused.

"That's right. I can collect information from the kind of people I encounter normally, Mr Foxe, as you can. But neither of us can pick up much from any source beyond the gentry, the middling classes and their servants. Charlie, on the other hand, is forced to live and move amongst the poor. Might he not hear something useful, if we ask him to keep his ears open? He's a bright lad, for all his dirt and poverty. Even better, many adults would ignore an urchin like him and go on talking as if he wasn't there. I know it's a long shot, but if servants see all their employer's dirty linen, the poor often know much more that their betters may think."

Foxe was dubious, but he was learning never to dismiss Mrs Crombie's ideas out of hand.

"Hmm …" he said. "You may be right. It can do no harm, I suppose. I agree with you that Charlie is bright. I have also found he can be relied upon to keep his mouth shut, if you tell him to. Very well, these servants Mr Morrow threw into the street must have gone somewhere. Perhaps we could find one or two and see what they will tell us. I notice that the glint of silver acts as a powerful inducement to speech amongst people of that sort. Moreover, we're not trying to get them to testify or anything like that. The man's dead, whatever he did."

Suddenly he stiffened.

"What's more," he said, "we know someone out there— someone uneducated—desperately wants us to know something very damaging to Mr Morrow's memory."

Foxe hadn't told Mrs Crombie about the note Mr Seager had given him, but did so now. She agreed it suggested somebody not only knew a good deal about James Morrow's death, but wanted to make it public.

"Good Lord!" Foxe said. "It's almost six o'clock and I haven't eaten. Nor have you, Mrs Crombie. No, no, I cannot send you home at this hour with a meal still to prepare and cook. I insist you stay and eat with me. Mrs Whitbread, my cook, is well used to sudden changes in my demands on her kitchen. I am sure there will be more than enough for both of us. Look, we won't stand on ceremony. Tonight, as most nights, I will ask for food to be brought to that table by the window there. It is quite large enough for two people. My dining room is daunting in scale, unless there is a large party. There's no use in making excuses. You will dine with me, then I will have Alfred call a chair and accompany you to your home. By the time we are finished, it will be too dark for any respectable lady to be abroad on her own."

"But propriety ..."

"Remember that my servants will be present most of the time, Mrs Crombie. Besides, I will be sure to send you to your home at an hour that will preclude any salacious gossip. Forget propriety for once. I assure you, I rarely think of it at all."

"That," Mrs Crombie said, shaking her head, "I can well believe."

8

DISASTER!

Foxe's morning began quietly, as he liked. That was not destined to last. Alfred found him seated in the coffeehouse, enjoying the meagre sunshine that filtered through the window beside him and scanning the London paper to see if there were any comments on Kitty's latest role.

"Excuse me for bothering you, master," Alfred said, "but a messenger has come from Alderman Halloran. He requests that you wait on him at his house with all the speed you can muster. I thought it best to speak to you at once on the matter."

Foxe let out a groan. Whatever could have stirred the good alderman into yet another frenzy? There was little option but to go to find out.

"Thank you, Alfred," Foxe said. "You were quite right to alert me at once. If the messenger is still there when you get back, tell him I will go to see the alderman right away. Oh, and tell Mrs Crombie where I have gone. I promised to spend a little time in the shop with her this morning. It seems she has still more ideas to stir up business. Thanks to Alderman Halloran, that must now wait."

When Foxe arrived, his worst fears were fulfilled. He found the alderman suffering a monumental panic.

"Ah, Foxe. At last!" the poor man said. "This is a kettle of stinking fish and no mistake. What a sorry tale! How will the city survive? How will I survive? The mayor is wringing his hands and shaking and expecting me to produce an immediate answer to every problem."

Foxe sat in the chair opposite the alderman, even though, in his distress, Halloran had forgotten to ask him to do so. Then he spoke, using his calmest tone.

"Some fresh developments, sir?" he said.

"Developments!," Halloran cried. "Developments be damned! This is a disaster, Foxe. A catastrophe! A veritable cataclysm!"

"Perhaps if you tell me what has happened ...?"

Halloran took a deep breath and launched into his tale of woe. As he went, sprinkling the narrative with frequent exclamations of distress and shock, Foxe sat listening in total calm. Whenever Alderman Halloran paused, expecting some cry of horror or indignation from his visitor, Foxe said nothing. As a result, Halloran repeated himself several times. It was obvious he felt Foxe had not grasped the full enormity of the situation.

Stripped of the repetitions and digressions into dire prophesy, the facts were as follows.

Late the previous afternoon, the mayor had received a brief message from Mr Samuel Allday, the banker and merchant from King's Lynn. The one the mayor had called in to discover what was going on at Morrow & Son's bank. That letter explained what he had found so far. The news was bad. The bank was critically short of cash. There might not even be enough to continue its normal business for more than a week or so. Mr Allday explained there was nothing much wrong with the banking business itself. Joseph Morrow's conservative outlook may have kept profits low, but they also minimised the risks taken on loans. On the face of things, Morrow & Son should be one of the soundest banks in the city.

Allday had not had time to be certain of the reason why the bank's coffers were nearly empty. However, he had discovered that various sums had been loaned to the Morrow yarn business over the past six months or so. All these loans were made on the direct instruction of Joseph Morrow himself. None were large enough individually to excite suspicion, but, taken together, the total amounted to a substantial sum. Allday had not thought this more than slightly unusual, until he found himself unable to find proper records of the interest, repayment terms or even the loans themselves. Nor could he find any documents from the yarn business acknowledging receipt and promising repayment in due course. In fact, the only records of any of these payments were notes in the bank's daily ledgers. Each recorded that such-and-such a sum had been handed over, in cash, on presentation of a letter of credit signed by Mr Joseph Morrow.

For now, all that was enabling the bank to meet its daily needs for cash to pay out to customers was the inflow of deposits. Should these be affected by uncertainty about Mr Joseph Morrow's death— should any hint of problems leak out and cause depositors to demand repayment at once—bankruptcy must follow. Even at the current rate of deposits, the bank was technically insolvent, since it had insufficient cash reserves to support normal business. It could call in various loans, but that would destroy healthy businesses and create the very panic they needed to avoid.

The mayor had sent an urgent message at once to Mr James Morrow to see if he could track the money down. Better still, might it be possible for the yarn business to repay at least some of these loans swiftly, without drawing attention to what was being done?

That morning, the mayor received a response. It seemed no one at the yarn business had any knowledge of loans from Morrow & Son's Bank—nor were they needed. Business was more slack than it ought to have been, but that was all. This lack of orders was due to the paucity of interest from those in charge—especially the owners, Joseph and Ezekiel Morrow. There were no planned changes or improvements that needed to be financed. All normal bills and payments could easily be covered from cash on hand. The business remained sound.

"Mr James Morrow has agreed to meet with the mayor at noon, Foxe. If I request it, the mayor will then send him on at once to talk to you. Will that be convenient?"

Foxe nodded his assent. This was indeed a kettle of stinking fish, as Halloran had put it. Where had the money gone? Everyone believed Joseph Morrow to be a wealthy man. If he had need of money—for example to pay a blackmailer—he would surely have no need to steal. Why come close to ruining his own bank, which everyone agreed was his only true business interest?

Well, at least he could make good use of the time before Mr James Morrow put in an appearance, Foxe thought. If there was a blackmailer behind this—and he could now see no better explanation, despite his skepticism earlier—they must discover what he was threatening to make public. No disgruntled servant or employee would be likely to extort such large sums as the alderman was hinting at. There had to be a different solution. Brock was probably the man to find out what that might be.

As soon as he returned from this latest exercise in calming Alderman Halloran's fears, Foxe went into his shop. As he hoped, he found Charlie Dillon there, sweeping the floor. It seemed to have become his daily task and he approached it with touching seriousness, going into all the corners and trying hard not to raise a cloud that might settle behind him.

Apologising to Mrs Crombie, both for missing their appointment and distracting her helper from his work, Foxe sent Charlie running at full speed to find the Captain. Foxe needed to talk with him before James Morrow put in an appearance. That gave him perhaps two hours—provided Charlie could find Brock at once and Brock grasped the urgency of the summons.

Mrs Crombie decided, wisely, that with so much else on Foxe's mind now was not the time to share her plans for a circulating library. It would involve a substantial outlay of cash to procure the stock to begin and income would be slow to build up. When she had first come upon the idea, it seemed simplicity itself to convince Mr Foxe of its merits as a further side to the business. Now she was not so sure.

Luckily, two ladies entered the shop at that point, each in search of some remedy for several ills. Mrs Crombie turned to serve them and Foxe, after bowing politely to each one, made his escape.

Passing through the connecting door from the bookshop, Foxe entered the hallway of his house and went to his library to wait for Brock.

CHARLIE MUST HAVE EXCELLED himself in speed and cunning in tracking Brock down. The Captain arrived in barely twenty minutes. Foxe heard Molly answer the knock at the door. Then, as Foxe had instructed her earlier, she took Brock's coat and hat and directed him at once to where her master was waiting.

"What's the rush?" Brock asked. "Halloran wetting his breeches again?"

"You could say that," Foxe replied. "Take a seat first and catch your breath. I am most grateful for your haste. Would you like some coffee, or a glass of something stronger?"

"When that little imp found me, I had a pot of good, strong ale in my hand and my sights set on a man I know who had little love for Joseph Morrow. Twice he asked for loans, offering good security and a sound notion of how best to expand his dye works. Both times Morrow dismissed his request out of hand. If anyone has a good reason to share what might be harmful to Morrow's memory, he's the one."

"Don't worry, Brock. I won't keep you long. Molly! Molly! Where's that girl? Ah, Molly. Bring the Captain a tankard of the best strong ale. I won't join you, Brock. My insides are already full of that dismal brew the alderman tries to pass off as coffee."

Once Brock's ale had arrived, Foxe summarised what he had learned from Halloran. He also added what Mrs Crombie had picked up from Mrs Whateley the day before. At the end, he asked Brock what he made of it all.

"Not much we didn't either know or couldn't guess," Brock said. "Except for the business about money missing from the bank, of course. That's bad news and no mistake. No wonder Halloran and the mayor are full of woe. I'd usually say it has to be blackmail, but somehow that doesn't quite fit. Blackmail about what? Morrow was so damned pious it's hard to work out what it could be. At least, what anyone might believe he might have done."

"My thought as well," Foxe said. "Any other reasons for rejecting the idea?"

"No mere servant would be able to squeeze Morrow for money, for a start, whatever he'd seen or heard. Morrow's reputation and wealth would be proof against that. From what your Mrs Crombie found out, they'd know what would happen if they tried it. Morrow's word alone would be enough to send them for trial at the assize. It would be simple for him to plant something where they slept—say some handkerchiefs or spoons—and make sure they were found. Next thing, the poor cove would either be hanging at a rope's end or on his way to penal servitude in America."

"Exactly," Foxe said. "The sums of money are too much as well. A servant might demand a few guineas. Child's play for Morrow to raise, even if he didn't do what you said. We have to be looking at many hundreds of pounds, maybe even more."

"I agree," Brock replied. "If enough money is missing to put the bank in danger of collapse, it has to be a considerable amount. Would Morrow be planning to disappear? Change his name and set himself up somewhere new?"

"Why? So far as we know, he's done nothing—except possibly embezzled money from his own business. I suspect that, but for his death, we wouldn't even know he'd done that. It seems that the flow of deposits was enough to cover the bank's immediate needs, even if it was short of capital."

"He wouldn't be able to make new loans though."

"True enough. He didn't make many anyhow. All he had to do to avoid suspicion was find some reason to turn almost every application down. Just like he did with your dyer friend."

"Ah," Brock said, "but banks make their money by giving loans. Without enough good loans, he'd have no money to pay depositors their interest, would he?"

"Hmm … You've a good point there. I know his bank generally paid a lower interest rate on deposits than many of the others, but it would still need to be paid. Of course, there would be the payments from past loans coming in. Halloran said Mr Allday commented that the yarn firm, though sound, was doing far less business than it could have. This might be a problem. Perhaps James was propping up the yarn side of things secretly so his father didn't find out he was making such a mess of things."

"But is it a matter for blackmail?" Brock asked. "It's a poor way to do business, but hardly illegal."

"True again. Let's forget blackmail for the moment. Back to the banking. Several big loans gone bad?"

"Wouldn't Mr Allday have found information on those? He's a banker himself. That must surely have been the first explanation to enter his head. No, the real puzzle is these so-called loans to the yarn business that the people there deny knowing about … or even needing. The only other explanation I can come up with is that Joseph Morrow—and perhaps his father too—were paying themselves annual dividends far too large for the business to sustain in the tepid way it was being run. More incompetence than dishonesty. Ezekiel thinks he can take large sums to sustain an estate he doesn't know how to run and Joseph is fiddling the books to hide the fact the business can no longer sustain it."

Foxe perked up.

"You may be onto something," he said. "Old Ezekiel bought that grandiose estate and has been playing the country gentleman. I wouldn't be surprised if the income from his share of the businesses was now insufficient to match his aspirations? Most of his capital must have been used to buy the place. Even if he bought it—or part of it—on a mortgage, that would demand regular payments. Quite large ones, I imagine."

"Would Joseph do that for his father? Run the risk of endangering his own future to keep the old man from ruin?"

"He might have," Foxe replied. "Doesn't one of the Ten Commandments talk about 'honouring thy father and thy mother'? There's another point in favour of that explanation too. Joseph must have expected to inherit everything when his father died. James, you recall, has already taken his patrimony. Joseph was the only child left. Even Ezekiel's wife is dead."

"No sisters to provide dowries or portions for?"

"None to my knowledge. There's also Ezekiel's age. Joseph would not have anticipated needing to keep up the deception for that long. Look, Brock, this is the best idea any of us has had so far. At the very least, it gives us something to investigate. Why don't you leave the other matters for a day or so and do whatever you can to discover the state of Mr Ezekiel Morrow's finances. When landowners are in trouble, there are usually some good signs. Leaving accounts from tradesmen unpaid for long periods. Delaying payment of wages to servants. Even putting pressure on tenants to pay higher rents or refusing to give them alleviation of payments due to poor weather and bad harvest."

"As you say," Brock replied, "it's the most promising area for investigation we have. I'll see what I can do."

"When Mr James Morrow comes here—and I very much hope he will—I'll try to find out what he knows of the matter. I suspect much will depend on whether he had enough time to think about anything beyond trying to pick up where his brother left off. He already told me he doesn't need money—though I take that state-ment with a pinch of salt. Still, it's quite likely that he hasn't felt any urgency to pry into what his father might have left. He may not even know the terms of the man's will. No! His brother's will. That's assuming the father is leaving it all to Joseph. With his eldest son dead, the father might well decide to do something else—endow a school or a hospital or something. Certainly brother James must have expected nothing so long as his brother was alive. They didn't get on, remember? Joseph would hardly make a will leaving most of what he possessed to his brother."

"So long as Joseph was alive ..." Brock said.

"Oh Lord, Brock. Surely not! That's a most tortuous path. Younger brother knows father will leave a fortune to his eldest son, kills that son and hopes the father will now leave it all to the only son left. Mr James Morrow didn't strike me as a murderer."

"Can't rule it out, though."

"I suppose not. Oh, I do hope that isn't the answer. Fratricide is a horrible crime, even if the brother in question is totally vile. Look, let's keep that as a last resort. I'm much happier with the idea of the dutiful son embezzling money to keep his elderly father afloat. Joseph Morrow was very much a slave to duty and the Ten Commandments, if what people say is correct."

"Aye, right enough. By the way, what's suddenly put the spring back into your step? Mrs Crombie, perhaps?"

"Mrs Crombie? What on earth are you raving about, Brock? Mrs Crombie is a respectable widow, with her husband dead barely four or five months. No. If you must know, I paid a visit to the theatre the other evening."

"Hah!" Brock cried. "I should have guessed. You're addicted to actresses, Foxe. Always were and probably always will be. Bring one home did you? You know your servants call such … ladies …'the master's little pets'? Most people keep their pets until the critters die. You change yours by the week."

"Don't exaggerate, Brock. I was true to Kitty for several years."

"Amazing, isn't it? But then, people say she's an amazing woman, in or out of bed. You never remained true to any of them for that long before. Sometimes, as I recall, you had several on the go at the same time. I used to wonder if they came on separate occasions, or whether you all cuddled up together."

"Well you can go on wondering, Brock. As I said, I decided to go to the theatre …"

"Yes, you said that. What then …?"

"The manager came to greet me personally. He was, indeed, most attentive. He insisted I meet some of the latest additions to the Company …"

"All female, of course!"

"As it happens, yes."

"That manager is probably mightily relieved to see you back. You must have spent a fortune on seats and boxes over the years. No wonder he turned his hand to pimping."

"A very inelegant way of putting it."

"True, though. Well, did you fancy one? If you spent the night with some bewitching young thing in your bed, it's no wonder the old Foxe is back. Did she perform as you hoped?"

"You are becoming coarse now," Foxe said in his most disapproving tones. "For your better information—though you do not deserve it—I slept alone. I did, however, promise to return next week to see the new programme. In which, I believe, at least three of the young ladies I met yesterday evening have quite prominent parts."

"You always liked the ones with prominent parts, as I recall," Brock said, with a guffaw. "Couldn't make up your mind, eh?"

"You'd better be on your way, Brock," Foxe said. He was trying hard to avoid grinning at his old friend. "Yes, off you go. Hopefully Mr James Morrow will be here soon. He won't tell me anything unless I am alone. You have plenty to do. Perhaps it will stop you from dwelling on my affairs."

"Doubt it," Brock said, as he walked towards the door. "There've been so many of them!"

~

FOXE WAS TO BE DISAPPOINTED. He hoped to ask Mr James Morrow some specific questions, but it was not to be. Soon after Brock left, Alfred knocked on the door of Foxe's library.

"A footman from Mr James Morrow has just delivered a message for you, Master," he said. "Mr Morrow sends his apologies. He will be unable to call on you today as His Worship suggested. While they were still talking together, he received most distressing news. It seems his father, Mr Ezekiel Morrow, has suffered a severe apoplexy. Mr James Morrow must return to his father's house at once."

"Damnation!" Foxe said. "Thank you, Alfred. It seems all possible disasters are falling upon the family of Morrow at the same time. Well, I shall have to be patient. Mr James must attend his father, of course. What a perplexing situation all this has produced."

For the next ten minutes or so, Foxe paced up and down the library. He knew it was pointless, but he couldn't sit still. For Heaven's sake! An old man's life was hanging in the balance and here he was complaining it had upset his plans for the afternoon.

Twice he sat at the fine mahogany desk set by one window,

where the best light fell. Twice he got up again and sat in one of the two upholstered chairs by the fireplace. He picked up pen and paper, then set them down again. Not even the fine painting on the wall opposite the window—brought back for him by a grateful client whose book sales had funded an extended visit to Italy—brought him any pleasure.

What finally brought this animal pacing to a halt was the sound of someone knocking at the front door. Foxe could hear Alfred attending whoever it was. Then there came a low mutter of voices, one of which sounded like a woman. Who on earth could it be? Not James Morrow, clearly. A maidservant he had sent?

Foxe's speculations might have continued a good deal longer, but there was a sharp tap on the library door and Alfred came into the room.

"Beg pardon, Master," he said. "A lady has called asking if you might be able to receive her. She says she is Mrs Morrow—Mrs Joseph Morrow—and wishes to speak with you on an urgent matter. May I show her in?"

"Great Heavens!" Foxe said. "Is there to be no end to the surprises this day brings? Yes, yes. Show her to the small parlour at once, Alfred. Oh … and you'd better tell Molly to bring tea and some suitable accompaniments. Oh dear, I am hardly dressed to receive a lady, am I? Well, I suppose it will have to do. I'm sure she must have seen a gentleman in a simple day gown before."

Going to the small parlour after a suitable delay, Foxe found Mrs Morrow dressed in deep mourning and accompanied by her maid. Naturally, her face was veiled, so Foxe could not take the measure of this most unexpected visitor. Alfred had already seated the lady in one of the upholstered chairs while her maid stood behind her. What on earth was to be done with *her*?

Mrs Morrow solved the problem. "With your permission, sir, might I ask you to call someone to conduct my maid, Minnie, to your servant's hall? She may wait there until I need her again."

"Of course, madam," Foxe said. He looked round wildly for the bell to call Molly. His usual method of summoning her with a barely modulated bellow was far too coarse for this situation.

Happily, finding the bell proved unnecessary, for Molly knocked and entered with a tray of tea things. Minnie helped her to set everything out on a suitable table. The two maids then served dishes of tea and offered the small cakes to Foxe and Mrs Morrow before they left.

The moment she and Foxe were alone, Mrs Morrow lifted the veil from her face.

"Ugh," she said. "I hate this dismal thing! I hate the awful black clothes as well, but people would be exceedingly shocked if I allowed my true feelings to show. At least like this I can see you properly."

Foxe was astounded as much by the vigorous manner of the woman before him as by her careless dismissal of proper mourning etiquette.

"Now, sir," she went on. "To business. I understand from my late husband's brother that you are investigating the circumstances of my husband's death. I know he was murdered, but that is all. It seems my family are intent on shielding me from anything they believe might upset my delicate feelings. Hah! If only they knew. They believe I am a timid, fragile thing, quite unable to deal with the less savoury elements of existence. I ask you. Do I look fragile to you?"

Foxe hardly knew what to say.

"You … well … you are quite a small person, madam. Perhaps a little below the height of many. And you are … may I observe … delicate in your physical appearance."

"Short and thin, you mean. True on both counts. That's how my late husband liked women to be. Over the years, I came to believe my appearance—and my fortune—were the only two things he ever liked about me."

By now, Foxe was so far out of his depth that he could do nothing but remain silent. Surely this couldn't be the wife of that notorious puritan Joseph Morrow?

"I see I have startled you, sir. Well, that cannot be helped. I shall, I suspect, shock a good many people in this city before this year is out. It is not my intention to put you out of countenance, believe me. However, there are certain matters that need to be clear between us. For a start, I am rather glad my husband is dead."

"Glad?"

"That is the only word. For many years, he bullied and browbeat me into acting as little more than a mouse following behind him. The perfect wife for one of The Lord's Elect: dutiful, obedient and —above all—silent. You will wonder why I did not leave his house. Where would I go? I was raised in a family of strict Calvinists. They would have turned me away and insisted I returned at once to my lawful husband."

"I am still unsure why you have come to see me, Mrs Morrow," Foxe said.

"To find out what is going on, sir. To learn what happened to my husband and why his family are scurrying around like a nest of rats visited by an extremely large and hungry cat. I hope I may persuade you that the years of adversity have proved my strength and resilience. To put it plainly, Mr Foxe, I am curious. I know you mean to apprehend my husband's murderer. For myself, I would give the man ten guineas and wish him well."

"Mrs Morrow!"

"Is that so very shocking, Mr Foxe. I suspect by this point you know a good deal about my late husband. If what little I have been able to glean about you is correct, I can hardly think you would see him as other than the monster he was. My housekeeper, Mrs Whateley, told me of her conversation with a Mrs Crombie, whom I believe you know. It seems that lady was full of praise for your kindness to her. I also heard last year of your disgraceful behaviour in escorting two ladies of dubious reputation to the mayor's ball. Mr Morrow fulminated about it for several days, with frequent allusions to Sodom and Gomorrah. I thought it noble of you."

"How may I assist you, Mrs Morrow?" Foxe felt he must bring this conversation to a point before he expired through an excess of fractured expectations.

"I did tell you, Mr Foxe, but perhaps you were so transfixed with outrage that you did not hear me. I wish you to tell me all you can about my husband's murder and why so little has been said about it publicly. When you have done that, perhaps you will be kind enough to tell me why his younger brother is scurrying about looking as if the sky is about to fall on his head."

This was plain enough, but it confronted Foxe with a grave quandary. It was not his place to interfere in the private matters of the Morrow family; nor, perhaps, should he divulge information they had determined to keep from the lady before him. On the other hand, what reason did he have for staying silent? If he would tell her nothing, might she not seek for information elsewhere? If she started contacting all the people she could, demanding to know why she was being kept in the dark, that must provoke a spate of gossip and speculation—precisely what the mayor most wanted to avoid.

In the end, he could see no straightforward alternative to making at least a partial disclosure.

"The circumstances of your husband's death are obscure, Mrs Morrow. He was found near Fye Bridge. He had been strangled, but nothing seems to have been taken from him. We are puzzled about why he went to that part of the city at night."

Foxe decided he would say nothing about the smell of drink about the body. That seemed altogether too cruel.

"I cannot suggest an answer, sir. I knew nothing of my husband's dealings outside the house. Indeed, for many years now I have scarce left it, save to attend Divine Service with him."

"Since the circumstances of his death are so … unclear, the mayor felt it best to prevent the spread of speculation, in case it might prove harmful to the city's business interests."

"Cause a run on his bank, then others."

"Precisely. No one in an official capacity has confirmed his death was due to a footpad intent on robbery, but no one has denied it either. For the moment, we all feel the less excitement his death arouses, the better. For my part, I am trying to ascertain who might have wished to do your husband harm in this way."

"A Herculean task, Mr Foxe. Few liked him. Many had good grounds for hatred."

"Why do you say that?"

"My husband possessed a strong streak of cruelty in his nature. Oh, he could not see it, deeming his actions to be no more than the severity justice demanded. Others did not regard it that way. If he had cause to reprimand a servant—something that happened several times on most days—he would do so in a loud voice, making the poor person stand before him while he rained down a whirlwind of Biblical curses and injunctions upon them. How many times have I had to comfort the victim afterwards and try to persuade them not to leave? Sometimes, when we sat to dine, he would regale me with tales of some poor individual entering his bank to seek a loan, only to be met by a jeering refusal, accompanied by a lengthy sermon on living within your means. Though he was engaged in business, Mr Foxe, he did not seem to enjoy it—or ever to be more than a mediocre practitioner. I believe he tried to use his dominant manner to deflect the criticism his weak abilities plainly warranted."

"So you cannot suggest anyone who might be especially ill-disposed towards him."

"Aside from myself, no one. And—for I'm sure the notion has now come into your head—I did not kill him."

"Madam! I would never think that."

"More fool you then! A good many wives would gladly put an end to their husbands, if they had the strength and the courage to do so—and believed they could escape punishment."

Foxe shook his head in real distress.

"Oh, Mrs Morrow," he said. "Please do not say such things, I beg of you. I have told you all there is about his death. The business on which Mr James Morrow is engaged has to do with certain … irregularities … at the bank. That is all that is certain at present."

Mrs Morrow looked sad for the first time.

"So I am to be ruined at the very moment my chains have been struck off?" she said. "Well, Mr Morrow would have said it was only to be expected. Many times he reproved my conduct, saying that the Lord would wreak his revenge upon me. Had he known I attended service last Sunday at The Octagon Chapel, and not sat in my usual place amongst his strict Calvinist congregation, he would have wondered why no thunderbolt had crushed me out of existence there and then."

"I was told of that," Foxe said, relieved to be on safer ground. "It seems to have been the talk of the city for an hour or two."

Mrs Morrow rose and carefully put her veil back into place.

"Could you please summon my maid, Mr Foxe? Thank you for the fine tea and for indulging me as you have. Do not fear. I am well used to staying silent. I will do nothing to excite further speculation or comment. My apologies for shocking you as I have. To be entirely honest, the ability to speak my mind as I wish has affected me as much as a large glass of wine must affect one who has never taken it before. I am more than a little intoxicated with the wine of freedom, sir. You have my assurance that I will soon get used to it and guard my tongue more carefully. Ah, Minnie. I am leaving now. Thank you again, Mr Foxe. I may perhaps, if you will allow it, enjoy your company again under less melancholy circumstances. Good day to you, sir. Good day.

9

THE TRUTH WILL OUT

BROCK WAS AT FOXE'S HOUSE THE NEXT DAY BEFORE FOXE HAD finished his breakfast. It seemed someone during the night had posted up printed notices at various places around the market place and in the streets nearby. The text accused the mayor and other wealthy merchants of covering up the true facts about Morrow's murder. According to whoever had composed the notice, this was to avoid admitting one of their own was nothing but a drunkard and a lecher who forced himself on women.

Brock had brought one for Foxe to see.

"Hmm," Foxe said, after he had looked at it closely. "If this is the same person who pushed the note under Mr Seager's door, someone has corrected more than his spelling. Notice the Biblical ring to the words, Brock? 'He who descends into lechery and drunkenness, and forces himself upon any who resist him, deserves to be recognised for the sinner and the fornicator he is. He who profanes his faith with hypocrisy should be proclaimed a liar in the streets of the city.' I would swear whoever composed this learned his English phrases from the Bible, not on the streets."

"Could be the printer was making it read better," Brock said.

"Maybe. But it may also be the murderer himself speaking. Not only is he convinced Joseph Morrow committed the sins he lists, he also sees him as hiding behind a façade of false piety. Remember the only sentence spelled correctly in the earlier note was the one about the Lord's vengeance. Had the writer copied that from a religious tract or book?"

"See anything else?" Brock asked.

"Not really. I'm too remote from the printing business now to gauge anything from how the page is composed. What really puzzles me is precisely why anyone would want to stir up a fuss like this. Whoever's doing it wants us to believe he knows the true facts about Morrow's death. Is it the murderer himself? Calling Morrow a drunkard appears to suggest it may well be. But why call him lecherous and a rapist? No one else has suggested Morrow was anything but a most upright and rigid puritan in sexual matters, as in so much else. And why seek to blacken the man's name after he's dead and cannot feel shame—assuming any of these charges are valid?"

The two sat for a few moments in silence, each trying to solve the puzzle, but to no avail. In the end, they parted. Brock to see whether any of his informants had picked up something useful; Foxe to take his morning promenade and try to put his thoughts into some sort of order.

The only useful idea Foxe had was to ask Mr Seager if he could tell anything of the printer from the notice itself. Seager must know about all the printers in the city. He might be able to recognise something—the typefaces, the paper, the general layout—that would enable Foxe to track down whoever had produced the pamphlet. 'A Notice to the Citizens of Norwich' it called itself—a bare title indeed for such a scurrilous essay in defamation!

There was no need. When Foxe reached his favourite coffee-house, Mr Seager was there already, and with one of the pamphlets in his hand.

"Seen this?" Seager asked.

Foxe agreed that he had. He assumed Seager would try once more to wheedle information out of him.

"Desperate stuff, if you ask me," Seager said. "His note to me didn't work, so he's trying harder. Look, Foxe. I won't print anything you don't want made public, but please tell me if there's anything in what this notice says."

"Yes and no," Foxe said. "I'm going to trust your word to keep what I tell you now quiet, as much for the Morrow family as for any other reason. When Joseph Morrow's body was found, it smelled strongly of cheap brandy."

"So the writer is correct on one point. Morrow had been drinking that evening. I can hardly believe it."

"Nor can the rest of us," Foxe said.

"What about the other part; the bit about lechery and forcing himself on women?"

"So far as I know at present, that has to be the 'no' in my response. I have not a shred of evidence to suggest Morrow wasn't as puritanical in matters of carnal lust as he claimed to be. That's what worries me. Has the writer truly got distinctive knowledge of Morrow and his death, or is he just throwing out accusations at random, hoping some may stick?"

"Either way, he must have hated our Mr Joseph."

"That is for certain," Foxe replied. "Let me ask you a question. Can you help me identify the person who printed this?"

"Well, you can rule me out for a start," Seager said. "I think you may also exclude all the other reputable printers in the city. Aside from the content being libellous … Though, now I think of it, in law no man can commit libel against the dead. No, for a start, look at the printing and the paper. The typeface used is old-fashioned. Many of the individual letters look to be so worn they haven't made a clear impression on the paper. The printing press used must be old as well. Several people brought me copies, thinking I might not have seen one. Each one was aligned slightly differently on the page. With something small like this, most proper printers would set up at least four identical pages at the same time, then cut the paper afterwards. I'd say this was done on a small press that can only handle a single sheet."

"Any more?"

"The paper is of very poor quality. It's thick and absorbent. That's why so many of the letters are smudged."

"Has it been printed by someone who happens to have access to an old press; someone who knows little about printing?"

"I don't think so. It's of extremely poor quality, but whoever did the typesetting knows his job. There aren't many amateurs who could handle the regular spacing of lines and proper word-spacing like this. No, I would say this has been done by some back-street press of the type used to turn out scurrilous broadsheets and radical tracts. You know the kind of thing. Calls to overthrow the government and hang the members of the present ministry. Imaginary last confessions of felons, sold for a penny each to those thronging to watch them dance at the rope's end outside the Castle."

"Are there many such printers?"

"Aye, a good many, though I could give you few names. Disgraced journeymen, apprentices who ran away once they believed they had learned enough. Even master printers who drank or gambled their way to poverty. That sort will print anything for ready money. You'll never find who did this, so don't waste your time trying."

Another dead end. There seemed to be no way to tell who had paid to have the notice printed, who had done the job, or even precisely why. The only thing clear was the determination of someone to make Joseph Morrow's sins public knowledge. Even that had to include the assumption that the charges made by the notice were true. The only firm evidence to support any of them was the strong smell of alcohol given off by the man's body. Someone was pursuing a vendetta against Morrow. Maybe the murderer; maybe not. It was hopeless!

Foxe went home dejected. Since it was obvious he couldn't make further progress towards finding the murderer of Joseph Morrow, he turned his attention to the other maddening mystery confronting him: Halloran's missing books. On that matter too he needed more information. He therefore sent Alfred to Alderman Halloran's home with a message asking when the alderman would have time to talk more about his missing books. At least some progress might be possible in that direction.

While Foxe waited for his manservant to return from this

errand, he wandered into his shop. Today it was quiet. Bad for business, but good for asking Mrs Crombie if she had heard anything useful. Like everyone else, she already knew of the notices posted around the city. There had been ample chatter about them amongst the customers who had come into the shop. Most found the allegations impossible to believe, given what they knew of Joseph Morrow. The general consensus was that it must be some disgruntled former employee or servant trying to make trouble out of nothing.

Nevertheless, the heightened curiosity the notices were causing had loosened several tongues. It was generally agreed Joseph Morrow had been a tyrant at his place of work and at home. Because of this, most expressed sympathy for his wife. It was odd, one said, that they never had children. Mr Ezekiel Morrow had been heard many times saying he longed for a grandson who could carry on the business to another generation.

There was also speculation about who would take over running the bank and the yarn business. With Joseph dead and Ezekiel Morrow widely rumoured to be at death's door, that only left Mr James or Joseph Morrow's widow.

None of this was especially helpful, but Foxe made sure to thank Mrs Crombie for her efforts. It was a shame it was a quiet day, he said. If more people had come to the shop, she might have been able to pick up further gossip.

This was the chance Mrs Crombie had been waiting for. At once she put forward the first part of her scheme to make Mr Foxe's bookstore what she thought it should be: the premier bookseller in the city.

"New books are expensive, Mr Foxe, as you know well, even the unbound novels ladies purchase whenever they can. Nor is that often, for they must save enough from their pin-money each time. The volumes they have finished they pass around amongst their friends and family, so making other purchases less likely. If we had a circulating library …"

"Mrs Crombie!" Foxe said. "I am called Foxe, but you are far more cunning than I am. No, no. You cannot disagree, for I can see exactly how you mean to proceed. First you will suggest such a library would attract more people into the shop, bringing their gossip with them. Then you will point out that even modest charges for borrowing would cover the cost of each book several times over —assuming it lasted long enough for, say, six or eight people to borrow it. That means a good profit. And if none of that were to sway me, you would move on to suggest that the wealthier sort might still prefer to buy their own—which they could read at leisure without having to return them in a few days—while the growing numbers of the middling sort would certainly be able to spend a few shillings on a library subscription. Better to read, perhaps, ten or twenty books in a quarter, than buy a single volume. Now, confess! Was that not your intention?"

Mrs Crombie hung her head.

"I fear you have guessed my plan to its smallest detail, Mr Foxe."

"Well," Foxe said, "the answer is 'yes'. It is an excellent idea and you have my full support to undertake it."

"Truly?"

"Truly, Mrs Crombie."

"Oh Mr Foxe," the lady cried. "If we were not in the shop in full view of the street, I swear I would throw my arms around you and kiss you."

"Restrain yourself, I pray you," Foxe said, laughing. "I have no doubt young Charlie is about somewhere nearby. If he were to see us and report it to Captain Brock, your reputation would be ruined in this city by nightfall. I have none to lose, so all would believe it proved I had designs upon your person and you were now giving in to me."

"I will remember your words," Mrs Crombie said, laughing as well. "But I will not forget your kindness either. May Heaven reward you, sir!"

"Hopefully by producing some information to help me solve this wretched mystery," Foxe said. "Ah! Here is Alfred returned. I hope it is with the message that I may call on the alderman today."

It was. Foxe left at once.

∾

BEFORE FOXE COULD BEGIN to explain the reason for his urgent request to see the Alderman, Halloran poured out his own news.

James Morrow had sent the mayor a message, Halloran told him. He had managed to persuade the bank's former chief cashier to return to help sort out the problems. The man had worked there during the whole period the bank had been in business—nearly five years—and for other banking businesses before that. Indeed, Mr James Morrow would have turned to him at once, had he not been so suddenly dismissed.

"So," Foxe said to that. "It seems clear enough that Mr James Morrow does not have any suspicions of the man's honesty. Perhaps the cause for Ezekiel sending the poor man away was as simple as it appears. He raised a matter no one wished to deal with. It does not seem to have been for darker reasons."

"All the man did was warn his master of his concerns," Alderman Halloran said. "But what if what he warned of was already known or suspected? Oh … this gets us nowhere. All is supposition without fact. Let us just hope the man can prove useful now."

Alderman Halloran pressed on, explaining how the mayor and various city bankers had talked late into the night to develop a plan to save the Morrow bank from default. After many hours, they agreed a proposal to put to Mr James Morrow. They assumed he would be the only person able to make decisions, since Ezekiel Morrow was said to be hovering uncertainly between life and death.

The plan was this. A consortium of local merchants and bankers would make a large enough short-term loan to Morrow & Son to keep them solvent. That would allow time for more permanent arrangements to be put in place. According to Mr Samuel Allday, if the capital was replaced, and no more money disappeared in secret payments, the bank could continue to trade without problems. However, paying back the loan would require selling more or less everything owned by Ezekiel and Joseph Morrow, including Ezekiel's house and country estate and the yarn business. Only if a good amount of the missing money could be recovered was there a possibility of retaining anything in the family. The losses were, sadly, likely to include the jointure for Joseph's widow. It was regrettable, but there it was.

Foxe agreed it seemed a sound plan. It would also be helpful to him, since working out what caused the crisis was obviously going to take time. He loathed facing so much pressure to get a quick result.

"I feel great sorrow for Joseph Morrow's widow," Foxe said. "She has done no wrong, yet must bear a hard punishment. Could we not establish a fund to help provide for her? I would gladly contribute to such a cause."

"I agree," Alderman Halloran said. "I will speak with the mayor about it. Of course, much will depend on the amounts raised by the sale of the estate and the businesses."

"Will you be interested in the yarn business?" Foxe asked. Alderman Halloran was a yarn merchant on a substantial scale. Probably the foremost such merchant in East Anglia.

"Perhaps," Halloran said. "Perhaps."

He would not be persuaded to say more.

Now it was Foxe's turn. He showed Halloran the printed pamphlet Brock had given him earlier, then added a summary of his conversation with Mr Seager of *The Norfolk Intelligencer*. Halloran was horrified and began at once to show signs of panic.

"Compose yourself, alderman, I pray you," Foxe said. "This is good news. It proves how much you and the mayor have been able to keep private until now. Whoever had this notice produced is becoming desperate. If you dismiss what it contains as claptrap, written by a person sorely afflicted in his wits, little harm will follow. Who will believe the ravings of a disgruntled employee or servant over the evidence of their own eyes? The people of this city have seen for themselves how strongly Joseph Morrow cared for his reputation for unbending virtue. He did not just live the puritan life, he gloried in it."

"I suppose there is that." Alderman Halloran did not sound convinced.

"Indeed there is," Foxe said. "Reputation is powerful for good or ill. I should know. I'm sure the greater part of the citizenry of Norwich believe they know all that is significant about me. Yet less that a hundredth part of their number have ever spoken with me for five minutes. Most would probably not recognise me in the street."

"I doubt the latter," Alderman Halloran said, laughing. "They might not know your face, but they would be sure to know your style of dress. Why, I do not believe there are many in London or Bath who could rival you in elegant—not to say most richly decorated—clothes. Amongst we drab, provincial gentlemen, you shine as does a diamond shoe-buckle amongst pewter."

Foxe decided to disregard this remark.

"What most puzzles me," he said, attempting to draw the conversation back to safer topics, "is who is so desperate to discredit Morrow? Why? The man is dead. He cannot be sensible of any slurs raised against his character. If we knew the answer even to one of those questions, it might point us to the murderer. As it is, I begin to think we will never find him."

"The mayor does not want either of us to concentrate on that matter, Foxe. His main priority is to find where the bank's money has gone. Have you any notion of how to start on that?"

"The three most obvious reasons for missing funds are theft, blackmail or bad business decisions," Foxe said. "In this case, theft seems unlikely. Morrow was a rich man, as well as the principal partner in the banking business. Why steal what you already own?"

"Blackmail?"

"For me, alderman, the sum involved seems too great. Even if it was taken in smaller amounts over a considerable period, it is more than most servants or employees would ever ask for. An individual blackmailer might be greedy, but surely not enough to empty the coffers of a bank? A group might do it. Yet in neither case does it take us past the most obvious problem. We have discovered no avenue for blackmail. Nothing that points to a secret dark enough."

"Certainly not in the case of such a confoundedly puritanical fellow."

"Precisely."

"Could be bad loans the man wanted to cover up," Halloran said. "Seems the other merchants who act as bankers in this city had a somewhat low opinion of Joseph Morrow as a banker and a businessman. Mr Allday says that only the man's rigid conservatism kept the bank afloat."

"Well," Foxe said. "If that is so, it must go against the suspicion of a long series of risky investments, all producing significant losses. No, alderman. Were that the case, we would have heard long ago of the resulting business collapses. There must be an explanation, but I cannot believe we have hit upon it yet."

There matters must stand for the moment, they agreed. Unless and until new evidence could be found, the investigation into Joseph Morrow's death had reached its end.

Alderman Halloran was just about to call a servant to see Mr Foxe out when the bookseller recalled what had, in many ways, been the main reason for his visit.

"Ye gods!" he cried. "I will forget my own head next. alderman, Mrs Crombie asked me to enquire whether Mrs Halloran might condescend to bring your two nieces to visit our bookshop. It would please her greatly to be able to show them what she has done, then offer them a dish of tea as refreshment."

"I'm sure they'd enjoy that greatly," Halloran replied. "I'll ask my wife. Please thank Mrs Crombie and tell her the invitation is much appreciated. Excellent woman you have there, Foxe. You ought to marry her before someone else does. Much better for you than those showy creatures you normally display on your arm."

"It is unlike you to play the matchmaker, alderman. The lady's husband is not yet six months dead and she has mentioned no pressing wish to marry again. In addition, my reputation would weigh heavily against any suit I might press upon her. Common opinion, sir, is that I am a seller of the most choice and disgraceful pornographic books, for only thus could I raise enough money to pay for my clothes and my women."

"I know that isn't true!" Alderman Halloran protested.

"Hush, alderman. I have worked hard to establish my dubious reputation. It serves me well to be dismissed as a dandy of light morals. Who could imagine such a man would be employed by yourself and the mayor in matters of importance to the city? It is my disguise—and a decent one too. If Mrs Crombie were foolish enough to accept my offer of marriage, that disguise would be threatened. Why, for me to be seen to have acquired a sensible, respectable wife would undermine all I have built up with such care."

"Well, you know your own business, I suppose. Have you advanced any further in finding my stolen books or identifying the thief?"

"I may have, alderman, I may have. One notion has occurred to me, but I have lacked the time and the opportunity to test its worth. Bear with me. I hope to be able to bring a speedy conclusion to that matter at least."

"I would be most grateful if you could," Halloran said. "Only so great a problem as the murder of Joseph Morrow and the loss of his bank's funds could distract me from my grief over my lost books. I swear it feels as if close members of my family had been snatched away."

"Patience, alderman. Do not lose hope. Now, you will remember to ask your wife to send word by a servant of her intention to visit? And please make certain she is accompanied by your nieces. I believe they would find such a visit of particular use for their future education."

FOXE RETURNED HOME feeling as frustrated as he had when he set out. Yet again, his investigation had reached a dead end. The efforts being made to cope with the mess Joseph Morrow left behind were interesting, yet none concerned him directly. Perhaps he should step aside and confess himself beaten? However much he hated to leave a puzzle unsolved, the reality was that, without fresh facts, there were no avenues left to pursue.

Foxe removed his outdoor coat, dressed once again in a comfortable day gown and retreated to his library. It was his favourite room for thinking, shut away from interruption but not too remote. He might hear the servants moving about in the kitchen and scullery, for those rooms projected from the house behind the back stairs, but he could not see them or be seen; not even if they went into the garden. The library windows gave a view only of the narrow space between his house and the next one in the street.

No one disturbed him for nigh on two hours. Indeed he was quite lost in gloomy reflection on his lack of progress when Molly knocked and startled him into wakefulness.

"Beg pardon, Master," she said. "Captain Brock is here to see you."

"Send him in, Molly," Foxe said, "and bring a jug of good ale." Here at least was someone with whom to share his woes.

Brock appeared remarkably cheerful, despite his first report being that Ezekiel Morrow was not expected to last the night. The apoplexy had robbed him of both speech and movement on one side of his body. Even if he lived, he was likely to have little ability to cope with the world. In the meantime, James Morrow was acting on his behalf in all matters. With his elder brother dead, it was generally assumed he would inherit all Ezekiel's property. How Joseph had disposed of his wealth—even if he had made a proper will—was still unknown.

Foxe brought Brock up-to-date with what he had learned from Alderman Halloran that morning.

"So you see, Brock," he concluded. "The matter of testaments and inheritances is probably moot, since all the property and wealth of both Ezekiel and Joseph will be needed to repay the loan required to keep the bank afloat."

"A bad business all round," Brock said. "We still do not know the cause. I have been about the city talking with all I could find who have dealt with Joseph Morrow. The merchants and shopkeepers who supplied the Morrow household, as well as those who purchased yarn. The only change over the past few months was that those presenting their accounts found payment to be unusually tardy. Mr Joseph Morrow was hard to please, but usually paid on time."

"He could no longer conceal his problems," Foxe said. "His losses must have been growing too fast. Still, this confirms only what we know. It takes us no further forward. I do not mean to be ungrateful for your efforts or belittle what you have achieved. However, the fact remains that we know Morrow was in financial trouble, yet still have no clear notion of its cause."

"I have not yet finished," Brock said. "Indeed, I have kept the best to last. I suddenly remembered to visit Miss Hannah and Miss Abigail Calderwood."

Foxe groaned and banged his forehead with the heel of his hand.

"I am thrice an idiot!" he cried. "Thank heavens for your good sense, Brock. Over the years, those sisters must have taught most of the children of this city. Did Joseph and James Morrow pass through their hands?"

"They did and the ladies remember them both."

"Of course they do! They may be old, but I wager neither has forgotten anything in the whole of their lives. What did it cost you to loosen their tongues? I never knew them give out information without a price."

"A bottle of good French brandy," Brock said. "You know, Foxe. What amazes me is that they rarely leave their house, yet know more of what is happening in this city today than I do. They told me of Ezekiel Morrow's state and I do not doubt that it is correct. They even know about your sadness over the loss of Kitty and Gracie—and of Mrs Crombie, her past history and the effect she is having on your bookshop."

Foxe laughed.

"Of course they do. I suspect they even know what I ate for breakfast and what Mrs Whitbread is cooking for my dinner. I swear to you, Brock, if any in this city could rightfully be suspected of witchcraft, it would be those two. Did you look around for broomsticks and black cats?"

"Now you mention it," Brock replied. "There was a cat on Miss Abigail's lap, but it was not a black one. Maybe it changes colour with the time of day?"

"I would not be surprised at anything that happens in that house. Now, tell me what those two were willing to share with you. I warrant it is not all they know. It would require more than a bottle of brandy to cause them to be that open. However, I'm sure whatever they have revealed is most useful."

"Before you ask," Brock said, "even they do not know who killed Joseph Morrow—or so they claim. Yet they expressed no surprise at his murder. They said they believed it must happen at some time. When I asked why, they rambled into a lengthy story about the Morrow boys as children."

"Your question was too direct, Brock. Remember they were schoolteachers. They always want those they instruct to find the answers for themselves. The most they will ever offer are hints and nudges in the right direction. If they told you of the Morrow boys' childhoods, they must believe the reason lies there—at least in part. Tell me all you can recall of their words, I beg you."

Brock related everything he could remember. So far as possible, he left nothing out, however trivial.

Joseph, as everyone knew, was the first child of Ezekiel and Katherine Morrow. He was followed by a daughter, who died in the first year of life. Then, four years after Joseph's birth, Katherine became pregnant again, this time with James. To Ezekiel's immense sorrow, his wife died giving birth. Indeed, Ezekiel was so affected by Katherine's death that he determined never to show love for anyone again. He never remarried and his attitude towards his sons was always cold and distant.

Thus it came about that Joseph was nearly five years his brother's senior. He too must have suffered greatly from the death of his mother, for he developed an odd mode of behaviour. One moment he would be sullen and withdrawn, the next loud and boastful. He also began to reveal an underlying element of cruelty in his character, especially towards any smaller or weaker than himself.

According to the Calderwood sisters, this cruel, bullying way of dealing with others extended to his younger brother. Perhaps Joseph blamed him for causing his mother's death. Perhaps it was no more than the inevitable rivalry between the boys in trying to gain some signs of approval from their father. Affection they could not gain, for Ezekiel had locked that emotion away.

All through their childhood and adolescent years, the rivalry between the boys continued. Sadly for Joseph, his father began to reveal a decided preference for the younger brother. However hard Joseph tried, his efforts were always judged inferior to James'. This was, Miss Abigail said, not surprising. James strongly resembled his father. He was quick-witted, determined and possessed of a good brain. Worse, he exhibited a decided aptitude for business matters from the youngest age.

In contrast, Joseph rarely revealed much concern for anything beyond seeking ways to draw attention to himself. He was not stupid. But if something failed to seize his interest at once, he could not be persuaded to concentrate. In the classroom, James shone while Joseph languished near the bottom. The same was true in their relations with the other boys. James was popular, Joseph feared and disliked. James would go around in a gaggle of others, Joseph was nearly always alone.

There was only one field in which Joseph was able to eclipse his younger brother, the Misses Calderwood had said. That was in religious duties and knowledge. Ezekiel had always been a pious man, much attached to a particular conventicle of rigid Calvinist dissenters. Both boys were made to attend services and Sunday school there. James soon showed too great a tendency to question the articles of faith. He was often punished as a result. Joseph, on the other hand, demonstrated the obsessive attachment to Biblical commandments and rules that characterised the grown man. In religious matters, Joseph was the star and James the one who lagged far behind.

Thus their lives continued until James at length told his father he could no longer live in the same house as Joseph. There were furious rows, but the young man could not be shaken in his resolve. In the end, Ezekiel agreed to give him the sum of two thousand pounds as his share of the family wealth and let him go. In later years, James and Ezekiel did become somewhat reconciled, but the boy's decision had broken Ezekiel's heart. He could never quite forgive what his son had done.

Worse was to come. Ezekiel Morrow's dissenting sect was fervent in their opposition to the taking of alcohol in any form. So when

James chose to apprentice himself to a brewer, they cut him off as an unbeliever and a damned soul. He probably did not care. By that time, he had established his own way in life and partook of many of its pleasures as freely as any other man of his age.

Joseph responded by becoming one of his brother's fiercest critics. He began to establish a reputation in the city as a most severe opponent of any kind of alcoholic drink. As James embraced a more secular style of life, Joseph became ever more the puritan. As James prospered in business, Joseph struggled to keep up.

Eventually, old Ezekiel determined to step aside and enjoy the final years of his life—at least as much as the last links to his religious background would allow. But putting Joseph in charge of the business was never going to work well. At his best, he proved mediocre. At his worst, he alienated customers and caused problems with the workforce. Ezekiel would not agree to dispose of the yarn business, so Joseph turned instead to an area where his knowledge could not be challenged by his father. Furthermore, banking demanded only a small staff and customers needing a loan were not in any position to criticise the man who might give it to them.

"It appears we may be right on one matter," Foxe said at that point. "Joseph was managing the profitable yarn business ineptly. If he didn't want his father to know that—which seems certain—he would need to make returns look better than they were. Even more so if his father was drawing large 'dividends' to support his lifestyle as a member of the gentry. The funds of the bank must have looked like the only solution."

Brock nodded in agreement, then continued his tale.

Poor Joseph! He tried harder and harder to be perfect. Of course, he failed, as any man must. Even other members of his sect began to complain of his behaviour towards them. Just as when he was a boy, he was only happy when he was the centre of attention. One or two of the elders warned him against the sin of pride, but he refused to listen. By the time he met his end, no one liked him or approved of his ways; neither his fellow dissenters, his employees, his servants, his customers—or even his wife.

"That was where they stopped," Brock said. "When I pressed

them for more, they said to look for the aspect of life against which Joseph set his face most strongly."

"Alcohol," Foxe said.

"That's what I said to them," Brock replied, "but they shook their heads. I should tell my friend Foxe to look harder, they told me. Then nothing else. They shut their mouths and smiled at me and made it clear I could ask until the Day of Judgment came and they would add nothing else."

"Oh, Lord," Foxe said. "Look harder. What can they want me to find? Well, I was thinking my puzzle over Joseph Morrow had come to an end, so I cannot be ungrateful that they have set me on yet another path. Brock, you've done a fine job and deserve my congratulations. First you recalled the Calderwood sisters, which I had not, then extracted at least some fresh information from them. Being unable, as yet, to make head nor tail of what they have told you is no reason for me to complain."

Brock was clearly pleased by this commendation from Foxe, yet he had not quite finished what he had come to say. This part, he suspected, would be less welcome.

"You will have to do without me for a time," he said. "Lady Henfield is called to attend her sister, who is at Bath seeking a cure for some female ailment or other. All is not going well and the family are gathering, just in case. From Norwich to Bath is a long journey, and perhaps a dangerous one. Lady Henfield therefore asked me to attend her and her maid to see they reach their destination safely. Naturally, I agreed. I have never been to Bath and will be most interested to see what people make such a fuss about."

"Will you be away long?" Foxe asked.

"Some two weeks at least. I can hardly see the ladies to Bath safely, then leave them to make their way back home alone. I have therefore undertaken to stay in the town for as long as they do, so as to attend them on the journey back. Lady Henfield has the private belief that her sister is making a fuss about nothing, but still means to satisfy herself on the matter. She estimates that to be in Bath for eight or ten days should suffice."

"I'll miss you," Foxe said. "I'll have no one to talk this matter over with."

"No one?" Brock said. "No, my friend. I leave you in safe hands, of that I am sure." Then, like the Misses Calderwood, he closed his mouth firmly.

10

"QUICK-FINGERS FLO"

Foxe slept badly that night, dozing, waking, rolling over and then back again as the hours of darkness crept past. His mind refused to let him rest. Instead, it kept scrutinising the meagre facts he had about Joseph Morrow's murder, looking for anything to provide a clue to why it happened. Some fact he had overlooked; some oddity or anomaly he had disregarded. Find it and he could move forward again.

At last, after yet another period of troubled half-sleep, marred by dreams of failure and disgrace, Foxe opened an eye and saw daylight behind the shutters. Perversely, now the morning had come, his exhausted body clamoured for him to remain in bed. He could hear distant noises showing that his servants were busy about their morning tasks. Once or twice he noticed soft footsteps outside his bedroom door, followed by a pause, then the sounds of the person retreating again. Molly was trying to discover whether her master was awake and ready to leave his bed. Once she was sure he was, she would hasten to bring him a jug of hot water, so that he could wash his face and attend to the business of shaving. Many gentlemen had their valets or menservants shave them, but Foxe preferred to make his own toilet.

If he sat up, he could see the dial of the clock on the mantle. Not much before eight. Well, by the time he was dressed and went down, his breakfast would be ready for him. He was not an early riser, getting up with the dawn, drinking a cup of coffee and attending to who knew what until the proper breakfast hour. Foxe preferred to stay in his bed as long as he could—especially when he was not alone.

That thought reminded him he had promised to attend the theatre next week. One or two of the young actresses the manager had introduced to him showed definite possibilities. The chance of putting them to certain practical tests of their suitability as future companions cheered him enough to make him set his feet on the rug by the bed and commence the lengthy process of starting out on another day.

At nine-thirty, Foxe took his place at the table in the small parlour and Molly brought him rolls, warm from the oven, home-made jam and fresh coffee. As he ate and drank, his mind remained as busy as ever, reviewing once again the few bits and pieces of evidence available to him.

Of course, a good part of his frustration came from having no one to talk with—no one to help him test his ideas and chart a firm path. Kitty and Gracie were gone. No help for that. Brock too would be leaving this morning—maybe had left already—on his way to Bath in company with Lady Henfield and her maid. Foxe wondered idly how Brock would behave himself. Would he preserve a strictly decorous relationship with the object of his affection? Would the lady tire of his scruples and make it clear that differences of rank would soon be lost if they both removed their clothes and gave way to their desires?

Well, time would tell. In the interim, he had work to do. And if no other solution presented himself, he could always talk with Mrs Crombie. She had shown herself an adept listener, even if she would be unable to offer the insights and criticisms Brock could. How odd that he had never considered until now how much he depended on this process of clarification and challenge.

After a few more moments, Foxe's mind circled back to what

little he knew. He remembered what the Misses Calderwoods had said. 'Look for the aspect of life against which Joseph set his face most strongly,' and 'tell your friend Foxe to look more deeply.'

Not drink, it seemed. Something else. Something that demanded looking at Joseph Morrow's life harder. What could that be? What else would either produce huge demands for money or form a basis for blackmail sufficient to cause Morrow to pay whatever he could scrape together?

Not gambling. That too could be dismissed. You could not wager your money alone. You needed other players as reckless as you. If you lost heavily, someone must win a correspondingly large amount. People might try to conceal the extent of their losses, but winners were certain to boast. Word swiftly got out of who was winning or losing at the tables.

Given the extent of the monies taken from the bank's coffers—and the relatively short period in which the fraud must have been taking place—the stakes at these imagined gambling-tables must have been immensely high. There were, so Foxe believed, people who would wager a fortune on the turn of a single card. Yet they would not be people willing to admit a person like Joseph Morrow into their midst. Not a sour-faced Puritan with a reputation for religious cant. Those who played for large stakes were the members or dissolute offspring of an opulent and aristocratic elite. To them, Joseph would be irredeemably vulgar, whatever his wealth—a person of the middling sort trying to join a playground reserved for the upper classes. He might—just—be tolerated once, so that they could take as much of his money as they could. They would never welcome him into their regular games. Even if Foxe assumed Morrow's luck had deserted him totally, or his companions at the tables had cheated outrageously, it was still impossible to believe he could have lost so much money so quickly.

Making a run of bad loans at the bank had already been ruled out. If enterprises requiring loans on that scale failed—whether by bad management or fraud—everyone would know. It would be reported in the newspapers and be common gossip in the coffee-houses. Many had money invested in the city's businesses. You were a fool if you did not take care to keep your eyes on what your money might be doing. Even the depositors in the bank would take careful notice of the general level of business success.

Besides, Joseph Morrow was well known to be ultra-conservative in banking matters. He preferred to limit his profits if the alternative involved taking on significant risk. That was how he managed to persuade depositors to accept a half-percent lower return on their money than the others bankers gave. Morrow & Son offered the ultimate in safety for your surplus capital. Only investing in 'The Funds', bonds guaranteed by the government, gave greater security —and they paid an even lower rate of interest.

The method used to get the money from the bank had been to register a series of fictitious loans to the yarn business. Mr James Morrow had been assured it had neither needed such loans nor received them. Whatever was written in the bank's ledgers, the money had been paid out in a mixture of bank notes, cash and cashable banker's draughts. Then it had disappeared. Foxe had already sent a message to Mr Samuel Allday to ask if the returned and cancelled draughts gave any clue to the destination of the funds. They had not. All had been exchanged for cash at other banks about the city, sometimes endorsed with the names of supposed suppliers to the yarn business. Many businesses paid their accounts in this way, making over a bill due to them to meet a payment they must make to someone else. Foxe had little doubt that these 'suppliers' would turn out to be another part of the fiction. The entire enterprise had been planned too carefully to fail on such an obvious point.

That left women.

If you assumed all that money had been spent on mistresses, there must have been far too many of them to hide easily. Expensive ones too. The kind who delighted in attending assemblies and balls dressed in rich silks and satins and sparkling with diamonds. Expensive mistresses expected a constant supply of magnificent gifts in exchange for suffering you to take liberties with their persons. Yet none Foxe had ever heard of hid those gifts away; or preferred cash to invest over jewels and gold to wear. That sort always liked to parade what their beauty and skills in the bedroom had brought them. Besides, he could not imagine any would submit to a Puritan provincial banker, even an unimaginably generous one.

Whores?

Foxe made a rough calculation of the number of the most expensive whores who would be needed to absorb money on such a scale. It proved to be colossal. Far beyond the physical ability of even the youngest and most ardent of rakes. The only way to reach such a number was to assume the man paying assembled them in droves—then watched while they either pleasured one another or submitted to a platoon of sex-starved militiamen. It was beyond belief. Nor could the holding of such Bacchanalian orgies have passed unnoticed.

Of course, Foxe could once have been certain of what had or had not taken place, but Gracie was no longer available to share the knowledge gleaned from her contacts throughout the bagnios, whorehouses and common stews of the city. That thought caused him pain, so he moved on rapidly.

Blackmail was the only explanation left, especially if the Morrow businesses were already declining under Joseph's lackluster management and he was trying to hide that fact from his father. It could have become the proverbial straw to break the back of a once-prosperous family firm.

Foxe supposed it must be so. Yet that solution too was as full of problems and unbelievable assumptions as all the others. Who would be able to extract such an amount of blackmail money? What secret would be so precious to Joseph Morrow—what action so shameful—that he would bring all to the brink of collapse rather than see it revealed? If he had such a secret, would he not protect it with such care that no one could have come upon it?

Suppose he drank in the concealment of his own home. The servants would know at once and it would have been spread abroad within hours. He might be embarrassed severely, but he would hardly have paid a fortune to keep it quiet. Besides, given his reputation, he could have relied on any who spread such gossip first being ridiculed as fools.

The same applied to keeping a secret mistress (not one who wore his gifts openly) or spending large amounts on collecting pornography. Indeed, to spend that amount on pornographic books, even if he hired naked women to read them to him, would have demanded a library to keep them in larger than many of Norwich's palatial parish churches.

Did he abuse his position to demand his servants submit to his sexual needs? Many a master did as much. The world was littered with maids dismissed for trying to tell the world what their master did to them, or those made pregnant by various male members of the household from master to butler or footman. Joseph Morrow's reputation would surely have been proof against a charge of rogering his maids. The reality was, of course, none had ever been made to Foxe's knowledge.

If blackmail was the only possible answer to why Joseph Morrow robbed his own bank as he had, it was going to take a better brain than Foxe's to discover what the man was paying to keep secret.

THUS IT WAS Foxe left his house late, hid himself in a corner of the coffeehouse far from his normal seat, then walked amongst the crowds of hawkers, hucksters, jugglers ,mountebanks, whores and thieves in the great Market Place. He kept his face cast down and his eyes kept firmly on the ground, acknowledging no one who crossed his path.

He never noticed the person sidling up to empty his pockets until some fragment of his brain warned him of the slither of a stealthy hand moving beneath his coat.

Foxe was too wily to cry out that he was being robbed. Instead he clamped his coat tight to his body with one arm and stepped backwards sharply, pulling the pickpocket off-balance. Next he swept his foot out in the direction where it must meet the thief's leg and tripped him up. The result, as he had expected, was to tumble the thief in the dirt at his feet.

Looking down, he saw a scrawny boy dressed in an old, torn coat much too big for him, a filthy shirt and equally grubby breeches. The boy's arms, where they showed below the cuffs of the coat, were thin as sticks, as were his legs below the breeches. His feet were bare, filthy and—where you could see through the dirt—blue with cold.

Foxe's action had so much taken the young rascal by surprise that he waited for one or two crucial seconds before trying to spring up and escape. That delay sealed his fate, for Foxe's foot was already resting on his back just enough to pin him down.

By this point, numerous passers-by had gathered round Foxe and the boy. All were urging Mr Foxe either to hang onto the child while a constable was fetched or deal him a good beating there and then. The busy Market Place was infested with pickpockets. Any taken could expect no mercy from stall-holders or customers.

Foxe, however, had other ideas. He bent down, took a firm grip on the boy's bony arm to prevent his escape, and hauled him to his feet. Then he set off towards his shop, dragging the miscreant alongside him. Neither had spoken a word. Only when they were both safely in the shop, with the door shut tight behind him, did Foxe speak to the thief he had captured.

"My purse, if you please," he said in a pleasant voice. "You cannot run off with it, so I might as well have it back."

The boy reached into a pocket of his old coat and took out Foxe's purse. He still had not uttered a word.

"What's your name, boy?"

Still silent. It appeared the lad was set on a battle of wills with his captor.

That was when Charlie Dillon came into the shop, stopped, stared at the youth held fast by Mr Foxe, and supplied the answer to the matter of the boy's name.

"Hey, Mr Foxe," Charlie said. "Why have you got hold of 'Quick-fingers' Flo?"

"This Quick-fingers, as you call him, picked my pocket," Foxe said. "I caught him in the act."

Charlie gazed at Foxe in awe.

"You caught Quick-fingers Flo?" he said. "You must be real fast, sir. No one ever caught Flo before. No one."

"Why do you call him Flo?" Foxe asked.

"Well … 'cos Flo's an 'er, not an 'im," Charlie said. "It's a girl you've got 'old of. May not look like it, but it really is a girl, ain't it, Flo? Lor', I be … I am … ashamed of you, gettin' caught like that, even if it was by Mr Foxe."

Foxe, determined to find the truth of the matter, pulled the thief towards him and swiftly put out his other hand to feel under the shirt at chest height. The child jerked back, face scarlet with embarrassment and anger, but Foxe still held her fast.

"Quiet, child," Foxe said gently. "I'll not explore anywhere else. Nor will I hurt you."

They made an odd tableau. Foxe striving to be as gentle as he could; Charlie still staring at Flo in disbelief; and the girl straining to place herself as far away from both of them as she could.

"Mrs Crombie?" Foxe called out. "Are you back there somewhere? Can you come here and take this young lady's arm in a firm grip? I still don't trust her not to try to run away. No, no, Flo. Stay there. No one will harm you."

In a moment, Mrs Crombie came forward and would have done as Foxe asked if Charlie hadn't intervened.

"Do as Mr Foxe says," he said in a surprisingly commanding voice. "I knows 'im. He won't hurt you, specially now he knows you're a girl. 'Sides, I'm here, ain't I? Just stand still and answer his questions like a good girl." He turned to Foxe, smiling.

"Flo's not really wicked, Mr Foxe. She only steals because she 'as to. The poor thing's mother died a while ago and her father decided he couldn't afford to raise all the children left behind. So 'e keeps the boys and puts the girls into the orphanage. 'Cept for Flo, that is. She's the oldest—nigh on fourteen, I think, though you'd never guess it. 'Er father sold 'er to the bawd of a brothel to replace their previous so-called virgin, whose maidenhead had been taken too many times to trick anyone into believin' 'e was the first."

"Monstrous!" Mrs Crombie said. "Her own father!"

"Didn't 'ave much choice," Charlie said. "If she'd gone into the orphanage along of the rest, she wouldn't 'ave fared much better. Probably be sent out as a servant. Then either worked to the bone or used by the master of the house in the same way as the customers of the brothel. Least he got some money for 'er."

All the time Charlie had been speaking, Foxe had been formulating an idea.

"Well, Flo," he said, "I'll give you a real chance, if you'll take it. Mrs Crombie here will look after you while I go and call for my maid, Molly. I'll tell her to take you down to the kitchen, find you something good to eat and a warm place by the fire, then keep an eye on you there while my housekeeper gets you proper clothes for a girl and sees you have a good wash. Then, if you promise not to steal or try to run away, I'll give you a position as a maid to help Mrs Whitbread, my cook. You can sleep in the attic, where it's warm and dry, and start to learn the skills of cooking. You'll get regular meals, proper clothes and a safe place to live. I'll even give you some money of your own, once you show you can behave properly. And I won't, I promise, ever try to treat you as men would have done in the brothel."

"Gawd!" Charlie said. "Say yes quick, Flo! You won't never have a better offer'n that."

"What's the catch?" Flo spoke for the first time. If nothing else, her voice would have given her gender away. It was surprisingly gentle and sweet-toned.

"No catch," Foxe said. "You have my word on that."

"'Allus a catch," the girl said.

Mrs Crombie started to speak, but Charlie got in first. He walked right up to Flo and glared at her. Neither were as big for their age as they should have been—poverty had seen to that—but Flo was still a good three inches taller than the boy. In this case, however, it made no difference. Charlie was the one in charge—and he was angry.

"Right!" he snapped. "Listen to me, Flo, an' listen real good. Don't you never, *never* suggest Mr Foxe ain't tellin' you the truth. You got that? Never! Now, do as 'e tells you, give 'im your promise to behave, and be grateful for what you don't deserve. I'm warnin' you!

Do as I tells you, or no one in this city will ever lift a finger to 'elp you again, I'll see to that."

For a brief moment, there was silence. Then Flo began to shake and burst into a flood of tears.

"Don't be mad wi' me, Charlie," she gasped. "I'll do it, I promises. I'll be the best maid ever, swear I will. Only don't throw me out on me own, like you says. I'd rather die!"

At this point, Mrs Crombie came to her wits and gathered the sobbing child into her arms.

"Charlie Dillon," she said, "I'm ashamed of you, bullying the poor child like that. Now, now, dear, dry your eyes. Stay here and we'll all look after you. And that includes Charlie."

But far from looking abashed, Charlie was grinning.

"Nah, Missus Crombie," he said. "She knows as 'ow I wouldn't 'urt 'er. It's just that now and again you've got to show a woman who's boss, like. Keep 'er in order."

Mrs Crombie was too amazed by this to speak. It was Foxe who managed at last to bring matters to a point.

"Charlie," he said. "Go through the door into my house—that one over there—walk across the hall to the far corner away from the street and go down the stairs. That will take you into the basement. Turn right and go through to the kitchen, where you'll find either Molly or Mrs Whitbread. If Molly isn't there, Mrs Whitbread will call her for you. Then ask Molly to come back here with you at once. Off you go."

Charlie walked off in a kind of dream, for he had never before been allowed beyond the kitchen in the rear of Mr Foxe's house. He'd been that far a good many times, since Mrs Whitbread often gave him oddments to eat, but never further.

When he returned with Molly, his eyes were, if anything even wider.

"Gawd's Truth, Flo!" he burst out. "It's like a palace in there. I never see'd such a beautiful place. There's all patterns and colours on the walls —pictures too—and fine furniture. There's even a proper rug on the floor, without a mark or a burn or even a sign of the moth on it. It's a marvel. If you gets to live here, even in the servant's rooms, I swear you'll be a fine lady in a year and too 'igh and mighty to speak to the likes 'o me."

Foxe gave Molly his instructions, then turned once again to Flo, who had somewhat recovered from her tears, though she stayed safely close to Mrs Crombie.

"Now, Flo," Foxe said, as gently as he could. "I need that promise from you. Not to steal, not to run off and not to be cheeky to those who will be trying to help you. Do you promise that?"

"I swears it, sir," Flo said earnestly. "Cross me 'eart and hope to die if I lets you down. I swears it on me mother's grave, I do. Since she died, no one 'as been kind to me like you 'as."

"Your promise is enough," Foxe said. "I know I can trust you now."

With that, Molly took the bewildered girl away and Charlie went into the storeroom about some mysterious business for Mrs Crombie.

"Mr Foxe," Mrs Crombie said to him. "You have amazed me again. Everyone in the city thinks you a thoroughgoing rake and dandy and little more. They see your fine clothes and the beautiful women on your arm and think they have seen the real man. Now I know better. That girl is the second person I've seen you help out of the gutter, when most men would either ignore her altogether or send her on her way to the gallows."

Foxe blushed.

"Who was the first?" he asked to cover his embarrassment at being praised like that.

"I was," Mrs Crombie said. "I was."

For a long moment, they looked at one another, each afraid to speak for fear of disclosing too much. Then Mrs Crombie pulled herself together.

"Did you notice young Charlie?" she said. "I know you feel lost in your investigations without the Catt sisters and now Captain Brock. Don't ignore Charlie Dillon. That young reprobate would walk barefoot through flames for you. Oh, he won't tell you so. I've never met any male willing to own up to his feelings on anything so important to him. Still, it's true enough. Just now you saw a side of

Charlie you probably didn't know existed. He may be small and grubby and none too honest in some matters. But he's also quick-witted, brave and a natural leader. All the street children in this part of the city look up to him and do whatever he says—even those several years older than he is. If you were to ask him to help you in your investigation, I have no doubt you would find him invaluable."

"Charlie?" Foxe said. "You really mean Charlie?"

"Of course," Mrs Crombie said. "You saw how Flo didn't hesitate to do what he said. It's the same with all the rest. Think about it, I beg you. Who notices street children, save to throw them a penny or a curse? Who bothers to guard their words if they see any nearby? Who else can move unnoticed and disregarded in the inns, taverns and drinking dens—or even the brothels and common stews? Sometimes people use them to run errands, but mostly they're ignored. If Charlie knew what to tell them to look and listen for, you'd have scores of keen eyes and quick ears working for you."

"I believe you're right, Mrs Crombie. Can't imagine why I never thought of that. If you know where he's gone, let's call him in and I'll negotiate terms of payment."

"No, Mr Foxe," she said. "You can do better than that. You can offer him the chance to be your apprentice. You're a Master Book-seller, I'm sure, and have every right to take on apprentices. Charlie loves being in the bookshop. I know he can't read or write, but he can learn and I can teach him. I've even seen him looking over those old tools upstairs with longing in his eyes. You gave Flo a chance she didn't really merit. Give Charlie the chance in life he does. He can live in the attic and help me here, as well as being your eyes and ears in the rougher parts of the city. You'll even be doing his poor mother a good turn, for I know she struggles hard to feed him. One less mouth will be a blessing, so long as she knows her lad is safe and growing up as she would wish."

It didn't take Foxe more than a moment or two to make up his mind. They summoned Charlie and explained Mr Foxe's offer. Now it was his turn to stare in joyful bewilderment, blinking back the tears. When it came to the part about helping Mr Foxe with his enquiries, the boy's chest swelled with pride and any onlooker might swear he had grown two inches taller.

All was soon agreed. Mr Foxe said he would ask his attorney to draw up the proper papers, Mrs Crombie applauded them both and Charlie ran off to carry the news to his mother. After the gloom and disappointments of the past few days, it was wonderful to be at the centre of such a tempest of happiness.

FOXE THOUGHT to retreat at last to his library to draw breath and consider all he had done. It was not that he feared he would regret any of it, but such a mass of changes in so short a time clearly deserved a period of calm reflection. Mrs Crombie, however, detained him. Mrs Halloran and her nieces, she told him, had sent word they would take up his invitation to come to the shop and would arrive that day at noon. Would it be acceptable for her to take the alderman's lady into Mr Foxe's small parlour to entertain her with tea? There was nowhere suitable in the shop itself or the storeroom behind.

Foxe agreed at once.

"I will stay to welcome the lady to my house, as is proper," he said. "Then I will make the excuse that someone must look after the shop and make my escape. I expect the two girls will take tea also, but I have no doubt they will soon become bored with adult conversation. As soon as you notice that, ask their aunt if she will allow them to come to me in the shop. Say I have set aside some books for them, or something like that. Then keep Mrs Halloran talking for as long as you can. I'll attend to the rest."

"Very well," Mrs Crombie replied. "Oh … in all the excitement of this morning I quite forgot to tell you of another addition to your household—of a kind. My cousin, Miss Eleanor Benfield, has agreed to come to assist me in your shop. She is but little older than I am and has no experience of shop work, but she is honest, reliable and quite determined. After the death of her father, she found herself dependent on an elder brother for a home and the necessities of life. Neither, I know, are willingly given, and her brother's wife treats her abominably. She therefore agreed at once to coming to Norwich and earning her living. She will lodge with me. I know that undertaking paid work will ruin her status as a gentlewoman, but she assures me that is far preferable to spending the rest of her life as an unpaid servant to her sister-in-law. Her brother too will be glad to see her gone. He has tried pressing her to marry—to be rid of her, of course—but I happen to know she has no inclination towards the married state. She has therefore refused all the suitors he paraded before her. Now he calls her a worthless spinster and claims her maintenance will ruin his estate. Imagine that, Mr Foxe. Such cruelty!"

"I will be glad to welcome her," Foxe said. "When will she be coming?"

"On Monday," she tells me. "That will be time enough for her to pack her few possessions and make the journey from Beccles."

11

THE BOOK THIEVES

MRS HALLORAN TOOK SOME TIME TO ADMIRE THE WAY THE SHOP had been renovated. She also happily promised to be a regular borrower once the circulating library was established. Maria and Lucy, her nieces, rushed around the shop, exclaiming at finding various titles and bombarding their aunt with requests to purchase "just this one, please". Mrs Crombie, as she had planned before-hand with Mr Foxe, turned all these requests aside with the information that Mr Foxe had kindly sought out some special books as a small gift for each of them. They must be patient until they could come back into the shop. Then he would hand them over.

That done, Mrs Crombie led her little group through the connecting door into Foxe's house to take a dish of tea. Both girls were agog with anticipation of what books Mr Foxe might have chosen for them. Tea was the last thing they wanted. However, being well-brought-up young ladies accustomed to taking part in the necessary social rituals, however irksome, they followed their aunt, looking the picture of demure compliance.

Foxe was waiting to greet them all in the small parlour. He complimented Mrs Halloran on her fine gown, which he swore showed off the amazingly youthful figure she retained. This was truly outrageous flattery, since the alderman's wife tended towards a certain mature plumpness, thanks to a great deal of formal dining and a healthy appetite. Still, she seemed to revel in his attention, even managing to produce a fair imitation of a girlish giggle at one point. Fortunately, the expressions on her nieces' faces were hidden from her.

Once the welcomes were over, Foxe excused himself on the grounds that someone had to watch over the shop in Mrs Crombie's absence. As he left, he suggested to Mrs Halloran that her nieces might be allowed to join him after they had taken tea. This caused both the girls to smile broadly at him, turned anxiously to their aunt to see if she would consent, then returned to imitating the most well-mannered of young ladies. Each secretly hoped the tea would not be too hot. If they could drink it swiftly, they might manage to escape before too much time had been wasted.

Mrs Crombie, of course, was well aware of their barely concealed fidgeting and constant glances at the small clock on the mantel. She allowed just enough time to pass to convince Mrs Halloran that the demands of good manners had been met, then suggested—in as artless a way as she could—that it would be well to allow the two young ladies to return to the shop while their elders shared another dish of tea.

The girls stood at once, then tried to walk to the door of the room with becoming grace. Once outside, they dashed across the hall and into the shop with no thought but to get there as quickly as they could.

Foxe had chosen his gifts with care, based on what little he knew of the two girls' likes and dislikes. For the elder, Miss Maria, he had considered her stated love for scientific and similar subjects. The package he handed her contained a new volume relating to geological discoveries throughout the kingdom, together with an introduction to a systematic study of the stars and planets. From the look on her face, he could see his choices had been good ones.

The choice for Miss Lucy had been harder. He knew she liked stories, but too many of the books he knew contained tales which would be judged unsuitable for a young lady of her age. In the end, he had found a volume of suitably decorous tales from Ancient Greece and Rome. This he paired with one containing tales of King Arthur and his knights, again purged of anything likely to offend the strictest moralist. Since she could scarcely be restrained from beginning to read immediately, he breathed an inward sigh of relief. Those choices too had hit the mark.

At length, not wanting Mrs Halloran to appear before he had been given long enough to complete what he had planned, Foxe cut through the continuing expressions of thanks.

"I have a question for you both," he said. "One that I wish to ask before your aunt comes within hearing. Why did you decide to rearrange your uncle's books? Whose idea was it?"

Foxe's question produced complete silence. Miss Lucy seemed thunderstruck and on the verge of tears. Miss Maria was also struck dumb, though her expression was more of guilt than fear.

"You need not be afraid," Foxe said. "I shall not tell your uncle, for I am sure you did all with the best of intentions. But you have seen how distressed he is by what he imagines to be the loss of several books. I'm convinced you do not wish his unhappiness to be further prolonged. You must confess, you know. Until then, I can do nothing to help you."

It was Maria who spoke first.

"It was my idea," she said. "Lucy is guiltless of all save following my lead."

"That is a brave admission," Foxe said, "though there was no need to seek to exonerate your sister in that way. I am not interested in assigning guilt—still less punishment. I simply look for a way to restore the books without your uncle suspecting the true cause of their disappearance."

"I am as much at fault as Maria," Lucy said. "Indeed, I was the one who first exclaimed that it was a miracle uncle could ever find a single title he might desire. I though he would be pleased that we had helped him."

"You've been in his library, sir," Maria added. "You must surely have felt much as we did. There are letters, scribbled notes, even pamphlets and newspapers lying everywhere."

"I have noticed that myself on several occasions," Foxe said, "but it would have been most impolite to remark upon it."

"Our uncle gave us free access to almost all his books," Maria continued, "save only some he keeps locked away for some reason. The trouble was it might take us half a morning to find more than a single volume on any particular subject. All is jumbled together. When he has finished with a book, he simply sets it down wherever he was or finds an empty place on a shelf and leaves it there. I have watched him."

"You are quite correct, Miss Maria," Foxe said. "I too have wondered how your uncle ever finds a book for a second time. Yet there is a lesson for you in this. Your uncle is not a tidy man. What matters most for him is adding to his knowledge. When a subject is new to him, he will devote himself entirely to the hunt. Tidying up is of no consequence. Indeed, he would deem it time wasted. What he has finished with, he simply discards somewhere and moves on to the next item. I suspect he has grown to find the result reassuring—signs of an active and ingenious intellect."

"But my sister has such an orderly mind, sir," Lucy said. "I swear the very sight of such a muddle gave her pain. Neither of us imagined any scholar could tolerate working in such a tangled mess. Is that not true, sister?"

"Indeed," her sister replied. "Our aunt is always complaining the servants say the room is impossible to clean properly. Yet uncle gets angry if things are moved. He often promises to tidy his papers and books, but never does."

She sighed at finding yet another example of the innate disorderliness of a most imperfect world.

"But now the damage is done," she continued. "We planned to rearrange the books subject by subject, but those few were all we could move. How our uncle managed to notice the change so quickly we could not guess. Then he made such a fuss we were too afraid to confess what we had done. We thought and thought, but could find no way to put them back without exciting suspicion."

"Will you really help us?" Lucy asked. "You have been so kind already in giving us these wonderful books. It would be presumptuous to ask you to do more."

"Yes," Foxe said. "I will help you, I promise, and all will be as it was. Indeed, if I am as cunning as the animal whose name I bear, you may even find your uncle asking you to do as you once planned in secret. However …"

Their faces fell in expectation of the typical lecture adults give when they find a young person's behaviour wanting.

"Don't look so miserable." Foxe could not help laughing at them. "All I am going to say is that, for my plan to work, we must enlist the help of your aunt. That will mean confessing to her as well as to me. She may indeed give you the lecture you fear, but I hope she will accept my advice to do no more. I have conspired with Mrs Crombie to ask your aunt to remain in my parlour for a few moments after they have finished tea, so that I may speak with her on an important matter. That will be my chance to win her to our side. Ah, here comes Mrs Crombie to tell me all is prepared for the next stage of my plan."

Speaking to Mrs Halloran was the part of Foxe's scheme that carried the greatest risk. She might insist on telling her husband what his nieces had done. Fortunately she was feeling well-disposed to Mr Foxe—perhaps recalling his flattery when he welcomed her earlier. Mrs Crombie had also been singing his praises. She was also tired of listening to her husband's complaints and moans over his lost books. She therefore agreed to comply with Foxe's wishes, though not before she had spoken sternly to the two culprits.

"Young ladies," she said, when she came into the shop with Mr Foxe beside her. "I have agreed to assist Mr Foxe in his generous efforts to save you from the punishment you so richly deserve. Yet do not think you will escape entirely. I shall have much to say to you when we return home. Yes, and a good many tasks to keep you from such idleness as may lead you into concocting further mischief. Now, sir, what do you require of us?"

"Aside from turning a blind eye to what I am going to tell your nieces to do, Mrs Halloran," Foxe said, "all you need do is fall in with whatever explanation for the 'loss' your husband brings to you.

It may well be somewhat fantastic. I beg you to accept it none-theless. Someone or something must carry the blame for moving the books. If it is not to be the true culprits, it must be something that cannot be punished in their stead."

"Very well, Mr Foxe. I agree, though my curiosity is greatly aroused by such enigmatic remarks. Still, I have agreed to trust you, so I will be patient until all is revealed."

Foxe's instructions to the two girls were more elaborate. The weekend was approaching and it would be essential to act strictly according to the timetable he had set out.

On Friday evening, they must go to their beds as usual, but contrive to stay awake. Then they should listen until they heard their aunt and uncle retire for the night. After that, they must let another hour pass until all the servants would also be abed. Only then should they light a single candle each and steal as quietly as they could to the library. Once inside, the first task was to find the books they had moved. These must be taken from the shelves and placed on the floor all around the room, as if they had been flying about and suddenly come to rest. That done, the girls should return to bed and go to sleep.

Foxe explained that he was sure the alderman would be informed of the books on the floor by the first servant who entered the library, even if he did not go there himself before anyone else. None of them should enter before that. The alderman would at once send for Foxe to tell him this news and seek his ideas on an explanation.

The same process should be followed on at least two subsequent nights, with several days left between each. This time books should be taken at random and left in a muddle on the floor. After that, Foxe hoped it would all be over.

While Foxe had been outlining his scheme, Mrs Crombie had listened in silence. Now she had a question.

"But why should Alderman Halloran not take this for yet more evidence of a thief?"

"Because nothing will be taken," Foxe said. "All the books will remain in plain view. My wish is only to provide an explanation for the 'loss' and return of the first set of books. One that avoids the blame being laid at the door of anyone in the household."

"That I can see," Mrs Crombie replied. "Another thing. Why ask these silly young people to risk going to the library in the middle of the night more than once? Each time runs the risk of being detected by someone, probably one of the servants."

"The risk of being heard by a servant is not great," Mrs Halloran said. "The maids and the footman sleep in the attics, while the library is two floors below that. And the butler, housekeeper and cook all have rooms in the basement, two floors below again."

"Yet I still do not understand the need for any further occasions in which books are disarranged so," Mrs Crombie persisted.

"So that the alderman may be convinced of the presence of an unquiet spirit—a ghost," Foxe replied. "I shall tell him that is the explanation for the first rearrangement of his books. Thus, when the poor spirit felt it had not disturbed him enough, it returned to repeat its antics. Meanwhile, I shall recommend that he call upon someone I know who will exorcise the room and put a stop to further visits. A … Monsieur Glampard, I think. Yes, a French-speaking Swiss priest who has long studied the occult in the libraries of Europe. Most sober English churchmen would dismiss the idea of ghostly visits out of hand. My Swiss scholar, of course, will back up my explanation in every way. Then—most conveniently—he will leave our city for good in search of yet more forbidden knowledge."

"And you know of such a person?" Mrs Halloran said in wonder.

"I am going to invent him," Foxe said, "with the help of an actor I have long known. He will be ideal for the part. Oh … and Monsieur Glampard will refuse any payment for his work. I will not put the alderman to any expense in the matter. That would not be right."

The two girls had listened to Mr Foxe with expressions of increasing glee. Finally, Lucy could no longer contain herself.

"Oh, sir!" she cried out. "What a storyteller you would have made. Your invention would put even Mr Walpole's new work, "The

Castle of Otranto", into the shade. I have not been allowed to read it all, but my uncle has read certain suitable passages to me."

"Hmm ..." Mrs Halloran said. "It seems to me a brazen tissue of falsehoods perpetrated on my poor husband. If it were not for saving these silly girls from the consequences of their mischief, I would never be a party to it. You are indeed like the animal who is your namesake, Mr Foxe. Most cunning—but not to be trusted."

"I assure you, Madam, I will bring no harm to your husband. Indeed, I will counsel him most earnestly to keep the whole matter secret. To allow a Swiss Catholic to conduct a ritual in his home would not endear him to the good Protestant people of Norwich. I am sure he will see the sense of that."

"You seem to have thought of everything," Mrs Halloran said. "Very well, we will do as you say. I will most definitely keep this whole sorry matter secret, for it will reflect little honour on any of us. I will also make sure these girls do not blab either."

The look she gave her nieces at those words was enough to make clear it would go hard with them if they disobeyed her.

"Now, nieces," she said. "Let us leave before our host produces some even more outrageous set of falsehoods to entertain us. Mrs Crombie, thank you for your kind conversation and good company. Mr Foxe, thank you for letting us into your house. Lucy, Maria. Have you thanked Mr Foxe properly for his generous gift of books —and for rescuing you from the disgrace and punishment you so richly merit?"

"Yes, aunt," they chorused. With that they took their leave.

Mrs Crombie, however, was still not fully content with Foxe's plan. It was, she told him, altogether too fantastic to be credible. Why not tell him simply that he must have mislaid the books then, armed with instructions from the girls, conduct a supposed search and find them?

"Because," Foxe said, "such a plan would immediately invite some further suspicion on the alderman's part. He will not be convinced he mislaid those books, of that I am sure. He has too clear a mind for that. Then, when I find them easily—and after he has searched for them long and hard—he will be sure I knew in advance where to look. From there, it is a small step to working out they must have been moved by someone in his household. Someone I could have asked where to find them. He has no reason to suspect his servants, so the search for the culprit would focus at once on his nieces. Can you imagine either standing up for long under the questioning of a man who has been a magistrate for so many years? Then the fat would be in the fire indeed."

"But why something so fantastic as a spirit and a Swiss magician?"

"Ah, Mrs Crombie. You are an honest, plain-spoken Norfolk lady of unimpeachable integrity. I, on the other hand, am a rogue long practiced in deceit of many kinds ..."

"Especially the kinds that lead young women into lascivious ways, I do not doubt."

"Those in particular," Foxe agreed. "However, nearly all my occasions for deceit have arisen in pursuit of my investigations, not for personal purposes. You cannot walk up to some villain and ask him to explain how he committed his crimes. Nor can you expect him to offer himself up to the magistrates, filled with remorse and eager to make a full confession. No, you have to find how to make him betray himself and give you the evidence you require. You must study to be devious and cunning, since felons and rogues are well-practiced in deceit themselves."

"Even so ..." Mrs Crombie began.

"Even so, Mrs Crombie. Let me explain a little further. I have found that to ask someone to accept a plausible and straightforward deceit is useless. They will soon see through it. What you must offer them is some explanation so strange, so unusual, so far-fetched that they must either take it whole or reject it utterly. Better still, you need to make it exciting. People live dull lives. To be involved in some unexpected adventure—so long as it is not at any risk—is often too tempting to be refused."

"So the alderman will believe your tale of the ghost?"

"Why should he not? It fits the facts known to him. It accounts for all that has happened in the house, with no loose ends. It removes the anxiety he has felt about possibly harbouring a thief amongst his servants. Best of all, it will involve him in something unusual and thrilling. I am certain he will keep it secret from others. That does not mean he will not revisit it in his mind many times, savouring the sense of adventure."

"I have learned much today, Mr Foxe," Mrs Crombie said, "not least that you are even more cunning than I had imagined. If it were not for your kind heart, you would be a most dangerous man."

"Not at all," Foxe said, laughing. "You forget that I have a conscience, as you do. Mine, I admit, is probably of a somewhat less strict nature, but I do hold most strongly to certain principles. I try never to harm others, save those who deserve it. I will not cheat to obtain what I cannot get by fair means. And I will not use my … uh … other wiles on married women or any who will not find the results entirely to their liking. You see? I am the most principled rake and libertine you ever met."

Then both laughed.

12

REVELATIONS

On Saturday morning, Alderman Halloran came to Foxe's shop somewhere near eleven in the morning, all smiles and excitement. If it was not by chance that Foxe was there, talking with Mrs Crombie and helping her serve a small group of customers, the alderman would never know.

"I've got them back, Foxe!" he cried, ignoring everyone else. "Quite safe and unharmed. Ah … um … my apologies, Mrs Jackson, Mrs … um … Norton, Mrs Radcliffe … and Mrs Crombie, of course. Most impolite not to greet you at once. Can't think what came over me."

All these ladies responded with curtsies of varying grace and mutters of "Good morning, alderman". Then they fixed their eyes on him and waited for his next words. This promised to be rich nourishment for gossip.

Having done his duty, the alderman appeared to have forgotten about them again.

"Every one returned," he said. "Found them myself this morning. Scattered over the floor, the desk, the table … even one on the mantel."

"Good morning, Alderman Halloran," Foxe said calmly. "This is indeed good news. I suspected it might happen, but am still greatly pleased that it has."

"You ... suspected this, sir? How so? You said nought to me on the matter."

"Let us retire to my small parlour, alderman, where I will explain all. Follow me. I will call Molly to bring us coffee—or a glass of wine or ale, if you prefer."

The frowns of Foxe's customers were eloquent testimony to their annoyance at his suggestion of taking alderman Halloran where they could no longer hear what was said. However, they responded to the pleasant good-byes of the two men with what politeness they could muster. It really was too vexing!

Once he and the alderman were seated, each with his chosen drink, Foxe explained.

"I said I suspected the books would be returned, alderman, because I was almost sure I could guess who had taken them."

"Who was it?" Halloran demanded. "Blaggard deserves to be horse-whipped!"

"It was Jacob Addinall," Foxe said.

"Addinall? Addinall? Never heard of such a man. Who is he?"

"Rather you should say who *was* he," Foxe explained. "Jacob Addinall died some fifty years ago, I believe. He was a noted, if eccentric, bookseller in his time. His shop was in King Street."

"How can the man have taken my books if he's dead? You're not expecting me to believe his ghost was to blame."

"That is precisely what I am telling you. As you know, I visit a good many libraries in the course of my work. The ghost of Jacob Addinall has been at work in several of them. When I was able to rule out the obvious explanation of theft, I was forced to conclude he had been to your library as well."

"Stuff and nonsense!"

"Hear me out first. Jacob Addinall died in a terrible fire which consumed his shop. The place was always in a most decided muddle. People used to marvel the man could find anything. Books were piled everywhere, in no order. There were pamphlets, prints, even pages of damaged books spread on every surface. That was how the fire took hold, people believe, and why it spread so quickly. It's assumed he was reading by candle one night, fell asleep and knocked the candle over. It cost him his life."

"All very sad, Foxe, but what has this to do with me? Fifty years ago I was still wearing a dress."

"The fire itself has nothing to do with you of course. What matters is the aftermath. Quite soon after Addinall's death, reports came in that he had been seen. Sometimes his ghost appeared in the dark hours in the vicinity of his shop. Sometimes people saw him in broad daylight, wringing his hands and uttering fearful moans. For a time, few were brave enough to venture along that part of King Street, for fear of meeting the ghost."

"How is it I have never heard of the man—nor of his ghostly tricks?"

"I am coming to that, alderman. These manifestations lasted a few weeks then the ghost disappeared. All was quiet in King Street and people soon forgot about the old bookseller. But then he began to manifest again—only not near his bookshop but in libraries, grand or modest, throughout the county. Sometimes he was seen. Sometimes heard. But his presence was revealed most clearly by what he left behind."

"And what was that, pray? Footprints?"

"Missing books. At least, not so much missing as moved and rearranged. Papers tidied away. Sometimes these actions were seen quickly, sometimes not. Indeed, in the places where the ghost went most often, it seemed determined to add to the mess, not lessen it. Books would be scattered around and left in strange places."

The alderman was quiet now and seemed to be listening more intently. Foxe pressed on.

"All kinds of explanations for the ghost's conduct were considered. Then it was noticed that its attentions only occurred in libraries—and sometimes bookshops too—where there was muddle and disorder in the shelving of books. That was why the ghost's actions might not be noticed at first. Where there is no set order, it is hard to see what might have been moved."

"Why would a ghost move books?"

"You recall I said the fire that killed Addinall was thought to have spread too quickly for him to escape? That was because of the chaos of books and papers in his shop. If it had been properly arranged—and tidy—it is quite likely he would have woken at the smell of smoke and the heat from the flames in time to save himself. It is even possible the fire would not have started at all. A candle knocked over on an empty desk would scorch the wood, but little else."

"So his visits were …?"

"A warning … and a reproach. That's why people said nothing. To admit that Addinall's ghost was visiting you was as much as to admit you kept your books in a deplorable state."

The alderman looked thoughtful.

"It did seem to me to be getting more difficult to find the books I wanted," he said, "almost as if they were being moved."

"I imagine so. So when you did not notice its first efforts, the ghost turned to picking on titles you were sure to miss and hiding them away. Only we all thought at first they had been stolen."

"So far as I know, no one has ever seen a ghost in my home," the alderman objected. "Least of all me."

"Addinall rarely actually appears these days—or so I've been told."

"Hmm … all sounds very far-fetched to me, Foxe. You may be honest in your opinion on the matter, but I will take a good deal of convincing that some unquiet spirit has busied itself moving my books around just because of the fire risk."

"Well, time will tell," Foxe said, looking quite relaxed. "If I am right, you will have more nightly visits and each will cause more chaos than the last. I knew one person who resolutely refused to believe in the existence of ghosts of any kind."

"And what happened to him?"

"Eventually he entered his quite extensive library one morning to find every book on the floor. The servants reported much banging and noise during the night, but none were brave enough to investigate. They did not share their master's scepticism. Indeed, several maids swore they had sensed something in the room or caught sight of movement out of the corner of an eye. One even claimed the ghost had come up behind her and fondled her breasts. However, that was soon dismissed as either a combination of hysteria and wishful thinking or a quick-fingered footman. The mess itself, however, seemed to admit of no other explanation."

"Did the man tidy everything after that?"

"He did. He even employed a man to come and devise a proper scheme of ordering. After that, there were no more visits by night."

"I will consider what you have told me," Alderman Halloran said, though his voice added a grudging edge to his words. "It is far from what I expected. Still, the most important matter is that I have got my books back. As for the rest … I remain unconvinced. I know many credit the existence of supernatural beings, ghosts, witches and the like, but I have never seen anything to convince me they are right. Well, good day to you, Foxe. I have much to do, as I imagine you have. I will tell my wife what you have said. She has a better brain in practical matters than I and may well show me where your thinking has gone astray."

I very much doubt it, Foxe said to himself.

When Monday morning came, Foxe found himself once again apprehensive, for he needed to meet yet another addition to his extended household. If it went on growing like this, he would require a larger house.

The young pickpocket, Flo—now to be called Florence in deference to her new status as a respectable kitchen maid—had settled in and been given more appropriate clothes. They had transformed her appearance from an undersized, male guttersnipe into a young woman; still painfully thin, of course, but otherwise revealing a surprising prettiness. With Mr Foxe she remained shy, though Mrs Whitbread, the cook, told her master the girl could be "quite the chatterbox" when she wished.

Miss Eleanor Benfield, Mrs Crombie's cousin and now her assistant in the bookshop, turned out to be a tall, handsome woman in her late twenties, though somewhat masculine in her manner. When she smiled—which fortunately seemed to become easier as they spoke together—she showed hints too of a less prim side to her character. If she was shy in coping with Foxe's practiced gallantry, a certain wariness was to be expected given the lady's recent troubles with her family. Mrs Crombie assured Foxe privately that "dear Cousin Eleanor" would soon regain a more light-hearted outlook.

Foxe was sorely tempted to head for his favourite coffeehouse as soon as possible, but he knew that could not be. He had received a message asking him to attend on Mrs Morrow at eleven. Although he expected a welcome warm enough, he was still nervous of the encounter. There were important questions in his mind that only she could answer. Yet they were of such an intrusive and personal kind that he dreaded having to ask them. However delicately he phrased his areas of interest, they were not the subject for an acceptable conversation between a gentleman and a lady on anything less than the most intimate terms.

When he reached the house, Foxe was admitted by a silent maid and shown into what he assumed to be a parlour or morning room. It was neatly appointed, though the furnishings and decorations were spartan in their simplicity and restraint. The walls were painted in a pale colour—whether a creamish white or pale yellow Foxe could not tell. Aside from two mirrors, the only decoration was a dingy painting of a severely religious nature. The furniture was also extremely sparse—a central oaken table, with matching chairs and two slender, upholstered chairs with wooden arms on either side of the fire.

Mrs Morrow was already seated in one of these and indicated that Foxe should take the other. He hoped it would hold his weight without breaking.

His hostess was still dressed in deepest mourning, of course, yet her expression was not what he had expected. If anything, she looked hostile to her visitor. Coffee was brought and served in silence. By this time, Foxe was feeling extremely nervous of what might ensue once the servant had withdrawn.

"I had thought you my friend," Mrs Morrow began. "Sadly, I seem to have been proved incorrect in that."

"But I am your friend, madam," Foxe protested. "I assure you I am."

"You do not act like one, sir. On the previous occasion we met, I asked you to be completely open with me about whatever you discovered regarding my late husband. You agreed. Yet you immediately broke that promise."

Foxe knew what was coming. What he had restrained himself from telling her before was only to save her still more suffering. Now he feared that it was likely to destroy the fragile trust between them. The only possible course of action was to confess at once and seek her forgiveness.

"Mrs Morrow," he said. "I own my fault and humbly beg your pardon. It was foolish of me, I admit, but no more than that. Instead of taking you at your word, I made the usual assumption we men make about women. I treated you as weak and unable to withstand harsh realities, when you had shown me ample proof that day you were not."

Mrs Morrow said nothing.

"I assume someone has shown you the notice that was circulated in denunciation of your late husband. In my defence, I assure you I had not seen it when we spoke. Afterwards, I hoped it might not come to your notice. That too was stupid of me and demeaning to you."

"You are correct," Mrs Morrow said. "Certain 'friends'— though they little deserve that name—hastened to bring me a copy. Oh, they were loud in their concern that I should not allow it to upset me. Of course, I could see through that feeble subterfuge. What they really wanted was to know whether it was true and perhaps gain further details from me. They were disappointed on both counts. I have no notion of why my late husband was accused of such hypocrisy. These charges seem more general than specific to him."

"There is some evidence for the charge of drunkenness, I fear," Foxe said. "That is what I do admit to concealing from you. When your husband's body was found, he smelled strongly of liquor, probably cheap brandy. So strongly that he must have consumed a great deal and spilt the rest over his clothes. The mayor wished to conceal this from everyone, both to spare his family—you—from more pain and to act as a trap for his killer. Anyone who knew the state of the body had to have been there when he died, or shortly after."

"My husband did not drink, Mr Foxe. I am sure of that. Someone in this house would have smelled it on his breath or on his clothes. The scent of alcohol does not dissipate quickly and my husband was rarely away from the house for any length of time, save when he was at his counting-house or with his father. He preached the dangers of alcohol so loudly and so often that many people would have been only too happy to be able to declare him a hypocrite on the subject."

"I believe you, Mrs Morrow," Foxe said. "No one I have spoken with has any information suggesting your husband was not utterly sincere in his rejection of all alcoholic drinks."

Now came the most difficult part. Foxe had hoped to be able to introduce his other questions gently and in an atmosphere of relaxed openness. Nothing to do now but plunge ahead and hope for the best.

"And the other charge?" he said. "What of that?"

"Lechery? That too is completely unbelievable," Mrs Morrow said. "There was never any trouble with our maids that came to my notice. No, nor the slightest suggestion of inappropriate behaviour by my husband towards any woman in this household. Two, as I recall, became pregnant during their time here, but neither suggested my husband had any part in that. Indeed, though he dismissed them at once, I understand both married the father. I sent them a little money in secret—all I could afford from the slender means my husband allowed me. I could do no more for them."

"And outside this house?"

"I have no idea."

"I was told many servants left your employment before their period of engagement was completed."

"That is certainly true. Some fell into theft, I was told. Others simply ran away. But even that was not likely to be because of my husband's actions towards them in any amorous sense. If they ran or left, it was usually because they disliked the strict and oppressive religious atmosphere about him. Or because he dismissed them for infringing one of the host of petty rules he tried to enforce. If I could have gone, I would have done so too."

She leaned forward now, eager to impress her words on her visitor.

"Nearly all our servants were taken from the orphanage, sir," she said, "save for the most skilled and experienced ones. The same applies to the apprentices at the yarn business. Oh, there were many fathers eager to see their sons learn the trade with us when my father-in-law was in charge. My late husband was not well thought of in the yarn trade, so requests for apprenticeships ceased. Yet apprentices were still needed. My husband took them from the Poor Law Overseers and the superintendents of various orphanages. Quite a few ran away, of course, probably for the same reasons as our maids. When they did, I believe they tried to get as far distant from Norwich as possible to avoid being captured and brought back. Their punishment would doubtless have been severe. No, Mr Foxe. As I told you before, I believe my late husband was far too strict with himself to get involved with any of the usual vices that wealthy gentlemen indulge in. His sole ambition was to be perfect."

Foxe tried one last time.

"So all that was said in that printed notice was false?"

"So far as I can tell, it was," Mrs Morrow said. "Oh dear! You put me in a great quandary, sir. There are matters I now feel the need to disclose to you, but they are of such an embarrassing nature I hardly know where to start."

The lady seemed so genuinely distressed that Foxe was sorely tempted to find some way of taking his leave without putting her to any more pain. He started to rise.

"No, sir. Stay seated, I beg of you. If I do not do this now, I may never find the courage again. Yet there is one promise I do most earnestly ask you to make—and keep without fail, this time."

"Tell me," Foxe said gently. "If I can make that promise I will.

Nor will I fall a second time into the error of underestimating your seriousness in what you ask."

"I need you to promise that what I tell you will not be repeated to anyone else—especially not to our pompous mayor and his aldermen cronies. I realise that may be difficult, but I am sure you can find a way. Without your solemn oath on this, I can speak no further."

Foxe did indeed feel himself to be in a difficult position. Without knowing what she was going to tell him, he must undertake not to divulge it even to those who might most need to know. His head told him he could not give such an undertaking. His heart urged him to give his word, whatever problems it caused him. He chose his heart.

"You have my most solemn promise," he said. "What you tell me now I will carry unspoken to my grave."

Mrs Morrow gave a great sigh and sat back in the chair.

"I cannot help but trust you," she said, "even though you have let me down once. Nor was that such a great matter in the end. I'm sure you only thought to save me pain. Alas, the pain has been inflicted long ago, Mr Foxe, though it sometimes feels as sharp as it ever was. Now, stay still and silent, I beg you. If you interrupt me, I may not be able to begin again."

"In some ways," she began, "my husband and I were barely husband and wife at all. Indeed, I often wondered why he married me. I expected he would want children, but I was wrong. I hoped in my innocence he would want me. I was wrong again. Oh, at the start of our marriage he made some efforts to consummate our union, but he clearly found it hard. Only if I lay totally still and silent could he achieve release. Trying to encourage him made it worse. He became very angry and accused me of acting the harlot. Once he burst out that women were all the same: shameless, filthy creatures.

"As you can imagine, I suffered great misery through this. I knew he disliked women who are plump and full-bodied. The ladies who took the opportunity of assemblies or dinners to show off their ample bosoms disgusted him, for he told me so often enough. Yet such a description never applied to me. I am small, with nothing about me of the voluptuary. That made my misery worse. I came to believe there was something specially revolting about me. Some sick flaw of nature that he had not expected, but which rendered him almost impotent. Was I indeed so unattractive, so maimed or withered? Was I doomed by nature to be an old maid, even though I was married?

"I blush to tell you this, sir, but I must. The only time he ever revealed any passion towards me was one day when I had exasperated him more than usual on some matter. I do not remember what it was. We were in his library, that I do recall. First he hit me hard about my face, several times. Then, without a word, he spun me around and pushed me face down onto his desk. In a moment, he had lifted my skirts and begun to beat my naked flesh, first with his hand, then with something he must have picked up. It hurt so much! After that, he … oh … oh, I cannot go on!"

"Please do not distress yourself, madam," Foxe began, but Mrs Morrow held up her hand for silence. Then she swallowed hard and continued her tale.

"Afterwards I kept away from him whenever I could and he stopped coming to my bed. All I felt was relief. I had accepted my fate and assumed he would seek what he needed elsewhere. Perhaps he would take a mistress. Perhaps he would frequent some discrete house of ill repute. For I assure you my late husband was not impotent, sir. I had proof of that, even if I knew that I was not the one who could stir his desire.

"Yet even this I came to believe was untrue. Oh, not that he was indeed impotent. I knew that to be false. But I saw no sign of him seeking out any other outlet for his natural needs. In many ways, he resembled a monk, bound by a vow of celibacy, more than a normal, healthy man. That is why I am so sure he never fumbled the maids. It was as if women were beneath his notice. They were not desirable or attractive in any way. Still less did they possess minds that harboured intelligence. When he could not avoid them, his behaviour was never more than polite and distant.

"And before you jump to another conclusion, sir, let me say that I saw no sign of close or remotely inappropriate relationships with men. It was as if he had no need of anyone, male or female. No need of closeness, affection or intimacy of any kind.

"So here I am, Mr Foxe. I was married to Joseph Morrow for eight years. We had no children, since the few times one might have been conceived, none came. I must describe myself as almost a virgin, even after all this time. Not quite so in the physical sense, but completely so in knowledge of what I imagine to be the normal relationship between a man and a woman who have shared the same bed.

"There. That is all."

Foxe was dumbfounded.

"But does not the Book of Common Prayer state that the first purpose of marriage is the procreation of children?" he stuttered. "What of that? Your late husband was, by all accounts, a most religious man. Would he not have seen that as something demanded by his faith?"

"You forget that he was a Calvinist and a Puritan. The prayer book of the established church meant nothing to him. No, less than nothing. He called it the perverted doctrine of a church tainted with heresy, error and Popish superstition. Yet that would not have mattered, since I am sure all the elders and ministers of his own sect would have echoed the same notion. Better to marry than to burn! At least marriage sanctioned intimate relations when children were the desired outcome."

"I cannot understand it," Foxe said. "You are very far from being an unattractive woman. Most in Norwich regard me as a libertine who has enjoyed the favours of more women that I deserve; nor are they so far from the truth. Believe me, madam, I am a connoisseur in such matters."

"Thank you," Mrs Morrow said. "Perhaps one day I may come to believe what you say."

"To speak truly, I am bewildered. Try as I may, I can find no reason why your husband should have been murdered. Nor why he should have taken as much money from his bank as he did. There I am completely at a loss. Might he have wished to conceal the poor profits from the yarn business from his father? Might his father have assumed all was as it had been in his day and demanded dividends greater than the present level of business could sustain?"

"I have little idea, Mr Foxe. To seek to hide his failings from his father—and everyone else—would definitely fit with my late husband's character. Would he perpetrate some kind of deception to do so? Yes, I think he would. Yet even he must have seen it could not work for long. Besides, who would murder him on account of it?"

"There you have hit the point fair and square," Foxe said. "That explanation might explain some of the financial losses, but nothing else. So long as I can see no clear cause for murder, I have little chance of finding the person or persons responsible. Nor can I see the murder as a random event; an act by a madman or a robbery gone terribly wrong. That will not explain the drink that saturated his clothes. The taking of a life in the way you husband was killed cannot be dismissed as a chance event. There must be a reason. Sadly, I still have no idea what it might be."

"I can give no answer either," Mrs Morrow said, "though I have made my head ache many nights recently trying to find one. All I can suggest is that you look to the parts of his life he valued most: his religious faith and his belief in his own excellence. If there was something which would destroy either or both of these, if revealed to the world at large, he would have paid any price to keep it secret. His whole existence until his death was devoted to proving himself a better Christian than anyone else. The ten commandments say we must not worship false idols. What if the idol you worship is the faith itself? I have done with that kind of religion, sir; maybe with all religion. I have seen for myself how destructive it can be when taken literally."

"Did your late husband hit you often?"

"Not often, Mr Foxe, but enough to make me afraid of him. When he did beat me, he would easily become violent. I soon learned the best way to avoid worse punishment was to stay as still as I could and not to cry out. If I did that, he would lose interest. At first, he apologised to me after and promised not to do it again. In time, he no longer bothered. He was a dictator, sir. If you obeyed him without question you were safe. If you crossed him he would punish you. If you stood up to him he would not cease tormenting you until he had broken your will."

As he walked home, Foxe found his mind seeking a way around her words like a mouse trapped in a corner by a cat. How could you use a man's religion as a source of blackmail, especially when you knew he followed the commandments of his faith to the letter? No drink, no gambling, no loose women—indeed virtually no women at all and no men either. All Joseph Morrow could be accused of was excessive zeal. That and a cruel disregard of any who failed to live up to his standards. Neither was cause for paying a blackmailer. Nor was beating your wife.

He must be missing something. Morrow was not killed at random, he was certain of that. Stealing all that money was certainly a deliberate act, carefully planned and carried out over many months. To believe that these two events were not connected stretched credulity to breaking point. What had he overlooked? What was he too stupid, too fixed in his mind or too narrow in his outlook to see?

It was time to step back and spend some time in relaxation. Time to attempt to empty his mind; to hope some pattern might be seen in events when he returned. Only now was he realising how important his intervals romping with one or other of the Catt sisters had been to his previous investigations. They were gone, no help for that, but if romping were needed, the theatre was still there. His promise to attend this week had not yet been fulfilled.

Thus it was with a renewed lightness in his step and a firmness of purpose that Mr Foxe returned to his house. That very night he would dress in his finest attire and go forth to see if might find at least one lady willing to provide him with the distraction he needed so much.

13

CHARLIE GETS INVOLVED

THE NEXT MORNING, FOXE FELT IN FINE FETTLE. HE HAD GONE TO the theatre as he had planned. For part of the evening he sat in one of the best seats, enjoying the performances as he usually did. He had missed the rest of the programme. A young servant brought him a note during the first gap in proceedings, inviting him to step backstage and meet with one of the young actresses he had met on his last visit. She hoped, she wrote, that he might convey his views on her performance. She was not to appear for the rest of the evening.

Foxe went, of course, but did not return. His comments on her abilities on-stage proved so charming to the young lady that one thing led to another and Foxe found himself enjoying quite a different performance in a suitably deserted area of the theatre.

Nor had his evening ended there. When the whole programme was ended, he thought it only right to speak with the other four actresses and give them his congratulations. As matters turned out, only one remained. One was indisposed and the remaining two had decided to allow other, more ardent admirers to walk them home. Still, one was enough. Foxe offered her his arm to escort her to her lodging and she accepted. But once they left the building, the night being so cold and dark, it seemed an act of cruelty to make the poor girl walk so far, especially since Foxe's house was but a few streets away.

Thus it was that Foxe had woken to the pleasant sight of a tousled head on the pillow next to him and the even more enjoyable sensation of a warm body alongside his. Leaving his bed had to be delayed until proper greetings and thanks had been given and received. Only then did the pair of them take breakfast together, under the rather baleful eye of Molly. Foxe was certain that by the time he bid his overnight guest farewell, everyone in the house would know that the master had returned to his former ways.

What Mrs Crombie thought of such goings on, Foxe did not discover. When he finally entered his shop, almost at the noon hour, she was far too eager to tell him that young Charlie wanted to speak with them both. Earlier, she said, the lad had been called outside the shop by two filthy and disreputable boys. After some minutes he returned, much excited by what they told him. To her frustration, he refused to divulge any of it. All he would say was that he would tell them both later, when the master had "finished playing with his new pet" inside the house. Since the lady did not ask Foxe whether this was a cat or a dog, he assumed she knew very well the nature of the creature involved. He even had the grace to feel a twinge of embarrassment. It soon passed.

Charlie was cleaning in the storeroom behind the shop, making space for all the new books that would arrive soon as stock for the circulating library. Several days before, Mrs Crombie had drawn up a list of suitable titles and Mr Foxe had sent it to several London booksellers and publishers. The total cost proved somewhat shocking, but Mrs Crombie assured him it would soon be recovered through the subscriptions and payments for individual loans made by those who wished to borrow them.

At almost any other time, Foxe would have enjoyed a visit to the capital to deliver the orders himself. He might even have hired a large enough chaise for his return to allow him to bring back those books that were readily available. Now he had been glad of the excuse that he was too much involved in his investigation to spare the time away. He could hardly visit London without calling on Kitty and Gracie Catt. It was what he might find if he did that worried him. To guess they had moved on and sought consolation elsewhere was one thing; to see it for himself was another. After his last evening's activities, he would not even be able to tell them that he had remained true, even if they had not.

Still, it was doubtless all for the best. After such a long period of gloom and loss of appetite for life, it was time he looked to the future. Though moralists might shake their heads, Foxe knew he had done what was right for him, the spring in his step and his eagerness to press on with the search for Joseph Morrow's killer proved it.

"Very well, Mrs Crombie," he said. "If Miss Benfield feels she can look after things here in your absence for a few minutes, we will talk with Charlie together."

"Oh, I shall be fine," Miss Benfield said at once. "Cousin Susannah here has been instructing me most diligently in all that needs to be done. It is high time I faced a few customers on my own."

"I assume Mrs Crombie has also told you of my interest in the death of Mr Joseph Morrow," Foxe said to her. "Have you heard anything of interest in this connection? Perhaps from those who have come in for books or stationery?"

The two women look at each other, undecided which should speak first. In the end, it was Miss Benfield.

"Little enough," she said. "The topic is now past the stage of generating great interest. What people are discussing is what will happen to the Morrow businesses, especially the yarn manufacture. It provides work for a good many, men and women, who work as spinners in their own homes. It is assumed Mr James Morrow will inherit all when Mr Ezekiel passes away. Yet he has his own, quite different business in Great Yarmouth to attend to."

"That's right," Mrs Crombie added. "Surely someone must be interested in purchasing the yarn manufacture, if Mr James does not want it? The demand for yarn is strong, I believe, and Morrow's yarns used to be regarded highly in the trade."

"You would think so," Foxe said. "To be honest, I have no better idea on this topic than anyone else."

"I did hear one rumour," Miss Benfield said. "'Tis said Mr Joseph Morrow had taken to walking late in the evening through the streets by Tombland, heading towards the Fye Bridge. It seems an odd place for such a person to be. Several people claimed to have seen him, for he was always distinctive in his attire."

Foxe was alert on the instant. This was indeed of great interest. He should have realised it would be impossible for a well-known person to be abroad in the city without someone recognising them. Few others wore the Puritan garb favoured by Joseph Morrow. He was unlikely to be confused with anyone else.

"They said he had been seen several times. Is that correct?" Foxe said.

"Yes," Miss Benfield replied. "But only in recent months, as I heard. No one knows where he was going. It cannot have been to The Maid's Head Inn, and the other buildings by the river there are warehouses or places of manufacture, not the kind of destination such a man might be seeking after dark. He could have been going over the water to Colegate, of course."

"After dark, you said. You are sure of that, Miss Benfield?"

"Always, as I heard," she said. "Not late at night, mind you. More about seven or eight o'clock."

"And several times?"

"So I was told. 'Tis all second-hand information though. One person telling another and so on."

"Thank you, Miss Benfield," Foxe said. "It is most useful information, even though I have no notion as yet quite what to make of it. Can you add anything more, Mrs Crombie?"

"I'm afraid not," she said. "Cousin Eleanor has a most beneficial way of talking with our older customers. To speak the truth, I am never sure whether some of them have still their right wits. Yet she sits them down and listens to their ramblings with the patience of Job."

"Many of them live alone, cousin, save for perhaps a maid near as old as them," Miss Benfield said. "They love to talk when they get the chance. Nor are they as lacking in their wits as you may think. 'Tis true they sometimes wander a little, but if you are willing to sort the wheat from the chaff, it's a marvel what they notice. Those of us who are still young have little time to spend on watching or listening. They have nothing else to do for days at a time. I feel sorry for them, Mr Foxe, and do what I can to make them feel less useless in this busy world."

"I am very glad you do, Miss Benfield," Foxe said. "See how useful it has been. Even if that were not the case, it shows a generous heart, willing to carry out a simple good deed. Would that more were of your mind. I guess none here has yet come near to our thirtieth year, save for me. When I am old, I can only hope there will be someone like you prepared to listen to my ramblings."

"Lah, sir! You are quite the flatterer," Miss Benfield said. "Cousin Susannah told me as much. What you say is true of my little cousin, but my own thirtieth year is not so far off. I shall have to take care that you do not turn my head with such silken words."

"Little chance of that," Mrs Crombie murmured.

MRS CROMBIE and Foxe found Charlie busy with broom, mop and bucket. Foxe was amazed in the change that had come over him through the simple expedient of making him an apprentice. Someone—Mrs Crombie he guessed—had found him better clothes, washed his face and tidied him up. Now he was working away at his tasks with surprising vigour.

"Ah," he said as they entered the storeroom. "G'morning again, Missus Crombie. Good morning to you too, master."

Foxe was glad to see the cheeky grin was still firmly in place, despite the formality of the lad's words.

"Good morning, Charlie," Foxe said. "I believe you have news for us."

"Right enough, master. That I do."

It seemed Charlie was intent on relishing his new position by referring to Foxe as 'master' as often as he could.

"Sit you down, master. Missus. I rubbed the seat of these two old chairs with a damp cloth, so you've no need to worry about soiling your fine clothes."

Foxe could see Mrs Crombie was struggling not to laugh, as he was. It would be most unkind to react to Charlie's sterling attempts to act in the right way by giving in to mirth.

Once they were seated, Charlie took a place in front of them, much like a teacher before a class—something he could never have seen—and prepared to pass on what he had discovered.

" I put the word out as you said, master," he began. "Everyone to see if they could find any trace of that Joseph Morrow cove where a gentleman like that ought not to be. Never mind where it was, so long as it wasn't the kind of place suitable for a wealthy gentleman and a rantin' Bible-puncher like 'im."

"That's disrespectful," Mrs Crombie said sternly.

"True though," Foxe said. "Go on, lad."

"Two on 'em came this mornin' to tell me what they found," Charlie continued. "Basically, it ain't … isn't … much. No sign of 'im in any of the ale houses, taverns or inns. No sign in the gambling-hells. Then they tried to find if he'd been seen goin' with any of the whores."

"Had he?" Foxe asked.

"Not sure," Charlie said. "Trouble is, you see, someone got there afore us."

Foxe sat up very straight.

"Someone else has been looking for traces of Joseph Morrow? This is news indeed. Could your … ah … associates find out who it was?"

"Aye," Charlie said, "and you ain't … aren't … goin' to like it, master. It were 'Gentleman' Jack Beeston's men."

"Beeston! Are they sure?"

"Right enough. No mistakin' those people. They're well known —and rightly feared—everywhere. 'Twas them for sure."

"They were following the same trails?" Foxe said.

"More or less. Didn't bother with the drinkin' places, I was told. Visited a few of the gambling-dens, then seemed to leave them aside too. But they definitely went to most of the stews and brothels. What's really odd is what they did at two of them."

"What was that?" Foxe asked.

"They took some girls away. That's why I said I wasn't sure whether or not that Mr Morrow had ever been to any of 'em. Seems Beeston's men put the fear of God into the madams. No one was willin' to say anythin'. All I know for certain is the ones they took away haven't been back."

"Who may this Jack Beeston be? The name I have heard, I think, but nought else." Mrs Crombie asked.

"Just a moment, Mrs Crombie," Foxe said. "Charlie. You're quite sure Beeston's men were on the trail of Joseph Morrow."

"Sure as I can be, master. Not as how I'd call it a trail. They were definitely asking about 'im and whether anyone 'ad seen 'im. It was more as if they were casting about, like a dog does before he picks up the scent of a rat. Lookin' anywhere a rat might be in the hope of turnin' one up."

"Do you know how long ago this was? Was it recently?"

"Nah! Should've said. It were nigh on five or six months ago."

Foxe whistled.

"As long ago as that? Well, for a start this proves there is, or was, something to find. Beeston wouldn't waste his time if there wasn't. Something that he could use against someone, most likely Joseph Morrow himself. If his men found it, that could explain what Morrow wanted so much money for."

He fell silent.

"Jack Beeston?" Mrs Crombie prompted.

"Ah … 'Gentleman' Jack himself," Foxe said. "I'm glad you haven't encountered him, Mrs Crombie. He's probably one of the worst criminals in Norwich, with a hand in every felony or vice that goes on here, just as long as there's money to be made. He's cruel, ruthless and—God damn him!—extremely sharp. Always works through others, while he sits safe in his house, laughing at the law. The sad truth is, everyone in authority knows who he is and what he does. Yet so far as I know he's never once stood in the dock before magistrate or judge."

"Is he that clever?" Mrs Crombie said.

"Indeed he is. Now I must be off as soon as I can to ruin Alderman Halloran's day, as he will doubtless ruin the mayor's afterwards. This is appalling news. If we are up against Beeston as a blackmailer, there'll be precious little chance of seeing any of Morrow's money again. Yet Mrs Morrow said she'd never known of any woman or girl being bothered by her husband. I can't make sense of it. Now Charlie ...!"

"Yes, master?"

"You've done extremely well and I'm proud of you. See if you can do even better."

"I'll do me best, master," the lad said. He seemed to have grown several inches more under Mr Foxe's praise.

"I need to know more about the girls Beeston's men took away and, if possible, where they took them. Can any of your ... people ... find that out for me?"

"That's 'ard, master, that is. As I said, all the madams and the whores are mortal afeared o'Jack Beeston."

"Never mind then. I don't want anyone to get hurt."

"Just a minute! Whass 'er name? Mary? No ... Eliza! Got it! She'd probably be able to do it. If what the lads and girls on the streets says of 'er is true, if'n any old goat slipped his 'and up 'er skirts, she'd only smile and charge 'im sixpence!"

"Charlie!" Mrs Crombie said sternly. "Don't be coarse!"

"No, Missus. Sorry, Missus," Charlie said. But when she looked away he winked broadly at Foxe. "There you are, master. Eliza could go and talk to some o'the whores, I'm sure. Most likely she knows a good many o'them already."

"What is the world coming to?" Mrs Crombie said. "That girl needs her bottom spanked."

"Aye, Missus," Charlie said. "Reckon she might enjoy that too, even if it was a lady what did it!"

"Charlie Dillon!" she exclaimed. "I'm ashamed of you ... "

"No, Mrs Crombie," Foxe said. "Don't scold the boy. I admit what he said isn't really fit for a lady's ears, but what we're involved in here isn't anything most ladies should ever encounter. If you're going to help me, as you said you wanted, I'm afraid you must get used to dealing with the worst aspects of human beings—even if, as I hope and pray will be the case, only ever at second or third hand. If Charlie has to censor what he says, there's a danger he'll miss out something vital."

"I suppose you're right," Mrs Crombie said. "Still, don't let me hear you speaking like this save on such an occasion as today, Charlie, or I'll box your ears for you. I'm glad my cousin Eleanor is safely out of hearing."

"You may be surprised at what your cousin is aware of," Foxe said. "I'm sure she would never talk openly of such matters, but I cannot believe she is as innocent of the pleasures of this world as you suppose. I detected quite a twinkle in her eye."

"Mr Foxe!" she said. "I declare you are quite, quite shameless. Eleanor Benfield has led a quiet and blameless life. Don't you go putting such ideas into her head. I brought her here and I won't have her ruin on my conscience."

"You need not fear, Mrs Crombie," Foxe said with a grin. "I think Miss Benfield's honour is quite safe from me at least. As for others …"

"I'm glad to hear it!" Mrs Crombie said quickly. Her stern look was in sore danger of being replaced by something else. "Come, let us return to the shop and be about our business. Do not corrupt this young man even more. Charlie, go on with your work. You can seek out this … Eliza … later, if you must. And you, Mr Foxe, said you needed to go to see Alderman Halloran urgently, not linger here indulging in idle and salacious tittle-tattle."

"But that's the most useful kind," Foxe protested.

ALDERMAN HALLORAN RECEIVED the news about 'Gentleman' Jack Beeston with surprising calmness.

"If Beeston is involved," he said, "we can forget about recovering any of the money, as you say. Bad news for the Morrow family, but makes little or no difference to the city."

"Why is that, alderman?" Foxe said.

"The matter of Morrow's businesses is solved. Oh, I forgot to tell you. Ezekiel Morrow died last night. Just as well in the circumstances."

"Who inherits?"

"His half of the yarn partnership to James. His share in the banking, the house and its estate to Joseph. Seems old Ezekiel never really gave up hoping the two might come together one day and share the original family firm. Joseph was already an equal partner with him in all the businesses, so all he was left in addition was that fancy house and estate. Won't matter much anyway."

"Why's that?"

"Both Ezekiel's and Joseph's executors must first settle all the outstanding debts. Fortunately, there are no significant mortgages to be carried on, but all the money that's been loaned to the bank to keep it afloat has to be repaid. That's going to take pretty much everything in the estate."

"And Joseph's bequests?"

"Everything to that damned, dissenting chapel he attended, save for the agreed widow's portion for his wife. The chapel is going to get nothing, I expect. Thanks to the generosity of Mr James Morrow, the widow may have about enough to live on."

"Can you explain?" Foxe asked. "I'm getting lost in all these transactions."

"Simple," Alderman Halloran said. "The cost of repaying the loans to the bank doesn't fall equally on both partners. Because Ezekiel was very much alive when the deal was struck, the lenders agreed to let a frail old man keep his home, at least during his lifetime. Thus three separate loans were made. One to Joseph's estate, covering the major part of the money. The second included an amount secured against Ezekiel's house and land, but it was agreed there would be no repayment of that part during the old man's lifetime. A third loan was linked to the value of Ezekiel's partnerships in the banking and the yarn firm. James is only affected by the segment of the loan attached to the yarn business. When the yarn business is sold, he may even have a little left. Joseph's estate certainly will not, despite the house and land passing to him. However, James says he doesn't need the money. He'll use it to make up any of the widow's portion Joseph's estate is not able to supply."

"Most generous of him," Foxe said. "So that's that, as far as the city is concerned?"

What Foxe said proved to be correct. The yarn business would be split up and sold to various other merchants, the largest part going to Halloran. The spinners were all out-workers, working from their homes and paid on piece-rates for what they produced. As long as someone wanted their output, it would mean no change for them. Aside from that, the business had few physical assets. A warehouse, a stock of raw materials and another stock of finished yarn. Those would be shared out, as would any current contracts to supply master weavers. After that, the business would disappear, its activities merged with those of the purchasers.

The bank would also be wound up in an orderly manner. The outstanding loans would be sold to a group of rival businessmen in the city who operated banking businesses. Deposits would be returned. Morrow & Son would be forgotten.

With the city saved from financial confusion and loss, neither the mayor nor Alderman Halloran felt much urgency over finding Joseph Morrow's murderer. Foxe was certain both would relish any possibility of seeing Jack Beeston handed over to the hangman, but that was most unlikely to happen.

Halloran enquired briefly whether Beeston might be the murderer.

"Most unlikely, to my mind," Foxe said. "How would he benefit? He was, I imagine, extracting large sums of money from Morrow. Even if Morrow suddenly refused—or was unable—to pay more, there would be no need to kill him. Beeston would take much greater pleasure in revealing to the world whatever he had been using as the basis for his blackmail. That would extract a cruel revenge and tell any future victims Beeston would not hesitate to destroy them if they did not pay."

"Any closer to knowing who did kill him?" Halloran asked.

"Not much, if I am to speak honestly. I have one or two ideas, but while they might explain the 'why' of the murder, they have little bearing on the 'who'. It may be that we'll never know."

"It's a dreadful thing for a magistrate to say," Halloran replied, "but I don't much care if the man is never found. Joseph Morrow was a canting Puritan and, from all you have told me, a cruel bastard as well. Sending someone to the gallows for killing him may be the law, but it would give me little pleasure."

Foxe agreed. The more he learned about Joseph Morrow, the less he wanted to discover the identity of his killer. Only two things kept him in the hunt. The first was that whatever sins Joseph Morrow had been paying a fortune to keep quiet must not come suddenly to light to cause misery or ruin to his brother or widow. The second was Foxe's insatiable curiosity. To leave a mystery unsolved pained him; he would not do it unless there was no other option. Whether he would share the solution with the proper authorities was another matter.

As Foxe was about to leave, Alderman Halloran detained him.

"Back to your normal self, Foxe, I see. Fancy clothes, spring in your step, full of questions. Did you have a good night? Sleep well? I always feel better for a quiet night and plenty of sleep."

"It was a good night, alderman, though I cannot claim to have slept that much."

"Too much going on in your head, I expect. That's your trouble, Foxe. Always thinking about some scheme or other."

"Not last night," Foxe said. "I can say with total honesty that I had only one thing on my mind."

"Well, now you can forget about Joseph Morrow for a day or so."

"Was your night a quiet one?"

"Hmm … if you mean did I sleep well, I would say yes. For the rest … Look here, Foxe. No use beating about the bush. Went into my library this morning and there were books everywhere. Thirty or more on the floor, more on the desk, on the table, even some on the steps of the ladder I use to get to the highest shelves. Terrible mess. Papers strewn about too."

"I did warn you."

"That's what my wife said. Told me I should have heeded your advice. Even warned me that if the servants thought there was a ghost they'd leave. Got quite cross with me. All stuff and nonsense of course. Don't believe in ghosts. Never have."

"A bad mess for you to clear up, then."

"Got my nieces doing it. Couldn't tell the servants, see? I must say those girls are tremendously sensible and brave. A good many young women would go off into hysterics at the idea of going into a haunted room. But they simply said ghosts didn't come in the day-time, so there was nothing to be afraid of. Level-headed, both of them."

"I certainly agree that they are admirable young ladies," Foxe said. "and I have some experience of the fair sex. Most are not nearly as empty-headed as they are made out to be. Those two certainly aren't. You know, alderman, I almost think that we men are to blame for a good deal of the feminine behaviour we complain about. If you expect women to be silly and frivolous and make it clear that's what you like, they can hardly be criticised for acting that way."

"Rubbish!" Alderman Halloran said. "Good Lord, Foxe, I hope you're not getting strange ideas. Haven't been dallying with any of those unnatural women called 'bluestockings', have you? All philosophical discussions and other things quite unsuitable for their minds. Good many doctors seem to think behaving like that will make them infertile, and then where will they be? Not your style, I would have thought. I always had you down as the kind of man more interested in women's bodies than their minds."

"Both, alderman, both, I assure you. You have no idea what a beautiful body, linked to an inventive mind, can produce in the way of … interesting recreation."

"Whoa, Foxe! Another time, perhaps. Can't risk my wife coming in and hearing you telling me things like that. Pads about the house like a cat sometimes. Never know where she'll appear. Off you go, sir. I've much to do, even if you haven't. Don't really want you to give up looking for our murderer. That would never do. Just not the same urgency, that's all. Sure the mayor would agree."

14

THE FEMALE FACTOR

ON THE WAY BACK TO HIS HOUSE AND SHOP, FOXE FOUND HIS BRAIN working at a feverish pace. The attentions of the two young actresses had aroused his mind as well as his body. If this was the effect of such nocturnal dalliances, he must repeat the dose at regular intervals. Not that he had been in any doubt about that.

He found himself drawn inexorably into his shop in search of Mrs Crombie. With Brock away, he had perforce turned to her to listen to his ideas and supply much-needed correction to the wilder ones. She wasn't as experienced in such matters as Brock, of course, but she did seem to have a mind of remarkable keenness.

He found both ladies busy serving. Miss Benfield was helping an elderly clergyman find a fresh set of Scriptural commentaries to enliven his sermons. Mrs Crombie was counting out sheets of writing paper for two young females, both of whom sounded as if they used it a great deal to enlighten their friends on their hopes and dreams.

"Do you have diaries as well?" one of the young ladies asked her. "A number of my fashionable friends keep diaries nowadays. They say they will make admirable reading in future years. I dread to imagine how many important matters I have forgot already, simply from the lack of writing them down."

Mrs Crombie had indeed a small stock of diaries. Foxe would never have thought of having such things in his shop. Yet here she was, selling one to each of the young women at two shillings a volume. Even better, they were assuring her that they knew of others who wished to record their daily thoughts and actions. Now they had found where the necessary volumes of blank pages could be purchased, they would be sure to recommend the shop to their acquaintances.

Once the young women had left with their purchases, Foxe asked Mrs Crombie to step aside with him into the storeroom where they could talk.

"Mr Foxe," she said. "Are you not forgetting how improper that would be? What if anyone glanced through the window and saw you taking me aside into a back room? Who knows what they would imagine?'

"I think we both know very well, Mrs Crombie, but you are quite correct," Foxe said. "There are times when the demands of propriety are altogether a nuisance, you know. I could always talk alone with Kitty and Gracie whenever I wished. That was, of course, because one was an actress and the other kept a bagnio. No one expected them to be respectable."

"I quite see your point," Mrs Crombie said. "However, I have not yet lost my reputation—though I find working with you means I have to exercise constant vigilance on the matter. Now, let us think. You wish to tell me something and I wish to hear it. The problem is that it is improper for the two of us to go off alone together. Cousin Eleanor cannot leave the shop. Very well. We are due to close at three today. You eat at four, I imagine?"

"About then," Foxe agreed. "I am not very precise about the hour to dine. When you live alone, as I do, there seems little reason to keep strict hours. My cook is very understanding about it."

"She probably has little choice," Mrs Crombie said severely. "However, here is what we will do. My cousin and I cannot prepare our meal until we arrive home, which we normally do together since she has come to work here. If she has no objection, I will arrange for her to stay with us after the shop is closed. With her as chaperone, there can be no difficulty if the three of us retire to the storeroom. You will have about an hour of our time, sir, if that will be enough."

"It will have to do," Foxe said. "Very well. I will return at three."

Back in his study, Foxe swallowed his annoyance and spent the time turning over again what he knew. What bothered him most was why Beeston's men had been combing the city and what they were looking for. He had asked Charlie to spread his net far and wide because he didn't know exactly what to seek out. Beeston would never waste his time fishing for a basis for blackmail like that. Morrow's reputation for strictness in behaviour was far too strong. Only when you had something suitable for blackmail would that reputation work in the other direction. It gave Morrow a great deal to lose and a strong incentive to pay whatever was demanded.

What about the business of taking certain girls away. What could that mean? It would hardly be because Beeston's thugs fancied them. If that had been the case, they could have demanded their favours right away. Since everyone knew whom the men worked for, the girls would have been too frightened to refuse and the madams not so foolish as to expect payment.

Perhaps they thought Beeston himself would want to talk to the women? That was more likely. But why keep them? Charlie had been told all this happened five or six months ago. If Beeston simply wanted to question the girls, they would have returned the same day. They could have been killed of course. Beeston was capable of having anyone killed if he thought it was to his advantage. But how could that have been the case here? What could the girls have done to warrant their deaths? Beeston was looking for something he could use to blackmail Morrow. Unless he could make it look as if Morrow killed the whores, having them disappear made no sense.

Round and round went Foxe's mind until his reflections became so far-fetched he grew disgusted with himself. Fortunately, it was now three o'clock, so he could seek out Mrs Crombie and her cousin.

Foxe decided the storeroom was unsuitable as a place to talk with two respectable ladies, so he insisted they came through into his house. There he seated them in his small parlour and sent for Molly to bring tea and something suitable to eat.

"I am bound to delay your meal, ladies," he said, "and I would not have you go hungry for my sake. Ah, here are Molly and Florence with the tea things. This is Florence, Miss Benfield. She is new to my household and has joined us to help in the kitchen, where I am sure she will be an asset."

Florence blushed furiously at her master's words, though she remembered, just in time, to make a rather sketchy curtsy to the two ladies. She was unsure what an 'asset' was and hoped it didn't mean Mr Foxe was regretting allowing her to stay. Anything was better than living on the streets and picking pockets—especially the obvious alternative available to a young female without money, home or family—and she had come to feel safe in Mr Foxe's house. She had never had a home before. It would be horrible to have it taken away now.

Fortunately for her peace of mind, Mrs Whitbread, the cook, knew what an asset was and reassured her that their master was paying her a compliment, not planning to send her away.

Once tea had been served, Foxe explained his dilemmas. Mrs Crombie resolved the one and Miss Benfield the other with such speed that he felt foolish for having been puzzled about them at all.

"As to why this wretch Beeston was sending his men to search widely," Mrs Crombie said, "the answer must be the same as it was for you. He suspected something, but did not know exactly where to look for evidence to back it up. That probably means he already had a clear notion of the basis for blackmail but his proof was too weak to be set against Mr Morrow's reputation. You told me some time ago that an attempt at blackmailing the man needed a strong enough basis to survive general disbelief. Everyone in the city thought Mr Joseph Morrow to be a man of unimpeachable probity. Most common accusations against him would have been dismissed as ridiculous."

"If extracting money from Joseph Morrow began soon after the events you described, Mr Foxe," Miss Benfield added, "such evidence was obviously secured. If, as we must assume, it came from these … women of ill-repute … the most likely explanation for them being taken away is simple; it was to keep them where they could be at hand if they were needed. Since the proof behind a charge plain enough to cause Mr Morrow to cheat his own bank lay with them, this foul Beeston man must have feared they might be silenced."

"You are both right and I am an idiot," Foxe cried. "Beeston would not search before he knew the basis for blackmail. He searched because that basis was not enough to convince Morrow the mud would stick. If Beeston himself faced a threat because someone could testify against him, he would have that person killed in an instant, so he feared Morrow would do the same. We always assume other people will act as we would."

"Where does that take us?" Mrs Crombie asked.

"Sadly, not very far. Unless we can find out what these poor girls knew, or guess at it from something else, we can proceed no further. Mrs Crombie, do you know where Charlie is? I did not see him in the shop. Might he still be in the storeroom?"

"I allowed him to visit his mother this afternoon," Mrs Crombie said. "He went to his old home briefly last week to tell her about his change of status; to assure her he is well and has a place to live. I gather she is frightfully proud of him. I sent him there today to take her a few victuals Mrs Whitbread was going to throw away. I hope you do not object."

"Not at all," Foxe said. "Had I known, I would have added a shilling or so."

"That would be well meant, Mr Foxe, but it would not have been wise. Charlie's mother drinks, I'm sad to say. With gin available at barely tuppence a pint in some places, a shilling would keep the poor woman drunk for a day or more. Far better to give her things she cannot sell, like food. Even giving her cast-off clothing is a risk. There's a ready market for such things."

"I was not thinking," Foxe said. "Indeed, though I used to pride myself on my knowledge of the lives of the poor and the labouring classes, I am coming to realise I know much less than I did. Money does many things, ladies, including cutting you off from the lives of those who have little or none. Without the help of others, my investigations would never succeed; unless they took place amongst people of the better sort, of course."

"There you have the advantage of us," Mrs Crombie said, "so we may make a good team. Is that all you wish to discuss? Thank you for the tea. Please tell Mrs Whitbread how much we enjoyed her small cakes as well. Time marches on and we still have our meal to prepare."

Although Foxe had to sleep alone that night, he did not regret it so very much. He was tired out. Even his mind had become too fatigued to keep him awake with constant questions and hypotheses. From the moment his head rested on his pillow until well after dawn, he remained blissfully unconscious.

Eventually, sounds from the rest of the house filtered into his brain and he came awake. It was not too long after his usual time. Molly must have been listening for him as carefully as usual, for he had scarcely set his feet to the floor when she came in with his hot water and shaving things.

"Charlie asked me to give you a message, master," she said. "He's got something important to tell you as soon as you're up and about. A mass of excitement he is too. Said to say that he's had a message from someone called Eliza and you'll know who that is."

"Very well, Molly," Foxe said. "When you go down, tell young Charlie I'll send for him when I sit down to my breakfast and he can tell me then whatever he has heard. Oh, and you'd better bring one or two extra warm rolls, if Mrs Whitbread has enough. I've never known Charlie when he wasn't hungry. It would be torment to him to watch me eat and have nothing himself."

"Right you are, master, though I expect he's already had his fair share and more. He wheedles around cook something shocking, he does. Bad as the cat for always wanting food."

"He's a growing lad," Foxe said. "By the way, how is Florence settling in?"

"Very well, master. We was all a bit nervous about her at first, but she's turned out to be the most sweet-tempered, hard-working person you could imagine. She was quite open with everyone about her past, right from the start. Told us how she'd had to dress as a boy and learn the skill of picking pockets. That's why she's so neat and quick with her hands, cook says. Lots o' practice.'

"I imagine so," Foxe said drily.

"Must have been a terrible life, so it must," Molly went on. "Still, as she says, the only alternative for a young girl was to fall into vice and all that kind of thing. That she couldn't abide the thought of. All those dirty old men, pawin' her about. That's why she pretended to be a boy. Even on the streets, she'd have been taken for a ... well, I'm sure you know, master."

"Indeed," Foxe said solemnly. Molly was a nice child, but she came from rather a straight-laced family. Working for Foxe had shocked her badly at first. Nowadays, she had come to accept her master's ways, if not completely approve of them.

"Well, we all likes Flo ... Florence ... a good deal and we're very proud of you for helpin' her as you have. Real Christian, I calls it. Like that Good Shepherd in the Bible."

"Good Samaritan, I think you mean, Molly. I'm glad Florence is happy here. It was impulsive of me as usual to do what I did, but it seems to have turned out well enough. Now, be off to tell young Charlie what I said. If he really has got something important to tell me, he'll be in a frenzy until he knows I'm coming."

Later, seated in his small parlour, Foxe waited until Molly had set out his breakfast before telling her to bring Charlie in. She had set a plate for the apprentice opposite, with a single roll on it. It seemed he'd already eaten three that morning in the kitchen. Mrs Whitbread said he'd make himself ill if he ate many more.

In fact, the lad was too excited at first even to sit down. The moment he came through the door, he started on his tale.

"Master, Master," he said. "Eliza's done it. She's found what you wanted to know. Said she would!"

"Sit down first," Foxe said. "Then tell me slowly and carefully. I'm not at my quickest first thing in the morning."

"Gar!" Charlie said. "This ain't first thing. I been up for hours."

"Maybe you have," Foxe said. "That is of no consequence. I prefer to enter each day gently and with great care. You never know what might be waiting. However, we are wasting time. What has Eliza told you?"

Charlie was not going to be forced to tell his tale beginning in the middle.

"Well," he began, "she went round to the back door of the first place and sniffed about a bit. Looked to see if she might know anyone. I said she was pretty free with her person, if you know what I mean, but she ain't no whore and doesn't want to be one. It's just that she knows a good few. Eliza says she never minds a kind gentleman givin' her a nice present for what she 'as to offer, but she'd prefer to pick and chose who lifts up her skirts. When you works in one o' them places, she says, you has to do it with anyone who'll pay. Cor, she don't 'alf fancy you, master! When I tells her who I works for now, she said she'd let you 'ave anything you wanted anytime. Wouldn't charge you a farthing either."

"I'm sure that's most flattering, Charlie, but you still haven't told me what she said."

"I'm comin' to that. Well, after a little while she spotted a whore she knew comin' outside to 'ave a pee, so she nips over and starts up a conversation. At first, she said, she couldn't get nothin' out of her. Too frightened. Still she kept at it and the doxie tells her Beeston's men 'ad come looking for anyone who'd worked for that Joseph Morrow. Only she didn't know 'is name. Said "that preachin' misery what kept goin' on about drink", but it was clear enough who she meant."

"Did they find anyone?"

"They found two, she said. No one in the 'ouse knew they'd worked there. Seems they never mentioned it to anyone. That Morrow cove 'ad put the fear o' God into 'em to keep 'em quiet. It was only 'cos they was more frightened of Beeston than they were of God that they spoke up. Anyhow, Beeston's men just said their master would want to ask 'em some questions, then they took 'em away and no one's seen 'em since."

"Interesting," Foxe said.

"That ain't all. Eliza went to a second place she knew. Bit of a cheaper 'ouse, she said. More stews than a regular brothel. Seems Beeston's roughs 'ad been there too and taken away another girl who'd once worked as a chambermaid at Morrow's house. Like the first two, she'd been sent to 'im from the orphanage where she'd been put when she was born. Reckoned 'er mother 'ad been a doxie like 'er and she was born to it, like. She'd never told anyone she'd been at Morrow's either. Whatever 'e told these girls to keep 'em quiet worked real well, master."

"Any more girls Beeston's men took away?"

"Not that Eliza could find. Just those three. Course, there could 'ave been others what kept their mouths shut, even under threats from Beeston. Some may 'ave died or be workin' for pimps on the streets, not in a regular 'ouse. No way o' gettin' to them, I reckon."

"Never mind, Charlie. You've done really well. How much should I give Eliza as a reward, do you reckon?"

"Shillin' I should think," Charlie said.

"Here's three sixpences," Foxe said. "Keep one for yourself."

"Cor, thank you, master. I'll give the others to Eliza, promise I will. She wanted to come and tell you all this 'erself, but I says Missus Crombie would 'ave a fit if she saw 'er. There's no mistakin' Eliza for a respectable young woman. Missus Crombie says it's real important to make sure the customers realise we keep a suitable shop for ladies to enter."

"She's quite right," Foxe said. "Remember that. If any of your … less respectable contacts need to tell you anything urgently, set up some kind of signal they can use to alert you without seeming to. Then go to the gate at the back of the garden—the one by the old stables and coach-house—and meet them there. That will make sure Mrs Crombie doesn't see them and get angry with you. Tell her that's what I've told you to do, or she might think you're creeping off to avoid your proper work."

"I'd never do that, master!" Charlie cried. "Never. She knows that too. Still, I'll tell her what you said and that'll make things easy. Missus Crombie says she'll teach me to read!"

"Excellent," Foxe said. "We can't have an apprentice bookseller who can't read. Be sure to work hard for her, won't you?"

"I will, master. Real hard. Missus Crombie's like another mother to me. I won't ever let her down, I swear. I'd rather 'ang meself."

"Well, we'll hope it never comes to that. Now, eat the roll Molly brought for you—here's butter and jam—then you'd better hurry back to the shop. I'm sure Mrs Crombie has plenty for you to do."

SOME SIX HOURS LATER, as he sat eating his dinner, Foxe reflected that this investigation had already taken longer than most of those he had entered upon in the past. Not only that, he did not feel much further forward than he had at the start. It really was time to pull himself together and undertake some serious thought. He could no longer make the excuse that he had little information on which to base a hypothesis; nor could he take refuge for ever in mourning the absence of Kitty and Gracie.

That gave him a thought. He finished his meal, refused Alfred's offer to bring him a decanter of brandy in his study and went to his room to change. A single evening of dalliance had raised his spirits and spurred his energy. Perhaps a second would be enough to jolt his mind into finding a way out of his current confusion.

At first, Foxe thought he would be disappointed. There was no performance at the theatre that evening. He was turning away when the manager came up behind him and greeted him warmly. The man had come to spend the evening changing scenery and laying out fresh costumes for the new play beginning on the following day. There would be few of the company present, he said, but Foxe was welcome to come inside and see if any might be willing to entertain him for a while. It was not unknown for a few of the younger and more junior members of the company to use gaps in the programme to practice their lines together, or walk upon the stage to rehearse difficult pieces of 'business'.

Once inside, Foxe's luck still seemed to be failing him. Of the five young actresses he had met, only one was to be found—the one he had barely spoken with on that first occasion. That might have been because she seemed rather shy, where the other four had competed eagerly for Foxe's attention. She was, he recalled, amongst the youngest and least experienced members of the company, having joined at the start of the current season. Because of that, she played only minor roles. She needed more experience and confidence to undertake anything else.

Foxe found her alone in the actresses' dressing room, mumbling to herself and dabbing her eyes with a handkerchief that was none too clean. Seeing him, the girl jumped up and began to excuse herself for being there.

"Why should you not be here?" Foxe said. "You have more right than I. But you are crying. Sit down, I beg you, and tell me what ails you."

Lily—for that was her name—had been much taken to task by the manager and the other members of the cast for forgetting her lines the night before. That was why she had come to the theatre when she knew no one else would be there. She had been trying with all her might to drum her lines and the movements she must make in the new play into her brain.

"Oh sir," she wailed, "I do so want to be an actress, yet all is against me. My memory is not quick and I am so nervous on stage that I trip over things and forget what I am to say. The audience laughs and the manager becomes angry and …"

"How old are you, Lily?" Foxe asked.

"I am just seventeen, sir."

Foxe looked her up and down. She was a pretty little thing, with a surprisingly full figure for a girl of her age. She had even put on her costume for her private rehearsal. As she looked up at him standing before her, Foxe became very much aware that the bodice of her costume barely contained her breasts. It had either been made for someone smaller or the manager had decided to divert the audience's attention from Lily's inexperience. Only a thin kerchief would stand between her bosom and the eager eyes on the men present.

Foxe had never believed in the benefits of resisting temptation, so he bent his head and kissed Lily full upon the lips. At first, she started and would have drawn back, but he had slipped one arm behind her, keeping her close to him. When he kissed her a second time, she hesitated, then responded as he hoped she would. Indeed, she was so engrossed in kissing that she seemed not to notice his hand slip beneath her kerchief to rest gently around a firm, soft breast.

"Oh sir," she whispered then. "Would you take advantage of a girl thus?"

"Only if she wished me to," Foxe replied. "Only if she felt nought but pleasure—and a certain warmth arising, perhaps."

With that, he deftly slipped one breast free of all covering and moved his hand to do the same for the other.

Foxe was a skilful and considerate lover, who had received instruction from some of those most practised in the arts of giving and receiving pleasure. Thus, as he covered each of Lily's breasts with gentle kisses, he perceived a marked quickening in her breathing and a flush appearing over her pale skin.

"Oh sir," she said, "I do feel it is becoming quite warm in here. And …" But at this point Foxe's fondling seemed to make her too breathless for further speech.

Thus their love-making proceeded much as you might expect, until Lily quite forgot anything else but the world of pleasure Foxe brought her. At length, after a final flurry of small cries and gasps, both were still.

"You are not quite the first who has used me so," Lily said at length, "but I have no doubt you are by a long way the best. Please tell me, sir. Was this but a moment's lust?"

Foxe was always honest with the women whose affections he enjoyed. He had no taste for deception in matters of love. He kept that for dealing with criminals.

"At the start, it was," he said. "I saw an opportunity and I took it. Yet I do not believe either of us would have achieved such a height of passion if we had not begun to feel more than animal desire. Oh Lily! You are so beautiful and so passionate, once aroused. I truly do not want to let you go."

"Nor do I want this to be all," Lily said. "Will you come again, sir?"

"I certainly will," Foxe said. "But might I persuade you to come to my house? It will be more private and comfortable there."

"Tell me where that is and I will come whenever you wish. Oh, Mr Foxe. This has been the best rehearsal ever. I feel I can walk out on stage tomorrow and sweep the audience away."

As he walked home again, Foxe too felt almost light-headed with excitement. Occasional encounters with compliant partners were undoubtedly pleasant, but he could never help longing for something more—something that included real passion on both sides. That was why he had missed the Catt sisters so much. Kitty might have been wayward and eager for presents. Gracie might have been almost too polished in the arts of love, so that he always felt as if she was judging his performance. Yet he had found passion with both of them. He missed that more than anything else.

Lily had said she felt she could conquer any audience the next night. Perhaps he could conquer his demons as well and regain his ability to spot such patterns as would make sense out of the muddle of information to hand. He certainly hoped that might be true. However, for the moment he knew he was assured of another night of sound sleep. Then he would see.

15

FURTHER COMPLICATIONS

WHEN FOXE AWOKE, HE FOUND HIS MIND ALREADY ENGAGED ON A new and most promising hypothesis. Much of it was guesswork of course, but it would account for a great deal of what had puzzled him until now. This happened to him sometimes. It was as if his brain had continued working on a problem even while he was asleep; as if, free from the limitations of calculated judgement, it had been able to explore new and unexpected pathways. One of these proved to be of great interest.

During breakfast, throughout his time at the coffee-house and on his accustomed walk around Norwich's vast and teeming Market Place, Foxe went over and over his new idea. Try as he might, he could not find any faults. There were gaps of course, though he could see how most of those might be filled. The first thing he should do was send a message to ask Mrs Morrow if she would be willing to receive him again.

But when Foxe returned to his house, he found a message for him. Alderman Halloran wanted an urgent meeting. What a nuisance! Still, there might still be a chance that Mrs Morrow would agree to meet him after the noon hour. He despatched Alfred with a suitable note, then made his way to the alderman's house.

What he found there was a man near his wits' end.

"It happened again!" Halloran cried, the moment Foxe entered the room. "Books and papers everywhere. Terrible mess. I warrant it will take my poor nieces most of the day to clear it up. Now my dear wife is furious with me. She says I have been a fool and should have taken your advice from the start. Help me, Foxe. This cannot continue or I shall go mad!"

"Calm yourself, alderman, calm yourself." Foxe said. "I did warn you. However, that is water under the bridge. Here is what we shall do."

Foxe's 'plan' was naturally what it had been from the first. He would contact 'Monsieur Glampard' at once to arrange the required exorcism. Alderman Halloran must see all cleared up, then ask his nieces if they would be willing to help him by creating a permanent rearrangement of the library. That would prevent the difficulty arising again. If all went well, the ghost would be satisfied and the matter ended.

This time, Alderman Halloran made no objections. Foxe thought he would have agreed to dance naked in the street outside, if it might only bring the 'manifestations' to an end.

With this settled, Alderman Halloran had one final piece of news for Foxe.

"You must expect a visit from Mr James Morrow tomorrow, Foxe. He came earlier and in a fine state of anger and confusion. Someone—but we can guess who—has contacted him with an attempt at blackmail. Says he has information about his brother that would, if revealed, ruin the reputation and standing of the whole Morrow family. He wanted to know what he should do. I said to come to you."

"This is wonderful news, alderman," Foxe said. "Now we have a chance to catch Beeston; or if not the man himself, some of his henchmen. I will look forward to Mr James' visit and have a plan ready. I too have made significant progress. I have one or two pieces of fresh information to find, but I think I can explain what Joseph Morrow had done that made him a target for blackmail. Aye, and how Beeston might have discovered his secret. If I am right, we may be on the way to discovering the identity of the murderer; though I admit that still makes me uneasy. If I am right in my hypothesis, I find myself even less at ease in seeing the law take its course."

"I leave all in your hands as always, Foxe. You have never let me down yet. Like you, I am less than eager to see the murderer stand before a judge, but to assist Beeston and some of his foul associates on their way to Hell would give me nothing but pleasure. Now, Foxe, on your way! If I do not prove to Mrs Halloran at once that I am putting myself in your hands in the matter of the ghost, I can expect nothing but silence and angry looks."

Foxe took his leave and hurried back to his house, pausing along the way only to visit a jewellers of his acquaintance and choose a fine brooch of pearls and sapphires as a present for Lily. He had instructed Alfred to take a second message with him and deliver it on his way back, after he had received a reply from Mrs Morrow. The second note was to Lily, inviting her to come to his house the following evening to tell him how things had gone with her. The performance that night would end too late for her to be abroad alone. Foxe would have to be patient for news—and other things— for a further day.

NEXT MORNING, Mr James Morrow came as promised, bearing the note he had received. It had no signature, of course but it was neatly written in good English with a tone quite unlike the missive that had been pushed under Mr Seager's door. The sender stated plainly that he knew things that would, if revealed, be of great harm and shame to the Morrow family. A payment of 50 guineas, in gold, was required to prevent this happening.

Foxe was delighted. With Joseph Morrow dead, the blackmailer clearly thought to continue extracting payments from his brother.

"Has this anything to do with that offensive, libellous notice that was set up all around the city?" James wanted to know.

"Yes, it has," Foxe said. "It seems most likely that notice was printed and distributed by this blackmailer. He wished to make his threat seem more credible."

"Is there any truth in what this wretch claims?"

Fox was cautious. "That I do not know for sure. I am certain the money taken from the bank's accounts by your brother was not to cover bad debts or rash loans. I believe it began with trying to hide poor business management from your father. Your brother wanted everyone to believe all was well with the business under his sole direction, when it was not. Later, he too was in the grip of a blackmailer, Mr Morrow, probably the same one. Exactly what was threatened against him, I cannot be sure. Now the fellow expects you to pay as your brother did."

"The devil I will!" Morrow cried. "He'll get no money from me. Let him publish whatever filth he wishes. None in Norwich will believe it."

"That may be so, sir," Foxe said "Yet that would also be to miss a fine opportunity to catch the villain—or his henchmen—and put an end to the matter once and for all."

"You want me to agree to this blackmail?" James was incredulous.

"No, not that. I want you only to seem to be ready to pay. If you respond by bowing to his demands, the blackmailer must set a time and place for the delivery of the money. It will be at night, I imagine, in some lonely part of the city. You must keep the appointment. However, I will be waiting and we will seize the blackmailer when he comes to collect his money."

"It goes against the grain," Morrow said.

"Nevertheless, I am sure it will be for the best. The blackmailer forced your brother into payments—large payments. Whatever he is threatening to reveal must be of some gravity. Unless you can assure me there is nothing whatever in your brother's life that could be the basis for blackmail, we must take his threat seriously."

James Morrow thought for a few moments.

"No," he said. "That I cannot do. I have been too remote from my brother for too long. Very well, Mr Foxe. I agree to follow your plan."

"Good," Foxe said. "Be sure to speak of this to no one. Our blackmailer will be alert to a trap."

"How will you catch him then?"

"It is best that you do not know, sir. Please trust me. I have dealt with such people before."

"Very well. Tell me what I must do and I will do it. If you can apprehend this evil man, you will do myself, my family and this city a great service."

Foxe instructed Morrow to ask for 24 hours to obtain such a large sum of money in gold, as was demanded. This would give Foxe time to make his preparations.

"Then you must fill a suitable bag with anything that will clink like coins. Pennies or half-pennies would do," he went on. "Go to the place the blackmailer tells you at exactly the appointed time, leave your bag and walk away. Don't whatever you do look back or turn around, someone will be bound to be watching. You must in all particulars act as if the blackmailer has won."

"Then what?"

"Return home. Nothing else. Leave all to me."

"Can't you tell me what you plan, Mr Foxe?" Morrow begged.

"I fear not," Foxe replied. "That way, you cannot make any movement, or act in any manner, that might warn the blackmailer. If I am successful, it will put an end of this matter. No one will ever speak of it again."

"You are sure of that?"

"As sure as I can be."

"Very well. I will do as you say. Look to receive some communication from me once the blackmailer has told me where and when to leave the money."

"Do not write or send a servant here! Such a messenger may be followed, I fear. Go to the coffeehouse where I take my daily cup—you know which one that is? Good—and make sure you give your order only to Samuel, the owner. You must order as usual, then say something like this: 'I am still trying to get word to the friend I told you of. If he comes here, please give him this.' Samuel will hand the message you leave to me, and to me only. In it, you must write the time and place laid down by the blackmailer."

Morrow agreed, though Foxe could see he would much have preferred to refuse the blackmailer outright. That would invite Beeston to respond by carrying out his threat.

James Morrow might feel certain his brother had nothing to hide. Foxe was not—not at all. In his mind, paying out such large sums could only be explained by assuming Beeston had somehow stumbled on something truly shameful. He even suspected he knew what it was. During the night, his mind had supplied him with an important recollection of Mrs Morrow's words. If he was right, they pointed to the cause of all the trouble. It was why he hoped to speak with the lady herself in less than an hour's time.

Once again Mrs Morrow received Foxe in her parlour. She was still wearing mourning, but that was the only indication of sadness about the house. Since Foxe's first visit, there were many signs of change within. Several handsome ornaments had appeared. Fresh flowers stood on the table in the room Even Mrs Morrow's hair had been styled in a manner more like the current fashion. A hat and mourning veil would doubtless hide that change, should she need to venture out.

Foxe's hostess offered coffee which he accepted gratefully. Then he turned at once to business.

"Thank you for agreeing to see me," he said.

"It is a terrible thing to say, Mr Foxe," she replied, "but I find myself looking forward to any opportunity to hear how your investigation is progressing. After years of being confined to sermons and my late husband's diatribes against all forms of modernity, I am eager for news from the world outside. As soon as decency allows, you may look to see me going about the city as other women do. I even have a shameful desire to attend the theatre, for I have never been to such a place in my life."

"Then you must allow me to escort you there," Foxe said. "I am a devotee of plays and am well known at most of the theatres in this city. I can assure you of the best seats and even an introduction to the principal players."

"Oh, Mr Foxe! That would be so thrilling. I can hardly wait. But you have come here on more sober business than indulging the whims of a middle-aged lady, I am sure."

"Sadly, that is the case. Things are moving quickly and I need your help again. There are certain questions I need to put to you, Mrs Morrow. Though they may seem odd—even trivial—I assure you they are not. The first is: was your late husband ever particularly bad-tempered?"

"No, sir. He was *always* bad-tempered. It would have been more surprising to find his temper improved. That never happened."

"Was he ever particularly anxious?" Foxe asked.

"Again, no. He seemed to me always anxious. You will recall that he was set on proving to himself and everyone that he was truly one of God's Elect. He would do this by being perfect. Such a course of life prevented him from relaxing at any time."

It seemed Foxe's idea was going to be dashed. Then he asked another question.

"Was he ever especially diligent in his religious observances? More than usual?"

Mrs Morrow paused and thought hard. Then she sat up straight, looking almost eager.

"To that, I can at last say yes, Mr Foxe. It happened about every four or six weeks over several years before his death. I would suddenly find him shut away in his bedroom praying for hours at a time. You could hear the constant drone of supplications from outside the door. He even had a small scourge. I would hear the sound of it striking his flesh. To me, that seemed an oddly Popish practice for such a devout Calvinist."

At last Foxe knew he was on the right track.

"Now, Mrs Morrow," he said. "Please think carefully. Did these periods of extra religious strictness coincide with servants leaving or being sacked?"

"That's hard to say. Our servants and apprentices ran away or were dismissed so often. It might have done, but I cannot be sure. Oh, let me think! It may have been the case, but not always."

"It was just an idea," Foxe said. "Please do not distress yourself."

"I am not distressed, just annoyed at my fallible memory. There was one time when it did, of that I am sure, for it was not so long ago."

"Ah," Foxe said, relieved. "Can you tell me of it?'

"I recall it because it was unusual," Mrs Morrow said. "My husband had taken two children from the orphanage at the same time, a boy and a girl. They were twins and did not wish to be parted. The girl went to work as a chambermaid and the boy was set to be an apprentice in the yarn business. They stayed for perhaps six or eight weeks, I think. Then my late husband dismissed the girl —for stealing, he told me—and the boy ran away the next day. I imagine he wished to remain with his sister, even if it cost him his employment."

"Did you see or hear of either again?"

"No, that I am sure of. Runaways often fear to be caught and returned to their masters where they naturally expect punishment. In my late husband's case, I feel certain it would have been severe. On occasions I found him beating certain servants with a birch because they had angered him in some way."

"Is it possible you can recall the names of these twins? It would be extremely helpful if you could."

"The maid was called Minnie. Minnie Goodwin, I think. Her brother's name I do not know. I had little to do with the apprentices."

"Goodwin. That may be enough."

"Do you hope to find these two children, Mr Foxe?"

"If I can. Or at least to find something about where they went after they left and whether they ever told others what had happened. Runaways in small towns usually seek out a city where they may disappear amongst a large population. Norwich is the largest city for many miles in any direction, indeed one of the largest in the country. A runaway here would be more likely to avoid being caught by staying within its bounds than trying to make his or her way elsewhere."

THOUGH THE MORNING had already been busy, Foxe was far from finished. On his way home from Mrs Morrow's house, he called on Alderman Halloran, hoping to find him in. Unfortunately the alderman, Foxe was told, was attending a meeting of the Mayor's Court and might not return for several hours. All Foxe could do was leave a message saying he would call again, late in the afternoon, on a most important matter.

The alderman's footman also told Foxe that his master had been late leaving because he had been entertaining a "foreign gentleman" in the library for nearly an hour. The man had been expected, since he had received instructions to usher him directly to the library, where the alderman would be waiting. Such a thing had never happened before.

Foxe expressed the required surprise at this news, then went on his way. Alderman Halloran had clearly wasted no time in summoning the 'exorcist' Foxe had informed him about. Perhaps the threat of Mrs Halloran's displeasure at any further delay had been the deciding factor. Well, that cleared up the matter of the 'lost' books—and without Alderman Halloran's nieces needing to confess to him what they had done. Foxe could only hope that Miss Maria's scheme of rearrangement proved successful.

Back in his house, Foxe set aside his outdoor clothes and went at once into his shop, seeking young Charlie Dillon.

He found him being instructed by Mrs Crombie in the proper care of the books which were sold unbound. Binding greatly increased the price, so it tended to be reserved for volumes likely to be long-lasting and subject to heavy use such as dictionaries and bibles. For the rest, mere novels were almost never bound at all. The relatively wealthy men—men like Alderman Halloran—who bought books on serious subjects would have a bookbinder deal with them according to their specific instructions. They wanted their libraries to display a broadly uniform appearance. Noblemen often liked to have their family coat-of-arms printed on the cover of all their books.

Foxe was loath to interrupt this lesson, but his need was too great to wait until a better time. He therefore drew young Charlie aside into the storeroom where they could talk without fear of being overheard by any customers. It took more than 30 minutes to explain all his instructions and make sure the lad had them by heart, then the two returned to the shop together.

"Mrs Crombie," Foxe said. "My apologies, but I must take up even more of Charlie's time. I am sending him on two most important errands which cannot wait. Perhaps in a few days I may be able to explain to you what he is doing. For the moment, I must beg you to trust me. The fewer people who know what I am up to the better."

With that Mrs Crombie had to be content for Foxe returned at once to his house. He needed a little time to review his plan before speaking to Alderman Halloran. It might not be so easy to persuade the alderman to take the action he needed without asking questions. Foxe must be quite sure of what he could say and what must be kept hidden, so as not to jeopardise all.

As it turned out, Alderman Halloran was unusually compliant. He agreed at once to loan Foxe four parish constables whenever they were needed. The prospect of either catching or severely frightening 'Gentleman' Jack Beeston was a powerful incentive.

However, the main reason for his rapid agreement was his wish to tell Foxe about the visit of the 'exorcist' that morning.

"Very odd fellow," Alderman Halloran said, "even for an exiled Frenchie. You did say he was French?"

"Swiss, actually," Foxe said. "He grew up speaking French and was trained in France as a priest. That was where he learned the rites of exorcism. When the revolution broke out he returned to his native land and turned his back on France for good."

"Glad to hear it," Alderman Halloran said. "I made sure no one knew who he was of course or why he had come. Bad enough to have some sort of French—Swiss—magician in my house. A Popish priest would have made it worse."

"Did he tell you he was a magician?" Foxe asked. This hadn't been in the script he had agreed with the actor. He wondered what else the man had invented on the spur of the moment.

"Something like that," Halloran said. "Can't recall his exact words. Anyway, meant he studied all kinds of 'arcane mysteries'—do recall those words—and was an 'adept', whatever that meant. Not a freemason, anyhow. Sure of that."

Alderman Halloran was a prominent member of one of the oldest and most prestigious Masonic lodges in the city. He would have known at once if Foxe's actor had pretended to have anything to do with The Craft. Foxe breathed a quiet sigh of relief that the man had avoided such an obvious trap.

"Did you stay with him?" Foxe asked.

"Exactly as you said to do. Couldn't risk him making off with anything, could I? Can't trust these foreigners. Don't have the same sense of what's right and proper as Englishmen do."

"So what did he do?" Foxe had decided to leave the precise details of the 'exorcism' to the actor's imagination. He could only hope he had showed some restraint.

"Not very much, really," Alderman Halloran said. "Asked for a Bible, then placed it on the table and lit several candles around it. He'd brought a small bell with him and he kept ringing it at odd moments. Aside from all that, he mumbled a great deal in some heathen tongue, then cried out what I suppose were magic words and rang his bell. Then he put the candles out, stowed his bell away in his pocket and told me I would have no more trouble. That was it."

"Nothing else?"

"Only to hand me two white stones and tell me to make sure I kept them on the library mantle for the next few weeks … along with a piece of cheese."

"Cheese?" Foxe could well imagine the man telling this tale to all the other actors, but that would never do—at least until the company were well away from Norwich. He would make sure of that.

"Cheese," he said. "Said ghosts hated cheese. Something about the smell and the presence of mice. Seems mice can see ghosts and that upsets them."

"I never knew that," Foxe said, struggling to keep a straight face.

"Anyway," Halloran continued. "That's all over. I spoke to my nieces and they'll start on rearranging the books tomorrow. Just hope I can understand whatever 'rational' scheme they come up with. I gather they've discussed it with my wife and she approved."

When Foxe got back to his house, he found Charlie waiting in the hallway under the disapproving eye of Alfred. Samuel at the coffeehouse had a message for him, the boy said.

"I would have brought it meself, master" Charlie said, "but he wouldn't give it to me. Said you'd told him to give it to you and you only. Anyhow, he'll have it ready—and secret like—when you goes in tomorrow. And I did the other thing you wanted too."

With all that settled, Foxe felt at last that he could relax that evening and look forward to the promised visit from Lily. His plans were in place. All he could do now was wait. He might as well enjoy waiting as much as he could.

16

OUTFOXED!

FOXE WALKED LILY BACK TO HER LODGINGS NEXT MORNING ON HIS way to take coffee. All about him appeared as usual. He was dressed in his latest and most fashionable coat, richly adorned with embroidery, with matching breeches and fine silk stockings, all made complete by the expensive shoes on his feet. This was very much the old Foxe, debonair and relaxed, walking along the streets of his native city with a pretty girl on his arm and putting on a fine show for all to see. If anyone watching took him for a fop and a fool, with his head empty of all save display, so much the better.

It was nearly eleven before he returned home. At once he went to his room and changed his clothes. When he crossed his hallway to the door to his shop an hour later, you would not have thought it the same man. Gone were the expensive embroidered coat and the fashionable wig. In their place Foxe wore his own hair, tied up neatly, and simple, dark clothes suitable for moving about the city without drawing attention. Samuel at the coffeehouse had passed him the message from James Morrow. The money was to be taken to Pig Lane that evening at seven o'clock and left in the doorway of a warehouse behind The Maid's Head Inn; the one with "Downham & Buckland" painted on the wooden panels. The location where the money was to be left now explained why Joseph Morrow had gone to a part of the city where he should not have been. Whoever the blackmailer was, it appeared he was content to use the same spot as before.

Foxe passed the details to Charlie Dillon. He also told Charlie to ask his many contacts amongst the street children to seek out a lad of some 14 or 15 years old whose last name was Goodwin. He might be living on the streets or working at some employment where no questions were asked about your past. He didn't want Charlie himself distracted from the immediate task in hand. He was to leave this search to others, since it was bound to take time to check all the places where a runaway apprentice might be hiding.

Foxe's final task was to send a message to Alderman Halloran asking for the constables to be ready at five in the afternoon. He knew that was early, but there was every chance the location for the handover would be watched well before the appointed hour. The time was chosen carefully. At this time of year, it would still be light enough at seven to move about without a lantern. Once darkness came, it would be impossible, since carrying a light would show your presence to anyone watching. There would also be few people moving around on the wharves or in the streets. Pig Lane lay in a part of the city mostly inhabited by weavers who needed daylight to do their work. They rose before the dawn—around 3:30 or 4:00, Foxe guessed—and started work on their looms as soon as there was enough light to see. When you rose that early, you had little reason to do anything after your evening meal save go to bed. Elsewhere in the city, men might meet their friends in local inns or taverns for a game of cards, a few tankards of ale and a pipe or so. Not so amongst Norwich's many weavers, who were paid strictly by what they produced.

With all Foxe's arrangements made, it was back to waiting. Mrs Crombie hinted several times that she and Miss Benfield were agog to know what he was up to, but Foxe held firm. He would tell them afterwards.

Lily was not on stage that evening and Foxe was tempted to distract his mind from its worries by paying her a visit, but in the end stayed at home. He needed to be fully alert and could not afford to be tired by another of Lily's increasingly virtuoso performances on the mattress. She had already picked up a repertoire of moves guaranteed to encourage him to match her, pleasure for pleasure.

That thought sent Foxe to seek out one or two volumes from his library which might serve to refresh his own stock of pleasing diversions. The trouble with being a rake who was basically faithful to one or two partners for long periods was that he settled into what he knew would almost always work. With a new lady to please, he must branch out and seek fresh possibilities.

By four in the afternoon, Mrs Crombie was becoming exasperated by master and apprentice. They had been roaming the shop and storeroom area since soon after noon, getting in her way and driving Miss Benfield to distraction. Charlie had swept out the shop three times, forcing the few customers to keep moving out of his way and raising just enough dust to make Miss Benfield sneeze until her nose was red. Mr Foxe had wandered around, picking up various books, only to set each down after a moment or so with a frown or an angry shake of his head.

"Doesn't he think his own stock is good?" one lady asked Mrs Crombie. "Nothing seems to content him."

In the end, Mrs Crombie could stand it no longer. She banished both of them to the storeroom, forbidding them to emerge from there until the shop had closed and she had gone home.

"You can wander around raising dust and wasting your time in there," she snapped. "If you stay in the shop, our customers will leave and Miss Benfield and I will probably join them. Why is the male of the species so restless when there is nothing active to be done—and no females worth attempting to distract from their work? This is a bookshop. Sit and read a book, Mr Foxe. Charlie, get the master to read to you, if he has not the patience to read to himself. Either way, get out from under my feet, I beg of you!"

At last, the hands of Mr Foxe's watch crept round to five, the constables appeared outside and Charlie could slip away through the gate at the back of Mr Foxe's garden to play his own part in the coming drama.

When Foxe and the constables reached Tombland, with the great bulk of the mediaeval cathedral looming to their right behind the wall surrounding the Cathedral Close, they paused. It was time to put into place Foxe's detailed plans to conceal the three burly constables and their leader. Pig Lane was a narrow alleyway leading down to the quay from Palace Street. It was essential both ends of Pig Lane should be blocked, for Foxe did not want their quarry to be able to escape. At the same time, the constables must be well hidden. None could be near the spot where Mr James Morrow had been instructed to leave the money. Too close and they would be detected; too far back and they might not be able to get to their places before the blackmailer escaped.

After a little consultation, it was agreed that the chief constable and one other should continue down Wensum Street towards the Fye Bridge, then turn right onto the quay and hide as close to that end of Pig Lane as they felt would be safe. There should be enough places by the wherries where they could conceal themselves.

The other two would follow Foxe along Palace Street and hide at the other end of the lane. Foxe himself would go through the Maid's Head Inn and wait in the inn yard, which had its own entrance onto Pig Lane. He would be closest and best able to observe events in the failing light, as well as able to prevent anyone from escaping via the inn itself. He had equipped himself with a loud, wooden whistle. When they heard him blow it, the constables were to rush into Pig Lane from either end.

All was in place more than an hour before the due time. Foxe still believed the blackmailer or an accomplice would take care to check for a trap well before James Morrow was due. Now it was a matter of staying quiet and alert. Fortunately, the chill weather had lingered long this year. Though the calendar might indicate spring-time, the air was remarkably cold. As the sun dipped towards the horizon, a strong easterly wind was blowing over the city, which should keep them all alert.

At around half-past six, several small groups of street children arrived in Pig Lane and began to huddle together in the doorways and behind the few carts left in the street. It looked as if they had come to bed down together during the hours of darkness. The narrow lane, running roughly north to south, offered a little protection from the east wind. For the rest, huddling together would have to suffice.

Promptly at five minutes to seven o'clock, a man appeared at the Palace Street end of the lane. He was well-wrapped against the chill, his hat pulled down low over his forehead. As he walked down the narrow alley, it could be seen he was carrying a bag which occasionally chinked, as if it contained coins. The sound alerted several of the children, who sprang up and rushed towards the man with their hands out in the hope of gaining a coin or two. The stranger paused a moment and handed out a few pennies, then pressed on. The children must have realised he would give no more, for they did not follow. Instead, they moved back quickly to regain their places amongst the huddled figures of their fellows.

The man paused a second by one of the doorways in the street, then walked on smartly towards the quay beyond. Only the more observant would have noticed he was no longer carrying the bag of coins.

More time passed. By the time he heard distant church bells ring out the quarter hour, Foxe was beginning to wonder if this would all be for nothing. Had he or the constables been spotted, in spite of their efforts at concealment? Was the blackmailer hidden behind the door where the money had been left, ready to slip it open a crack and withdraw the bag unseen?

Then, footsteps, stealthy this time, coming up Pig Lane from the quay at the other end. Foxe risked leaning out a tiny bit from his hiding place to see what was happening. A man was approaching in the half-light, not walking confidently as James Morrow had done, but with the crouched stance and wary tread of the habitual criminal.

The street children must have had exceptional hearing, for at once several sprang up from doorways and yard entrances to run forward, hoping for some more pennies. This man, however, was made of crueller stuff than the last. As soon as the children came near, he cursed at them, telling them to keep away for he had no money to waste on "sewer rats and street-shit like them". When one lad persisted further, he received a sharp blow from the stick the man was carrying.

The children hung back, circling around him but staying out of range of any more blows. Ignoring their presence, the stranger went at once to the doorway where Morrow had left the bag of money. He picked it up and shook it. The sound of clinking coins rang in the street, but still the children held back. Only when the man seemed satisfied with what he had and turned away again did they move closer.

That was when Foxe blew hard on his whistle.

The man's head jerked up at the sound and he would have run off, but it was too late. Three of the girls leapt onto his back like cats, their hands scratching at his face and eyes. A boy bent down, scooped up a handful of mud and refuse from the street and thrust it hard into the man's face, crying "There's street-shit for you!" As their quarry tried desperately to shake off his attackers, several of the bigger boys ran up to join the fray. Yet, before they could get close enough, a small girl, perhaps only seven or eight years old, ran in front of the man, drew back her stick-thin arm, and drove her bony fist hard into his testicles.

The man cried out in agony at the blow to those parts of him most likely to feel it and bent down, his hands clutched between his legs. Now the bigger boys arrived. One took careful aim and delivered a hefty kick from a hob-nailed boot onto the man's backside, just where his spine met his buttocks. Two more struck his legs to trip him, so he fell full-length on his face. Finally, the boy he had struck with his stick walked up and planted several hard kicks full into the man's ribs.

All the fight had gone out of the man, who lay moaning and cursing with his face in the filth of the street and no less than five children sitting on his back to hold him down. That was when the two constables from Palace Street arrived, swiftly followed by the other two from the quay. They told the children to move aside and dragged the man to his feet. Though he cursed and tried to spit at them, his mouth was too clogged with mud to allow more than animal noises to come out. The chief of the constables stepped forward and peered into his face.

"Matthew Garvey," he said. "Even in this bad light I knows your ugly features. I ought to have guessed. We've been on the look-out for you since you bribed your way out of the court house in Ipswich. Now we'll 'ave the pleasure of sending you back to keep your appointment with the 'angman."

His words brought more muffled curses from Garvey and a final attempt to pull himself free of the strong hands which held him.

"Resisting arrest," the chief said to his men. "Silly."

The sharp blow he delivered to Garvey's head with his heavy truncheon must have rendered the man unconscious, for he slumped forward and would have fallen to the ground if he had not been held firm.

"Take him away," Foxe said. Then he bent forward and retrieved the bag Garvey had dropped. "I see you know this man."

"Garvey," the chief of the constables said. "Known as 'The Gut Burster' from 'is habit of driving 'is fist into a man's stomach again and again as an inducement to obedience. 'E was taken a while ago in Ipswich, when this 'encouragement' caused a man's death. Escaped from the court while 'e was waiting to be taken back to the jail to be readied for the 'angman. Two o' the guards was bribed, they say. Anyhow, they both 'ad to stand in the pillory for 'alf a day. One lost an eye and most o' his teeth. T'other can't walk proper any more."

"One of 'Gentleman' Jack's men?"

"Aye, thass right. One of the worst too. Scum o' the earth, believe me."

As the constables dragged 'The Gut Burster' away to the lock-up, Foxe opened the neck of the bag he was holding and peered inside. As he had hoped, it was full of pennies.

"Charlie?" Foxe called. "You there?"

At once, the excited gaggle of children parted and Foxe's apprentice stepped forward.

"Share these pennies out," Foxe said. "There ought to be enough for everyone to have at least a shillings' worth. If not, I'll make it up tomorrow. Well done, everyone. Now find somewhere better to sleep than this wretched alley. You can come back with me, Charlie, once you've handed round the pennies."

Well, they hadn't caught Beeston, but Foxe never believed the man would do his own dirty work. He must be content to have caught his henchman. If this Garvey knew he was facing the noose, he might well be tempted to try to turn King's Evidence to save his neck. Much good would that do him!

Then, as he and Charlie made their way back through Tombland and up Queen Street towards the Market Place, Foxe had another thought. It was hardly important whether Garvey tried to take Beeston down with him or not. All that mattered was that Beeston should believe his henchman had decided to betray him.

"Charlie," Foxe said. "Do you think you and your friends could start a rumour?"

"Easiest thing in the world, master," the boy replied.

"Good. Spread it around that, as Garvey was dragged away, he started cursing Jack Beeston and promising to make sure he would be hanged alongside him. Can you do that?"

"Aye, o'course I can. God! That won't 'alf put the wind up Beeston! 'E'll be shitting bricks!"

"Charlie!" Foxe said. "What would Mrs Crombie say if she could hear you?"

"She ain't 'ere, master, is she? Anyhow, it's true. Beeston ain't never been caught 'cause no one dares to give evidence against 'im. If 'e thinks someone who knows all 'is capers is really goin' to tell what 'e knows, that'll upset 'im good and proper. Beeston knows there's no magistrate nor judge who ain't longin' to send 'im to the gallows."

"That's what I'm hoping," Foxe said. "Now off to your bed, or Mrs Crombie will be clipping your ears for sleeping when you should be working."

❧

FOXE HAD PLANNED to forego his coffee the next morning in favour of visiting Alderman Halloran. He wanted to hear what had become of Matthew Garvey. However, even that had to wait, for Charlie brought him more important tidings.

He had found the boy. Tom Goodwin had indeed been an apprentice to Mr Joseph Morrow. He had run away and was now living rough on the streets on the other side of the river, surviving by petty pilfering. Charlie had yet to speak to him, but he hoped he could persuade him to come and talk with Mr Foxe.

Foxe was delighted.

"Tell Tom Goodwin I already know about him and his sister," he said. "All I want is to understand what happened after that. If it's what I think, I'll not be handing him over to the authorities or anyone else. Make sure he understands that or he may not come. Then, if he agrees, tell him to come to the garden gate tomorrow around noon. I'll be waiting."

Charlie's second piece of news was that the rumour about Garvey peaching on Beeston was already the talk of the city. If it hadn't already reached Beeston's ears, it very soon would. Even better, in the way people did when passing on rumours, the story was being embellished and added to. Someone had just come into the shop and told Mrs Crombie that "everyone knew" a large force of constables, assisted by a troop of Yeomanry, was being assembled to take Beeston and make sure he couldn't raise a mob to set him free. When captured, he was to be sent to London for trial. There would be no Norwich jury who could be bribed or intimidated. Once the authorities had Beeston under lock and key, they were determined he would dangle at the end of a rope.

Foxe listened to this with growing satisfaction. If that didn't frighten Beeston, nothing would.

"I don't know how the news about Garvey trying to turn King's Evidence spread so fast," Alderman Halloran said later that morning. "Someone amongst the constables, I suppose. Anyway, it will do the villain no good. Any half-respectable defending lawyer would have Garvey's evidence dismissed as untrustworthy—a wretched attempt to shift the blame. There's another point too. Garvey will never stand trial for blackmailing the Morrow family. That would be an invitation for him to vomit his foul accusations out in open court. No, he's already bound for the gallows for that murder in Ipswich. All we have to do is send him back, making sure he doesn't escape this time, and let the hangman do the rest."

"Nevertheless, it should be enough to worry Beeston a great deal. A most satisfactory ending, alderman," Foxe said. "It's a shame we didn't take Beeston himself, but we can't have everything."

"Agreed," Alderman Halloran said. "Even if it had been Beeston though, we probably wouldn't have brought him to court and risked him bringing accusations against Morrow. Still, he isn't to know that." He paused for a moment. "I don't suppose you understand what it was Beeston was using to blackmail Morrow, do you?"

"Almost," Foxe replied. "I am sure in my own mind what it was, but I would like to have proof before I tell you. If luck stays with me, I may have that proof by tomorrow afternoon. If so, this whole matter will be over for everyone."

"Amen to that!" Alderman Halloran said. "Now … when you have more news, come and see me again. The mayor is strutting around as if he had solved this crisis entirely on his own. Perhaps if we give him yet greater cause for satisfaction, he'll burst and allow the rest of us a period of peace and quiet."

17

THE END OF THE ROAD

FOR A WHILE, FOXE THOUGHT TOM GOODWIN WASN'T GOING TO come. Noon came and went without anyone coming near the doorway from Foxe's garden into the lane beyond. He was just about to give up and return inside, when he heard a faint sound of footsteps. The gate opened a small amount and a hand could be seen holding to the edge. Silence. Then a slight movement further and a face peered around the gate.

Foxe had positioned himself well back, where he could be seen clearly. He didn't want the boy to suspect a trap.

"There's no one here save me," Foxe said, keeping his voice calm. "Come in, but leave the gate ajar so you can get away if I am not telling you the truth. I will not stir from where I am now. All I want is to speak to you, not take hold of you. That I promise. When we are done, you will walk away as freely as you came."

Again a long pause. The boy's head was now fully clear of the gate, so that he could take a good look around. Foxe waited. Then the gate opened enough to allow a skinny body to slip inside the garden. Even so, as Foxe had suggested, Tom Goodwin held the gate open with one of his hands. His whole body was poised to run.

"What's it you wants, mister?" he said. "I was told you needed to 'ear somethin' about my sister. That right?"

"That's right, Tom. I know she's your twin ..."

"Was!" the boy spat out. "Was my twin sister."

Foxe kept his face calm and his words gentle.

"I'm sorry, Tom," he said. "Was your sister. I also know you both worked for Mr Joseph Morrow ..."

Again he was interrupted, this time by a string of curses and obscenities, delivered in a voice trembling with rage and hatred.

"I can see you had no cause to like the man," Foxe went on, "but why did you kill him?"

The boy's head jerked up and he half-turned at those words, ready to bolt back into the lane.

"Wait, Tom," Foxe said quickly. "I just want to understand. You have my promise I will not try to seize you or hand you over to the constables. If ever a man deserved a violent death, that man was Joseph Morrow. But I need to know what he had done that drove you to such violence. That is all."

The boy hesitated. Perhaps it was the chance at last to relate what had been devouring him from within for so many days. Perhaps it was some hope that this man would announce to the world how Joseph Morrow had been fine without, but foul within. Perhaps it was a chance to explain what had changed his sister from a cheerful, loving companion into a barely recognisable madwoman. Whatever it was, the urge to talk finally overcame the urge to run.

"That man ... that ..." Tom stammered, "... fiend from hell destroyed my sister. We both worked for 'im—and rotten work it was too. Only the orphanage said if we ran away they'd find us and punish us bad. I was supposed to be an apprentice, but 'e taught me nothin'. I was a nobody. A gutter-snipe to be worked 'til I dropped an' kicked awake when I did. Minnie—thass my sister—was a maid-of-all-work. She were lovely, mister. Small an' skinny, like, but the sweetest, finest sister anyone ever 'ad ... until 'e took 'er from me."

"She worked in the house then," Foxe said.

"Aye. In the 'ouse, the kitchen, the out-'ouses, anywhere there was somethin' filthy and 'ard to be done."

"What happened?" Foxe asked, as gently as he could.

"One day—'bout three weeks ago, I reckons—that … that … devil, Morrow, decided she'd done summat wrong an' needed to be punished. 'E were like that, mister. 'E had this great list o'rules what you 'ad to follow, an' if you didn't, you got a beatin'. Well, that day 'e claimed my Minnie 'ad broken one of 'is stupid commandments. Usually, the girls got a borin' lecture an' perhaps a cuff around the ear for their pains. But that time, 'e says, the sin was worse. That's the kind o'thing 'e said, mister. You never done wrong, you sinned. Fucking bastard!"

Foxe kept silent. They were coming to the crux of the matter and any foolish or inappropriate words might spoil all.

"So … 'e catches 'er in an out-'ouse where she'd been sent to fetch summat and pulls 'er inside. 'E had a bundle o' birch twigs in 'is 'and, she told me. A thick bundle it was too. Next thing she knows, 'e throws 'er 'ead first across an old saw-'orse standing there and ups her skirts over 'er head. That way, mister, if she shouts or screams, 'e's muffled the sound. Then 'e beats 'er—hard—across the bare arse and thighs. An' all the time 'e does it, 'e's callin' 'er a whore and scum and heaven knows what else. My sister was never a whore, mister. Never! Even when we was in the orphanage and some o' the older boys tried to tempt 'er to let them 'ave 'er in exchange for extra food, she wouldn't. She were pure, I swear it."

"I believe you," Foxe said.

"Well, Morrow beats my sister till she can feel the blood running down 'er legs and 'e's breathin' like an old, broken-winded nag draggin' a cart up an 'ill. Then 'e stops, and she thinks it's over. Then … then … I can't 'ardly say it …"

"I can guess," Foxe said. "No need to go on."

The boy ignored him, his face twisted with an almost inhuman rage against a world that had treated him so cruelly for the whole of his short life.

"That … Morrow …" he spat out. "That Christian man, as 'e claimed … 'e forced 'er, 'e did. Pulled down 'is breeches and raped my sister. Then, when 'e'd finished, 'e cursed her for a temptress and a harlot, dragged 'er down the garden, and threw 'er into the street. Aye, an' told 'er if she ever breathed a word of what 'e'd done, 'e was goin' to swear she'd been stealing from 'im—money and cloth and God knows what else. It'd be 'is word against 'ers and 'e knew who the magistrate would believe. She'd be taken to the hangman or transported. 'E would 'ave done it too!"

"Yes," Foxe said sadly. "He would."

"When my sister found me, mister, she were like a ghost walkin', she were so shocked and ashamed. It was as if that devil had eaten up her soul. So … she tells me what Morrow done—tells me calmly, like she might tell me one o' they tales she used to whisper to me to 'elp me sleep. I says we'll run away together 'cos I knew a safe spot to 'ide. It were in an old warehouse by the river, mister. Good place to 'ide up for a day or so, I reckoned. Just till we 'ad some sort o' plan."

The boy's vehemence was failing now and his face had gone deadly pale.

"I left 'er there on 'er own to go an' steal enough food to see us on our way out of the city. No more'n thirty minutes, it were. When I got back, I called out and she didn't answer. She'd managed to find a bit o' rope from somewhere and slung it over a beam. Then she'd 'anged 'erself."

He could not go on. For a moment he seemed stunned, then his body was torn by great sobs of pain and grief. Foxe's eyes too were wet with tears of mingled sadness and anger. No wonder Joseph Morrow had paid and paid again. If he had done this before—and Foxe was sure he had, every time his wife had seen him praying and lashing himself afterwards—what had those other poor creatures done? Mrs Morrow had told Foxe the only time her husband had seemed fully aroused sexually, was when he had beaten her on her bare bottom. He should have understood then.

Foxe's attention switched back to the boy before him. He was speaking again, calmer now.

"Minnie were 14 years old, mister. Just 14, same as I be. Once, in church, the minister read from the Bible and I remembered them as I cut my sister down. That minister read as 'ow Our Lord 'ad told 'is disciples it was better for a man to 'ave a great millstone tied about 'is neck and be thrown into the sea than 'arm a child. My sister was a child, mister! Nothin' but a pretty child.

"That's when I knew what I 'ad to do. I couldn't do no more for 'er. 'Ad to leave 'er there for someone else to bury in a pauper's grave. No, mister, my job was to be that great millstone waitin' to be hung round Morrow's neck. So I stole a bit o' leather strap and took to followin' 'im about, waitin' for my opportunity. I knows it's wrong to steal, mister, but I 'ad no choice. It was steal or starve—an' if I died, who was goin' to do for that bastard?

"Then, one evening around seven—just as it were gettin' dark— I spotted 'im comin' out of 'is 'ouse carryin' a little bag what clinked. Furtive, 'e looked, as if 'e were on 'is way somewhere 'e shouldn't 'ave gone. I follows 'im down towards Cathedral. Then 'e goes into an alley behind The Maid's 'ead. It was gettin' quite dark by then, but I could see 'im against the light at the other end of the alley. For a moment, 'e seems to stop, like 'e was lookin' for some-thin', then 'e goes on down to the quay.

"I knew that was my chance, mister. No one about and 'im without any idea I was comin' up to him. I 'ad that leather strap around 'is neck in an instant, then I pulled and pulled and choked the life out of 'im—just like that noose must 'ave choked the life out o' my sister."

"Why put him in the hold of the wherry?" Foxe asked.

"I didn't, mister. That weren't me. You see, when I was lookin' for food earlier in the day, I found this drunk man fast asleep. I'd 'oped 'e might 'ave a bit o' grub about 'im, but all 'e 'ad was a bottle o' brandy, 'alf finished. I took it anyhow. Thought it might keep me warm that night if I found nothin' to eat. As I looked at Morrow lyin' on the ground, I remembered 'ow much 'e used to go on and on about not drinkin' booze. So I takes out the bottle and pulls 'is 'ead around so as to pour some into 'is mouth. The rest I slopped over 'is clothes. Kind of a last insult."

"How did he get in the wherry then?"

"While I was pourin' the booze over 'im, I 'eard someone

comin', so I nipped smartly behind some barrels and 'id. It was a couple or three men, sailors I reckoned. One on 'em trips over Morrow. Then they smells the drink and thinks 'e's passed out wi' boozin'. One on 'em says as 'ow it would be a good joke if the drunk woke up next mornin' 'alf way to Yarmouth. So they ups and throws 'im into the wherry alongside the quay and I takes meself off."

"Simple," Foxe said. "Only I never thought of it."

"So what 'appens now," Tom Goodwin asked. "I told you everythin'. You still not goin' to 'and me over to the magistrate?"

"No, I am not," Foxe said. "I already half guessed much of what you've told me. No, boy. I shall tell only one person what I have learned today and he won't tell anyone else. I know the law says murder is murder, whatever the provocation, but the law doesn't always serve the ends of justice. Instead I'll give you two choices. You can run away now and I shan't come after you. If you do that, you'll need to live on the streets until someone catches you stealing —which they surely will. Then you'll be punished as Mr Morrow told your sister she would be if she opened her mouth. The second choice is this. You have to stay out of sight a while longer and make sure you aren't taken up by the constables as a vagrant or a beggar. To help you, I'll give you a few pennies now and send more by Charlie Dillon. That way, you can eat without stealing.

"I have a good friend who owns several wherries and some ships sailing out of Yarmouth. He's away at present, but he'll be back in a week or so. If I ask him, he'll find you a place on one of his boats where you can learn the trade of a sailor. Start a new life, far from here, and put this nightmare behind you. You can live as I'm sure your sister would want you to. Which is it to be?"

The boy took little time to make up his mind. He took the few pence Foxe gave him, promised to stay out of trouble, and was gone.

Foxe turned away too, back to his house. He needed a drink— needed it very badly.

≈

NEARLY A WEEK HAD PASSED since the day Tom Goodwin had told his story in the quietness of the garden behind Foxe's house. By rights, Foxe ought to have visited the alderman long before now, but he had been prevented by urgent business. Besides, no one hurries to bring news of the kind Foxe had brought today. Now, at last, everything was clear in Foxe's mind, so he had come to share his knowledge with Halloran. The two men had been shut away for almost an hour in the small parlour before Foxe finally reached the end of what he had to say.

"I would not have thought a professed Christian, an educated man—nay, until today I would have said a civilised man—could stoop to such terrible wickedness," Alderman Halloran said, when Foxe had related all he had discovered about the poor wenches Joseph Morrow had maltreated.

Halloran's face had turned a dark red with suppressed anger and his hands were bunched into fists at his sides.

"I am glad he never stood before me in my court to be sent to the assizes," he went on. "I doubt I could have kept the proper demeanour of a magistrate. I keep thinking how I would feel if such things happened to my nieces—God forbid! I would not trust myself to stay my hands from choking the life from the foul wretch who did it."

For a short while, both men were silent, then Halloran spoke again.

"One thing is still not clear to me, Foxe. How did Beeston discover what Morrow had been doing? It took you some time. Without you and your nose for hidden information, I doubt I would ever have found out."

"I cannot be certain, alderman," Foxe replied, "but I do not think my guess will be too far from the truth. The maid, Minnie, was not the first to suffer thus at her master's hands. Mrs Morrow told me that her late husband indulged in periods of frantic prayer and flagellation every 5 or 6 weeks over the past two years. At a rough estimate, assuming each such orgy of repentance followed an attack, that makes some 20 in all."

"Twenty!" Halloran cried. "In God's name, why did none of them come forward and accuse him?"

"He threatened them, as I told you, and they believed him. I would have too. Joseph Morrow paraded his piety around the city. Everyone thought him the most upright and puritan of men. Without any evidence but their own tales, who would have preferred the accusation of ignorant, unlettered children over the calm statements of an educated and respected man?"

"I suppose you're right," Halloran said. "Justice is supposed to be blind, but somehow she always smiles more eagerly on the rich and powerful than on anyone else."

"From all I have discovered," Foxe continued, "Morrow never tried to keep any of his victims in his household. He had no liking for them. Their presence only reminded him of what he had done. Once his frenzy had passed, we know he threw himself into a period of frantic repentance. Thus, whether they were thrown out or ran away, the victims had to go. So far as I know, the girl Minnie was the only one to take her own life. The rest had to go somewhere where they would be taken in or starve. We both know the most likely places in this city to welcome runaway girls or dismissed servants."

"Brothels. Of course. That's why Beeston's men looked there."

"Indeed. I doubt they knew at first just how many children had been sacrificed to Morrow's lust. All they would have wanted was to find one or two whom they could 'persuade'—not gently either, I imagine—that to defy Beeston was far worse than facing transportation to Botany Bay. These were children, remember. Our courts may be required to pass sentence of death on children, but the assize judges almost always recommend His Majesty to exercise clemency and commute the sentence to transportation. Beeston wanted to be able to tell Morrow he had a number of his victims ready to stand up in court and give their evidence, should Morrow fail to pay what he demanded."

"That still doesn't explain how Beeston found out in the first place."

"That's simple. 'Gentleman Jack' has a large network of spies and informers to keep him abreast of anything that might prove useful to him. It's likely one poor child had told another girl in the brothel what had brought her there. Thus it would have reached the ears of the bawd. Perhaps the bawd herself had wormed the truth out of her. Most of these children have never known a mother. Many madams in brothels are tender towards their girls, however hard-hearted they may be when it comes to money. Either way, such news would soon have reached Beeston's ears. The rest, we know."

"Yes, that must be right," the alderman said with a sigh. "Well, it's all over now."

They both kept silent again for a time. Only the soft, regular beat of the clock on the mantel broke the silence. Once, Foxe picked up his coffee cup, but found it was empty. He would have liked some more—talking was dry work—but his host was sunk into some kind of deep reverie and failed to notice.

At last, the alderman spoke again.

"By the way, Foxe," he said. "Where have you been this last week? I expected you here before now. Indeed, I called into your shop one day looking for you. Even Mrs Crombie said she had hardly set eyes on you for days. She didn't know what you were doing either."

"I was trying to find the last pieces of the puzzle, alderman. It was not easy either."

"There's more? Wasn't abusing and raping those poor maidservants enough?"

"That's exactly the point," Foxe said. "I kept wondering why Joseph Morrow had been willing not just to wreck his own life and business, but ruin his father and his wife as well. He must have realised Beeston would never be content until there was not a penny left. Yet he kept on paying. Why?"

"He knew the shame and disgrace that would follow if he did not," Alderman Halloran said. "You told me yourself he aspired to be perfect. Many people would have taken great delight in seeing such a self-righteous prig brought low. They would have laughed him out of the city."

"It still didn't seem to me to be enough. It is a sad fact that a good many masters treat their maidservants as playthings to appease their lust. No sane person approves, but the practice is widespread, believe me. Of course, most such men pretend to some fondness for the girl, but that soon evaporates should she be found to be with child."

"Morrow went far beyond using his servants as playthings."

"True. I suspect he had long been tormented with some inner demon of lust; a demon that required him to inflict pain as a precursor to finding release. I know—I will not tell you how, but it is certain—that Joseph Morrow could not experience real desire or passion without there being pain and cruelty mixed in."

"Well, there you have the answer to your doubts surely," Alderman Halloran objected. "The men you mentioned—those who seduce their maidservants—do them no physical harm. Such behaviour should not be condoned, but even wives will often turn a blind eye. Add violence, cruelty and rape and it is a different matter."

"Maybe so … maybe so. Yet I was not convinced. Then I realised I had also forgotten to clear up the reasons for two pieces of information. Do you recall the handwritten note to the newspaper editor? Who wrote that? Was it the murderer? Was it Beeston? And why had Beeston's men searched 'gambling hells' and taverns, not just brothels. If they had received information in the way I have guessed—if they were just looking for former maids—why look further? What has kept me busy is seeking out the answers to these two puzzles."

"Did you find them?" Alderman Halloran asked.

"Yes, in the end. I'm sorry, alderman. It is dreadfully impolite of me to ask, but I wonder if you might call for some more coffee? This will be a long tale, and my throat is parched already?"

Once he had quenched his thirst, Foxe took up the story again.

"I started with the matter of the handwritten note," he said. "Beeston, we presume, organised for the printed notice to put extra pressure on Mr James Morrow after his brother's death. Yet somehow I doubted the handwritten note was his work. The words smacked too much of anger and the writing and spelling were both too poor. There was also the matter of the Biblical quotation. I was convinced whoever wrote that note had learned their reading and writing—such as it was—in some religious circumstance.

"Beeston would not have pushed it under the door of the news-paper office either. He would have known no editor would print material from such a source. Newspapers are run by over-worked men and the margin for profit is usually tiny. None would have the time, or the inclination, to chase after what was little more than a malicious-seeming rumour. No. I came back again and again to the same conclusion. Either the murderer wrote it, or it was someone with a similarly close knowledge of Morrow's actions."

"So what did you do?" Halloran asked.

"First, I sent word to my ... informant to discover whether the murderer's sister was able to read and write. The answer that came back was 'no' to both, and since my source is ... was ... very close to the murderer I'm sure it must be true.

"But if the murderer's sister didn't write the note, who did? Was it the murderer? Was it one of those others Morrow had abused, trying after his death to bring shame upon him? Could any of those read or write?

"That took me to the Superintendent of the orphanage and the Overseers of the Poor from whom Morrow obtained his servants. Did they teach their charges to read and write? For the girls, the answer was a clear 'no'. There was no need, they told me. Their charges almost all became household servants. Such time as they could spend on their education was better directed to practical matters. In fact, they didn't teach the boys to read or write either at the orphanage. Once again, their emphasis was solely on practical skills.

"I received a slightly different answer from the Overseers of the Poor. They certainly did not teach reading or writing to the younger children in their care, save for a minimal introduction to their letters for the boys; just enough to be able to make out the words on a simple written note. However, some children came to them later when they were older. These might have been taught something of reading by parents or at Sunday School before ending up in the care of the Overseers."

"Not very helpful, then," Alderman Halloran said.

"On the contrary. You'll recall my second puzzle was why Beeston's men had searched gambling hells and taverns. Put that together with the earlier estimate that Joseph Morrow may have assaulted up to 20 children and tell me what you see."

"Little enough, Foxe. I suppose that there must be more victims of Morrow at large than we first accounted for."

"Exactly. Some had been missed. And who might you find in taverns and such places doing menial work or begging outside?"

The alderman's face clouded. He had the answer.

"Boys!" he almost whispered. "Boys as well!"

"Yes, alderman," Foxe said. "That was my conclusion. Especially since I recalled that Mrs Morrow had told me her late husband took so-called apprentices from the orphanage and elsewhere for the yarn business. When his father had been in charge, parents were eager to apprentice their sons to him. Some paid high premiums. Ezekiel Morrow was a man to seek out to set your child on the way to a prosperous future. His son, sadly, was a mediocre merchant and tradesman at best. Yet the business still needed apprentices. In the end, he had to get them where he could."

"Boys." Halloran still seemed in shock.

"I returned to the Overseers of the Poor and asked if they had sent Morrow many boys or girls," Foxe went on. "In both cases, the answer was 'no'. One or two girls only, who were, so far as they knew, still employed by Morrow's wife as maids. Only one boy in the past year. The man I spoke with remembered him for two reasons. First he was a little older than most—almost 16—though so badly nourished during his life he looked much younger, being very short and slight. The other reason was the boy's strange history. He was the child of a man who was said to have been notably religious. However, the man had, in time, lost his mind, thrown up his work and gone off as an itinerant preacher, abandoning his wife and children. The wife and the girls were sent to the House of Industry. At the time the boy was brought in, Joseph Morrow had been seeking a new apprentice, so they bound the lad to him. He worked at the yarn warehouse for about three months

—maybe less—then ran away. No one knew where he might be now."

"Damnation to the man!" Halloran cried. "Now it's clear why he was willing to pay anything to keep things quiet. The detestable crime of sodomy carries the penalty of death, even if it's with a willing partner. To do thus to a child, to add rape to buggery, would ensure universal condemnation and swift retribution at the hangman's hand."

"Yes," Foxe said. "Joseph Morrow knew that if this came out, he was finished. He was not just avoiding shame, he was trying to survive. Given how much he was detested by almost everyone he encountered, the man must have feared the mob would get to him before any trial. Their form of justice would have been far more prolonged and cruel than a hanging."

"But why did he do it, Foxe? Why risk so much—not just once, but maybe many times?"

"I believe he could not give up the Calvinist notion that being of 'The Elect' he would still be saved, just as long as he showed repentance. First he tried to conquer his temptations by willpower. His lust was too strong for that. Every time he inflicted pain by beating someone on their bare backside, the lust that seized him could not be resisted. Yet he was too much the severe judge to stop handing out punishment of that kind. Instead, he continually 'repented'. He punished himself and tried to believe it wouldn't happen again."

"If there is a just God," Halloran said, "there will be no question of salvation, whatever those fools of Calvinists believe. Joseph Morrow will be burning in Hell on the end of Satan's toasting-fork."

"Amen to that," Foxe said. "It's said Satan was an angel before he fell. This case has made me believe that whenever religion first turns rotten and then is linked to pride, more Satans are produced."

Halloran nodded.

"Right," he said. "It's absolutely clear to me that none of this should ever be made public. I won't even tell the mayor. The remaining members of the Morrow family are innocent and have suffered enough. This would destroy them. No, let us agree to say no more on the matter. It is over. Morrow's foul sin should go to the grave with him."

"I agree," Foxe said. "I heard this morning that Jack Beeston fled this city several days ago. You recall the rumour that his accomplice had talked to the authorities and laid bare many of his crimes. Beeston clearly thought it prudent to get away while he could. He may come back one day, but for the moment we are free of him."

"Good. That I *will* tell the mayor. Now, Foxe. Let no further search be made for this murderer, whoever he is. It is a terrible thing for a magistrate to say, but all our killer has done is save the hangman a job. If he came before me in court, of course, I would have no option but to send him to trial. The law is clear, even if justice might point another way. However, nothing in my duties requires me to search further, if I am convinced—as I am—that he must have fled the city."

"If he hasn't gone already, alderman," Foxe said, "I'm certain he will very soon. And even if he were found, without additional evidence there would be no basis for a trial, so long as he did not confess."

"True. So, Foxe, abandon your investigation. You have done well, as always, but to go further would serve neither justice nor humanity."

Thus the matter was dropped, never to be mentioned again. For a while, the two men once again sat in silence, then the alderman stood up.

"It is high time to turn to a better topic," he said. "My nieces are burning to show you what they have done in my library. If you can spare a moment, perhaps you would walk through with me and inspect their handiwork."

18

STARTING ANEW

Mrs Halloran was crossing the hallway as Foxe and the alderman came out of the small parlour. Foxe bowed to her with a grand gesture, provoking a smile and a wry comment.

"Mr Foxe," the lady said, "I thank you for your courtesy, but you have no need to treat me thus. I do not doubt there are a good many ladies eager to receive your attentions. Do not waste them on an old, married woman."

"Married you may be, Madam," Foxe replied, "but you are very far from old. I assure you that no courtesy directed towards you could ever be wasted. Why, you look the very picture of beauty and vitality."

"You, sir, are an incorrigible flatterer—even with my husband standing right beside you. Now, enough! Is the alderman taking you to his library? I know my nieces are waiting there, eagerly hoping you will praise and approve their efforts. They have worked with true dedication at this task. It is such a fortunate chance that they will be able to finish it."

"Surely they will be returning to their parents' home soon, Mrs Halloran?" Foxe said. "I understood from your husband that theirs was but a short visit."

"Hasn't he told you? No, I can see that he has not. Our nieces will be remaining here for the foreseeable future, Mr Foxe, and glad we are of it. Their father, who has a senior position with the East India Company, as you know, has so impressed his superiors that they have requested he take up the post of manager of the company's office in the great trading city of Canton in China. It is a great honour, which has also come at an excellent time. His wife found the climate of Bombay most trying."

"Damned hot and humid," the alderman explained.

"They communicated all this to us and asked if we would be willing for their daughters to remain with us for the duration of this posting. Naturally, we agreed. While living in China would be an undoubted experience, I doubt our nieces could find there sufficient polite society to help them become the ladies they should be; nor would they be in a position to meet suitable husbands. They will remain here with us in Norwich."

Foxe knew very little about China, but quickly assented anyway. He suspected the few Europeans about the Chinese Emperor's court would be elderly diplomats or traders eager to win concessions. None would be suitable company for girls of an impressionable age.

"So you will have their company for some time yet," Foxe said. "I do hope you and they will make full use of the circulating library Mrs Crombie is working so hard to establish."

"Never miss a chance for more business, eh Foxe?" Alderman Halloran murmured.

His wife ignored him.

"It will, I am sure, be of great benefit to us. Now, do not keep Maria and Lucy waiting any longer."

Foxe and the alderman walked together to the grand staircase which gave entry to the first floor, where his library was situated. As they reached the half-landing, Alderman Halloran paused to speak.

"Y'know, Foxe. I must confess I hadn't really believed what you said about ghosts and whatnot. I thought you were playing some elaborate trick on me. Never had any time for mumbo-jumbo about supernatural beings. Not so sure now. Since that Frenchie fellow ...

sorry, Swiss … did his exorcism stuff, there's been absolutely no trouble at all."

"I'm glad to hear it," Foxe said.

"I'm also delighted with the way my nieces have organised the books. You'd never believe how easy it is now to find any book I want to consult. In the past, it might take me an hour or more to find some things. I knew where everything was, of course, but the finer details sometimes slipped my mind. That's why I'm determined to keep the place tidy and follow the system of arranging the books the two of them have set up. Telling you all this because my nieces seem to have the very highest opinion of you, Foxe. If you approve of what they have done, it will make their day."

"I'm sure I will, alderman," Foxe said. "Miss Halloran sent me a draft of the scheme she proposed before they began the rearrangement. I was impressed and told her so. Indeed, I passed the paper to Mrs Crombie. Now she and her assistants will be using a very similar scheme to keep track of our stock."

"Did you say 'assistants'? I thought there was only her and Miss Benfield."

"There's young Charlie Dillon too. I have also agreed she may employ a second adult to help her with the circulating library, once that is in full swing."

"So it seems my ghost has done us both a good turn, eh? Wonderful woman, your Mrs Crombie. Not only has she transformed your shop, I can assure you she has a wonderful head for business. I should know."

"Yes indeed," Foxe said. "I feel much the same way about her."

"You ought to marry her, Foxe. Snap her up before someone else does."

"I never had you down for a matchmaker," Foxe replied, laughing.

"I'm quite serious. She's a fine figure of a woman. Young. Intelligent. Don't let her slip through your fingers."

"Alderman! The lady's husband is barely six months in his grave. Besides, I very much doubt she would have me. She has spent enough time in my company to know I am not good husband material."

"You mean all those actresses? They don't signify much in a wife's mind. Plenty of excellent husbands stray from time to time and are none the worse for it. Though I must admit that in your case the straying has been more persistent and wayward than most. No, you would give all that up, once you were married."

"Let us speak no more of it, I beg of you. I am not at all inclined to think of marriage at present, alderman. Maybe I never will be. Either way, Mrs Crombie is too good a person for me to trifle with. She deserves the best of husbands and I doubt that would ever include me."

"You do yourself an injustice, Foxe. I know you like to play the fop and the thoughtless dandy. I see you for what you are. However, I will say no more at present. Let us press on, so that you may begin your tour of inspection."

"So THAT IS the end of the matter," Mrs Crombie said to Foxe later that day. The two of them were standing in Foxe's shop and Mrs Crombie and Miss Benfield had counted the takings and locked up for the day. "I never liked Joseph Morrow, so I have little pity for him. It is his victims I feel sorrowful for."

"Quite so," Foxe said. He had given the two ladies a slightly edited version of his final discoveries. The full details would have been too upsetting.

"One question, if I may," Mrs Crombie said. "Why did you involve those children in your scheme? Were they not put in danger?"

"Yes," Miss Benfield added. "I thought that too."

"Not at all," Foxe said. "I could not place the constables too close. They would have been seen and disclosed my trap. Yet I feared the blackmailer might still find some means of escape before they could come up and seize him. No one ever takes any notice of street urchins. They may go anywhere and not raise the alarm. I simply asked them to detain our man long enough to let the constables take him. I did not specify how they should do it. As it turned out, Garvey's boorish cruelty in trying to strike one of the children when he arrived sealed his fate. By swarming all over him, they protected one another from serious blows. No, ladies. It was Matthew Garvey who came to serious harm, not the children."

"You are right, as always, Mr Foxe. It is only that I do not like to think of children being quite so knowing when it comes to handing out punishment."

"Well, it is, as you said, all over," Foxe said. "Thanks to some prompt action by the mayor and the more prominent merchants of the city, Joseph Morrow's businesses will be wound up or sold in an orderly manner. None who rely on them for their employment will be harmed. 'Gentleman' Jack Beeston has fled—at least for a while —and I gather that the young whores he had rounded up have all gone back to where he found them."

"I find that sad," Mrs Crombie said. "There are far too many young women in this city who must prostitute themselves to live."

"Thus it has always been, I imagine," Foxe said. "A very few who take that path prosper greatly. Some have even managed to marry aristocrats in due course. For the rest … what can you say? Even some respectable wives were once more or less sold to their husbands by families greedy for money or connections. It is a unhappy world."

"Let me give you some more cheerful tidings then," Mrs Crombie replied. "This morning, while you were with Alderman Halloran, Mrs Morrow came to this shop, accompanied only by her maid. We exchanged many pleasantries and even a little gossip. Since her husband's death, she has made a remarkable change for the better. Why, she has even paid her subscription for our new circulating library."

"That is indeed good news," Foxe said. "Her late husband treated her abominably. It is only due to the generosity of his brother that she will have a widow's portion upon which to depend for her future."

"She thinks most highly of you, Mr Foxe. A good deal of her

conversation was taken up in singing your praises. I understand also that you have agreed to take her to the theatre."

"I have. It quite amazed me to find that she had never been to a theatrical entertainment. Though, had I thought about it more carefully, I would have been less surprised. Back in the days of Oliver Cromwell, the Lord Protector, all the theatres were closed down. The Puritans considered them sinful: the very birthplaces of all iniquity."

"I have never been to the theatre either," Mrs Crombie said, "nor, I imagine, has Miss Benfield. Is that right, cousin?"

"Right enough," Miss Benfield replied. "The theatre is still not considered a suitable place for a respectable young woman—indeed any respectable woman—to venture on her own. It was quite impossible to go unless you grew up with brothers or other family members who might take you. Even then, your parents might forbid it. I gather the mob in the gallery can become quite offensive."

"Well," Foxe said, "they can certainly be boisterous. Yet I can see no great harm attending when the company are performing a tragedy by Mr Shakespeare or the like. Would you two ladies care to prove it for yourselves?"

Mrs Crombie and Miss Benfield looked at one another. Then, greatly daring, they both said they would.

"Then I shall take you also," Foxe said. "We shall all go together, including Mrs Morrow, and I shall take a box. It will, I assure you, be a most respectable outing."

"Will not your friend be disappointed to see you come with such a party?" Mrs Crombie asked slyly.

"My friend, as you call her, is an actress, Mrs Crombie. No player ever feels disappointment to see more people attending their performance. No doubt she may be surprised, but that is all. I must, however, warn you that it is not unknown for actresses to wear quite revealing costumes during the dances, pantomimes and burlesques. They tend to be more circumspect in a provincial city like Norwich, compared with London. Still, someone who has lead a very sheltered life, such as Mrs Morrow, may still find it shocking."

"It is now plain why you enjoy the theatre so much," Mrs

Crombie said. "But do not fear, at least for the two of us. We may be dowdy and provincial, but we both know how the world wags. Isn't that right, cousin?"

"In my family," Miss Benfield said, "I was considered to be rather daring in my dress. My father had to speak to me about it on more than one occasion. He told me that the French ladies might reveal their bosoms to an unseemly degree, but that was not an example to be followed on this side of the Channel. Then I would draw my handkerchief somewhat higher about my neck for a day or so, just to please him, before allowing it to slide back to where it had been before."

"I remember my mother warning me not to allow myself to be too much influenced by you, cousin," Mrs Crombie said with a laugh. "She imagined I had not already thought of such things on my own, though she confessed she had not been backward either in dressing to attract others. That was before she married, naturally."

"Naturally," Foxe said.

He was well aware they were hoping to convince him they were not such dry sticks as he might imagine.

"Many a pretty young actress has cherished hopes of attracting the eye of a rich patron by such tricks," he went on, "just as a number of high-born ladies have, well away from the stage. We poor men are beset on all sides. If we show an honest appreciation of female charms, we are accused of lechery. If we turn our heads aside, we are accused of being too scrupulous."

"That could never be said of you, sir," Mrs Crombie said.

"Hmm … we have exhausted that topic, I believe'" Foxe replied, not sure which charge was being laid against him. "It is also time you ladies returned to your home to prepare your meal."

"Do you know when Captain Brock is to return?" Mrs Crombie asked. "I thought he was to be away only a few days."

"He will be back soon," Foxe said. "Lady Henfield was delayed by a family matter and the good captain has waited to be able to escort her back safely."

"Do you think their friendship will ever deepen into something else, Mr Foxe?"

"Ah," Foxe said, "so that is the true subject of your question. I do not know, I assure you. The gap in status between a mere merchant—even a wealthy and well-respected one like Captain Brock—and the daughter and sister-in-law of earls is very great. Yet such gulfs have been bridged before. So long as they are content, the nature of their acquaintance seems to me to be entirely their own business."

"Alas," Mrs Crombie said, "you are sadly wanting when it comes to gossip, Mr Foxe. Never mind, Miss Benfield and I easily make up for your deficiency. I know you may laugh, but I am certain a good many customers come as much for the opportunity to gossip as to peruse the books. If that were not the case, they would surely send a servant in their place."

"So we would lose nothing," Foxe said.

"Mr Foxe! I declare I despair of teaching you even the most rudimentary aspects of running a successful shop. A servant carries out instructions only, since to deviate might bring criticism. When the mistress comes herself—or the master—her eye may light on something outside her original intentions. The longer she stays in the shop, the more chance for this to happen. I am quite certain that many—perhaps most—purchases are not on the customer's mind when leaving home. They result either from whims or the care taken by the shopkeeper to keep the customer standing where suitable items can be seen most easily."

"Such duplicity!" Foxe said, smiling.

"Such good business!" Mrs Crombie replied. "You will see it will be the same for our library. A servant will come to fetch a single book. The mistress will come on the same errand, yet return home with three."

"I am glad you are here to advise me," Foxe said. "Now I know why I never felt at ease even in my father's shop. I lack sufficient guile."

The two ladies now became so convulsed by laughter that they had to remain several minutes longer to compose themselves before leaving for their home. As for Foxe, he felt a great weight had been lifted from his spirits.

Later that evening, as he sat in his library with a glass of good brandy and an even better book, a further revelation came to him. He had not thought of Kitty or Gracie all day. And they say women are fickle, he thought to himself. Though I shall always cherish the memory of those two, it is good to move on. With that, he bent once more to the page before him.

ABOUT THE AUTHOR

William Savage is blogger as well as an author of historical mysteries. History has always been his fascination, but it had to wait for him to retire to have the time to turn this love into a popular blog about Georgian and Regency England and two growing series of historical novels.

You can find out more via his Amazon author page here.

For more information
www.penandpension.com

Printed in Great Britain
by Amazon

10890511R00144